MIRRORS OF TIME

A JINX HAMILTON ADVENTURE

JULIETTE HARPER

D0878811

1

The Druid Forests of Kent, 1590, Jinx

The human body responds to potentially harmful stimuli with involuntary reflexes. You don't think about what you're doing. You react. That's what I did. My skills as a catcher landed Glory and me in a world of trouble.

The wedding came off perfectly — in fairy tale fashion. Looking back, Lucas and I almost made a clean getaway. Then Morris Grayson called out, "A word with you, nephew?"

Lucas hesitated and looked at me. I knew he didn't want to speak to his uncle, but flush with the joy of the day, I generously thought Grayson's request might be a peace offering.

Silly me.

When I nodded, Lucas stepped away, barely missing a collision with Glory who rushed forward exclaiming to me, "I didn't get to hug you yet!"

It sounds awful now after everything we've been through, but I only half listened while she encouraged me to take lots of pictures in France so we could "scrapbook the honeymoon."

Out of the corner of my eye, I caught Morris making an odd

gesture. At some point during the next series of events, my reflexes kicked in. I put out my hand and caught a small, flat, elongated metal object.

I'm not sure if that happened before bright lights erupted inside the portal or when a powerful, sucking wind threatened to pull us off our feet.

Glory clutched at me, crying out, "Jinx. What's happening?"

Shouting to be heard over the gale, I said, "I don't know. Hang on."

Even with our combined weight, we couldn't stand against the cyclone. Lucas called my name before the roaring of the storm overcame all other sounds. I lifted off the ground, and we were sucked into a dark corridor.

My perception switched to roller coaster mode delivering terror-inspired glimpses of branching tunnels. I recognized Trafalgar Square in Londinium. The market in Istanbul where Lucas took me for Turkish food. The lair back home, but with the furniture in all the wrong places.

We tumbled through space for an indefinite period. Minutes. Hours. Days. I had no idea. Lulled by disorientation, I didn't process a cogent synapse until we slammed into a rubbery wall that sent our bodies plunging straight down.

The thought involved a reference to a certain human waste product.

No matter if you trip and fall in the kitchen or jump off a building, one certainty looms ahead. You will hit bottom.

Bracing for impact, I hastily tried to slow our fall with a braking incantation. I managed to mumble the opening words of the spell before we landed. The incomplete casting must have helped some. The impact stunned me, but I didn't lose consciousness.

A blast of frigid wind caught me full in the face, clearing my head. I sat up carefully and looked around. Glory lay sprawled in deep snow a few feet away. Not certain I could stand, I crawled to her.

"Glory? Are you okay? Wake up."

She groaned, swaying as she pulled herself into a sitting position, but otherwise, she seemed unharmed. Confused, she put out her hand and picked up a clump of snow.

"How is there snow on the ground?" she asked. "It's June."

"It was June in Shevington," I said, taking in the thick forest that ringed the clearing. "What parts of the world would have snow in the summer?"

Glory started rattling something about Patagonia. Under the rapid-fire torrent of words, I thought I heard noises in the woods. Hushing her, I strained to listen. There they were again. Footsteps.

We had nowhere to hide. Thanks to a bright, full moon overhead, we could see our surroundings. That was something.

"Get up," I said. "Someone's coming."

I stood up and shoved the object from the portal into my jacket pocket. Glory's legs were shaky, but she was on her feet and moving behind me.

"Someone coming could be good, right?" she asked nervously. "They could be here to rescue us."

I wanted to ask her when anything in our world ever worked out that easily, but I didn't have time. A hooded figured stepped out of the woods, stopping a few feet away.

Cautiously I probed along the internal pathway to my power. When I felt the familiar response, some of my fear receded.

"Uh, hi," I said lamely. "We're not supposed to be here. We don't know where 'here' is. Can you help us out?"

A slim hand threw back the cloak's dark cowl. I wanted to weep with relief. Glory had been right. Help had arrived.

"Oh, Moira, thank God," I babbled. "When the portal

malfunctioned I thought we were done for. Where are we? How do we get back to the wedding?"

The woman I thought I recognized looked at me with uncomprehending eyes. "Do I know thee? Your speech falls strangely on my ears, and your manner of dress is most unusual."

Glory still wore her bridesmaid gown, and I was in a summer dress. We did look like civilians who had been dropped head first into a Renaissance faire.

Even though warning bells were going off in my head, I wasn't ready to let go of the illusion that everything would be okay. Maybe Moira had enjoyed a little too much champagne at the reception.

"Of course you know me," I said, with a nervous laugh. "It's me. Jinx. You know, the Witch of the Oak. Kind of a big deal."

Her answer shattered my fantasy of normalcy once and for all. "Adeline Shevington is Witch of the Oak."

The hair on the back of my neck stood up. Dreading what Moira would say next, I asked, "What year is this? Where are we?"

Even in the midst of fleeting denial, I already knew the answer give or take a decade or two.

"The year of our Lord 1590. You are in the Druid forests of Kent."

Beside me, Glory gasped and then did what Glory does; she found the bright lining in calamity. "Oh my God!" she gushed. "This is so cool. We time traveled! You may not know us yet, Moira, but you will, and you'll like us. Honest. I can't wait to get home and tell Chase about this."

Glory's enthusiasm for history and love of novelty shielded her in the moment, but I did the mental math. By 1590, Adeline Shevington should have been dead. If she wasn't, we were indeed lost in time, but not our time.

Much later, when I had an opportunity to consider those opening moments in retrospect, I realized I'd made a considerable mental leap.

Before we landed in those woods, I'd never heard of alternate time. Without being able to put a name to the sensation, however, I intuitively understood that everything felt wrong.

The flavor of the night air. The frequency of my power. The pulsations of natural energy from the forest.

The sensation reminded me of searching for a radio station on Aunt Fiona's old wood cabinet Philco receiver. You could hear the music against a background of static before you hit the sweet spot on the dial that would give you a clear signal.

While Glory talked a mile a minute and I assessed our situation, I felt Moira's eyes on me. When I shivered — from the cold and emotional overload — the alchemist reacted with familiar kindness.

Raising the staff in her hand, Moira ignited a fireball, which she guided toward the ground. The snow melted as the flames approached, and stones rose from the earth to form a circle. Contained in its bounds, the fire grew into a warming blaze fueled by the force of her magic.

Next, the alchemist murmured, *"Formae pallium suum."*

A thick cloak descended around my shoulders while a second engulfed Glory and although I was still wearing strappy sandals my feet were no longer cold. I drew the heavy fabric close to my body and sank onto my knees beside the fire. Glory joined me reaching for my hand. I squeezed her fingers tightly and managed a weak smile.

Moira sat down across from us, the flames highlighting the angular planes of her face. "Perhaps your tale would best be told from the beginning," she said. "When I know from whence you have come, I will be better able to help you arrive at your destination."

I don't know how long I talked. Inconsequential details crept into the coherent narrative I tried to craft. But even with those meaningless asides, I managed to communicate two salient facts to Moira.

We were from a time and place 425+ years distant where we knew a different Moira.

Since that night I've learned a great deal about time travel. Temporal constants exist — events, people, qualities that manifest regardless of the time stream or its differences.

Any version of the woman I know as Moira Shevington could not help but be intrigued by what I was telling her.

"Who am I in your world?" she asked, leaning slightly forward as if drawn to me by the magnetic attraction of the things I might say.

Unsure of the consequences of sharing information, I dodged the most loaded revelations I could have made.

"You're the resident alchemist in a New World Fae community."

"The New World," she said, the words coming out with a kind of hushed excitement. "I harbor great curiosity about this far away place of which Raleigh and the others speak. How came I to those shores?"

"That's a really long story, and honestly, I'm not sure how many specific details I should give you," I admitted. "In broad terms, you were part of a colonizing group of Fae."

She considered the statement. "Were these settlers Druids specifically?"

"No," I said. "They were magical dissenters representing many Fae races."

The fire guttered as a gust swept over the clearing. Beside me, Glory burrowed deeper into her cloak. "Could we maybe have this conversation inside somewhere?" she asked. "I'm still freezing."

Moira dipped her staff toward the flames, bringing the fire to a higher level. "My village lies nearby in the woods," she said. "I have been abroad this night on an errand of healing and am on my way home. I cannot bring you among my people if you present a danger to them. Would you be willing to submit to a veracity spell?"

"Of course," I said. "We'll answer any questions you have for us."

Shifting nearer to where I sat, Moira held out her hands, which I clasped without hesitation. Our eyes met, and the alchemist whispered, "*Sed verbo veritatis et nemo ex ore cadere.*"

Let none but words of truth fall from thy lips.

The first question surprised me. "Are you Creavit?"

"I'm an Hereditarium witch."

"Do you know Ruling Elder Brenna Sinclair?"

If you ever have to pass a lie detector test, remember that you can tell the truth without telling the whole truth.

"I know a Brenna Sinclair, but she's not ruling elder, and she is no longer Creavit."

"Are you a Spanish agent?"

Frowning, I said, "No. Why would the Spanish be interested in England?"

"Oh," Glory said, "Spain was a Catholic nation, and they had competing maritime interests with the English. After Queen Mary died, her husband wanted to marry Elizabeth. She was a Protestant. Well, is a Protestant, I guess. There's this whole Reformation thing going on."

Moira let go of my hands and reached for Glory. The alchemist put a series of questions to my companion, which Glory answered with breathless enthusiasm.

"How did you gain familiarity with these events?" Moira asked.

"I'm an historian," Glory said. "Well, I was an historian, or

really an archivist. But it helps if you're both. I studied Elizabethan England when I was in graduate school."

Moira's dark brows furrowed. "In your time women are
allowed to attend university?"

"Not just attend, but teach," Glory said. "I wanted to do that,
too, almost as much as I wanted to be a singer like Elvis, but I
would have needed a doctorate. I didn't have enough money to
pay for tuition, so I went to work for the state, and then life took
over, and I never went back to school, but I wish I had."

For a Glory word burst that was fairly short, but Moira still
blinked a couple of times. Glory does that to people. She has a
loose relationship with periods, adores conjunctions, and never
seems to need a pause for breath.

"I do not understand all the things of which either of you
speak," Moira said finally, "but I detect no deceit in your words. I
know not what events brought you here, but I do believe you
have been removed from the stream of time in which you
belong."

I'll take progress where I can get it. "Then you'll help us?" I
said.

"I will," Moira replied, "but there are forces here that, were
they to learn of your unique origins, could present a considerable danger to you. I think it best to disguise your identities
rather than risk such an occurrence."

No argument from me on that one.

"What should we do?" I asked.

"Until we discover how to return you to your world, I will
hide you among our people," Moira said. "My dwelling lies at
the edge of our settlement. I will take you there now under cover
of darkness. Tomorrow you will be introduced to our Elder as
travelers sent to me from a colleague in a remote region of
France to study as novices."

Let's face it. We were not in a position to say no. We couldn't stay in the forest alone without proper clothing and supplies. We couldn't pass ourselves off in an alien world without help — and different time stream or not, this woman was still Moira. I trusted her.

"Thank you," I said. "We're grateful."

With a snap of her fingers, the alchemist extinguished the fire. The rocks sank into the ground. When we reached the edge of the tree cover, Moira turned and blew softly toward the clearing. The snow drifted smoothly over our tracks leaving the area pristine and undisturbed.

"Follow me in close order," she said. "Step only in the tracks I leave. Nowhere else."

I motioned Glory to go first, bringing up the rear. After we'd covered a few yards, I looked back. In the moonlight, I could see that our trail disappeared behind us. Whatever Moira was doing, there would be no evidence of our passage through the woods.

The alchemist led us with unerring confidence. She never stumbled or tripped even when the thick canopy over our heads blotted out all traces of the moon.

Without warning, a muscular wolf with a shaggy black coat stepped onto the path blocking our way. He regarded Moira with amber eyes, letting out a low, almost conversational series of whines.

"You heard the things of which we spoke. The strangers are under my protection," Moira answered. "They mean me no harm."

The wolf nodded and trotted into the trees, but he didn't leave us. I caught glimpses of his dark fur against the snow as we moved forward.

"Friend of yours?" I asked.

Instead of coming off light and flip, the question betrayed my fear.

"An old friend," Moira replied. "He presents no threat to you. He means only to guard us until we reach our home."

Something about the phrase "our home" made me gulp. "He lives with you?"

Moira chuckled softly. "I suspect Orion might tell you that I live with him."

After about 20 minutes lights appeared through the trees ahead. I made out a clump of several dozen stone buildings resembling beehives.

Orion trotted out of the woods and fell in beside Moira. He looked back at me and wagged his tail, which I took either as a sign of acceptance or anticipation over what a nice snack I'd make.

Moira led us to a solitary hut situated at the edge of the community. Orion held back while we passed through a small entrance chamber intended to keep out the cold.

When we entered the single, circular room, the wolf came inside, laid by the door, and put his head on his paws.

A low fire smoldered in the central pit. At a word from Moira, the flames sprang to life.

"Welcome to my home and workshop," she said, igniting a series of oil lamps that floated into the dome over our heads further illuminating the hut's interior.

Glory moved gratefully toward the heat, holding her hands out to warm them. I sank down on a nearby bench, suddenly overcome with fatigue.

"Are you hungry?" Moira asked. "I have fresh bread and cheese."

"Not for me," I said. "I'm so tired I'm about to drop."

While Glory helped herself to the food, which she fearlessly shared with Orion, Moira led me to a low sleeping ledge that ran along the wall.

A mattress covered in animal pelts for warmth softened the surface.

"I don't expect you to give up your bed," I protested.

"These pallets are for guests," Moira assured me. "I sleep nearer the fire with Orion."

While I slipped off my shoes, she took blankets down from a shelf overhead.

Settled under their reassuring weight, I began to drift asleep watching Glory as she fed bites of cheese to the black wolf. I remember thinking, "Wait until I tell Festus about this," before I imagined I heard Tori calling to me.

In that netherworld between consciousness and slumber, I searched for my friend, but her voice came to me from far away.

Barely able to hold a coherent thought, I tried to form a mental image of the village, which I sent out along our connection hoping to reach Tori.

Like Hansel and Gretel dropping breadcrumbs, the exercise made me feel less alone — and it pushed me over the edge of awareness into a deep, dreamless sleep.

2

Shevington, Tori

Nobody expects a wedding to come off like clockwork. You're stuffing the combined insanity of two families into a shared venue with free food and booze. What could possibly go wrong?

All it takes is Crazy Uncle Poindexter getting drunk and bringing up politics or the divorced parents refusing to play nice for the happy occasion to turn into a bad remake of *Family Feud*.

But compared to the complications at Jinksy's nuptials, I would've taken a wedding-cake inspired food fight among battling kinfolks in a heartbeat.

We didn't get that kind of family drama, instead, Lucas' Uncle Morris took an action that caused a cascading catastrophe.

But I don't want to get ahead of myself. Hours passed before we began to put the pieces together — before we focused our energies on finding a way to undo what Morris Grayson did.

Instead, I want to try to do for you what Jinx would have done had our roles been reversed. I want to try to tell you what happened. That very night, I began to write it all down. The exercise gave me a way to talk to Jinx while she was gone.

We said our farewells right before the accident happened. As Jinx and I hugged, I watched the swirling energy of the "going away" portal over her shoulder. Lucas stood just outside the opening, waiting patiently for his new wife.

I whispered against her ear, "You got your fairytale wedding, Jinksy. Perfect from start to finish."

Those words haunted me for days. I never should have mentioned perfection. People are mistaken when they think the greatest beauty exists in the absence of flaws.

The search for perfection leads down the sure road to disappointment. In the Fae world, random thoughts can have substantial consequences. Had I unconsciously triggered a negative result?

In the coming hours, my internal dialogue pinged all over the place. I'm ashamed to admit that in the immediate aftermath of the accident, one of my first thoughts bordered on being downright petty.

"You just had to take a portal to France. You couldn't let me drive you to the airport in Raleigh like I wanted to?"

From that fairly absurd position, I almost immediately plunged head first into a vicious round of self-accusation. One rational corner of my mind dug in its heels and said, "Quit being superstitious." Which only led my inner alchemist to launch into a lecture about how caution and magic must go hand-in-hand.

Newton's Third Law is central to the way we use our abilities. "For every action, there is an equal and opposite reaction."

I voiced an intention that spoke to perfection, and within a matter of seconds the most imperfect thing I could imagine — one over which I had no control — happened.

Looking back, I understand that I was experiencing the first stages of survivor's guilt. Thankfully, no one suggested that to me that night. I probably would have handed them their head on a platter.

To suggest that I was a "survivor" implied that my best friend was gone for good. That was *not* an acceptable interpretation of the events.

I refused to believe that Jinx, radiating with happiness, stepped in that portal and died.

Our last conversation played on a loop in my head. She asked me, "Was today as beautiful as I think it was?"

"More beautiful," I replied. "Right down to your Prince Charming complete with uniform."

We both giggled on cue. "Did you get a good picture of the Best Raccoon in all his splendor?" she asked.

"From the back, with his tail sticking straight out of his pants," I said. "I intend to plaster the lair with poster-sized prints."

Jinx impulsively hugged me again. "Hold down the fort while I'm gone, okay?"

"Don't you worry about anything," I said. "I've got this. Concentrate on having an amazing honeymoon."

I wish I hadn't said that either. Not the part about the honeymoon. The part about me having the situation under control. That fantasy had roughly two minutes of life left.

Jinx took a few steps toward the portal, stopped and looked back at me. "Tag. You're it," she grinned. "Get that brother of mine to the altar already. Then we'll be sisters officially."

"There's been talk," I admitted, "and we're already sisters. Now go on. You're going to be late for your own honeymoon."

Even now, I see the next sequence of events like a series of stop-action photos.

Jinx entered the portal.

Morris Grayson called to Lucas.

Lucas hesitated, but joined his uncle when Jinx nodded.

Glory rushed past me, eager to get in her farewell moment with the bride. I heard her rattling on about Jinx taking lots of pictures so they could scrapbook.

With one eye on Lucas and his uncle, and the other on Jinx and Glory, I didn't think I saw what Morris did.

Hours later something changed that perception.

I did see static electricity arc across the portal. Jinx frowned, leaning away from Glory's embrace, and extending her hand to the right. She almost looked like she might be trying to catch something.

Before anyone could react, the portal opening contracted like a living creature gasping for breath. The exhalation came with a hot torrent of air and blinding light.

On instinct, I put up my hands to shield my eyes. I recognized Connor's touch when he grabbed my arms and pulled me close, putting his body between me and the explosion.

As quickly as it had ignited, the blast extinguished. I opened my eyes to find Connor searching my face. "Are you okay?" he asked urgently.

I nodded numbly. "I'm fine. What happened? Where are Jinx and Glory?"

The dragonlets mirrored my confusion and concern, screeching low over our heads and landing in an agitated line where the portal had been. Minreinth's faceted eyes searched the empty air while his flock keened nervously.

Everyone started talking at once, but one voice rose above the din.

"What the *hell* did you do?" Lucas demanded, grabbing his uncle by the shoulders and shaking the man violently. *"Tell me what you did!"*

Grayson didn't answer. Although he arranged his face to convey careful neutrality, the DGI director looked almost

pleased to be the subject of his nephew's fury. I read smug satis-
faction in the set lines of his patrician features. I wasn't sure why,
but Morris Grayson looked like a man who was getting exactly
what he wanted.

Lucas wheeled toward Barnaby and Moira. "Get this damn
thing back open. *Now*."

Moira tried to calm her nephew. She laid a restraining hand
on his arm and spoke to him in soothing tones. I didn't hear
what she said, but Lucas' response made my heart clutch with
fear.

"You don't *understand*, Aunt Moira," he said desperately. "I've
seen that flash before. The day Axe died. We have to find Jinx.
We have to find her before it's too late."

Grayson chose that moment to break his silence. He shifted
out of neutral and into cloying paternalism.

"Lucas, dear boy, this type of portal malfunction cannot be
rectified."

The unctuous, fake sympathy in the words made me want to
throw up.

"You know that I am right," he went on. "We tried everything
when Axe was killed. I'm sorry, son, but your wife is gone."

Moira's brother, Owain Kendrick, shouldered his way
through the crowd. "That will be enough out of you, Morsyn," he
said. "Leave Lucas alone."

Grayson, who evidently believed he held an advantage in the
situation, bristled. "This is none of your concern, Owain. Lucas
is the Grysundl heir. His true family will comfort him as he
recovers from this tragic loss."

Whatever he hoped to accomplish, Grayson overplayed his
hand. Lucas lunged at him. I don't know what he might have
done to the DGI director if Owain, Chase, and Festus hadn't
managed to get between them.

Still not grasping the tenuousness of his position, Grayson

plowed ahead with maddening confidence. "Nothing will help you find Jinx," he said. "The Witch of the Oak is dead. You would do well to consider your position and gain mastery of your emotions."

Chase let out a low growl. He didn't shift, but his eyes took on the menacing amber glow of the large cat that lurked barely beneath the surface of his control.

"Shut up, Morris," he warned. "My girlfriend was inside that portal, too. Shut up, or I swear to God, I won't be responsible for my actions."

"Steady son," Festus counseled. "Ripping this guy to pieces will be fun, but we need him to talk first."

Grayson paled, but he refused to give ground. "Remember to whom you are speaking," he said. I will report the both of you directly to The Registry for your animalistic behavior."

Merle, Earl, and Furl, all three in human form, moved to stand with the men confronting Grayson. "Don't waste your time," Furl said. "We represent The Registry. Chase's behavior doesn't need to be reported, but yours is another matter."

The bickering exchange might have gone on for some time if Lauren Frazier hadn't stolen center stage.

"Jinx and Glory aren't dead," she said in a ringing voice. "Morris threw something into the portal. I saw him do it."

When the eyes of all assembled turned on her, Lauren's nerve faltered briefly, but then she gathered her resolve and confronted Grayson.

"You did the same thing to my brother, didn't you? You wanted Axe out of the way to ensure Lucas had a career with the DGI. Now you've gone after Jinx because you don't think she's good enough for your nephew."

Rippling anger spread through the crowd. Grayson opened his mouth to defend himself, but then thought better of it. He settled for glaring at his accuser with flashing eyes.

Reading the delicate balance of the situation, Connor took charge. "Merle, Earl, Furl," he said, "perhaps it would be best if you were to escort Director Grayson to the Lord High Mayor's house."

"Our pleasure," Furl said, jerking his head at Grayson. "This way."

Jinx's father had been standing on the sidelines of the confrontation with clenched fists. The idea that Morris Grayson would be ushered into protective custody didn't sit well with Jeff — at all. He asked for five minutes alone with the DGI director. Greer said she could get the truth out of Grayson in three.

Her threat carried teeth — real ones. At the sight of the baobhan sith's feral smile, Grayson came to the rapid conclusion that cooperation was in his best interest. No one with a functioning brain cell wants to spend three minutes alone with an angry Scottish vampire.

As the triplets walked the Director away, Lucas turned to Lauren. "What do you know about this?"

The fury he had unleashed on his uncle was gone now, replaced by a stunned shock that his childhood friend could have been a part of his betrayal.

"Morris wanted me to get between you and Jinx," Lauren said.

I admired her courage. She faced Lucas and told him the truth.

"That's what I came here to do," she said. "I didn't care if I hurt either of you. I was still angry about Axe's accident. But then I saw you and Chase. I remembered how we all used to be when we were kids. I couldn't go through with it, Lucas. I couldn't. When I told Morris that I was out, he threatened me. I made a deal with him. I wanted the Copernican Astrolabe. He said that if I didn't help him sabotage your wedding, he'd frame me for the theft of the artifact. I swear to you, I didn't know he planned to tamper with the portal. Now I realize that he must have done the same thing to Axe. I was wrong to blame you both all these years."

A man in the crowd yelled, "She's in league with Grayson! Justice for the Witch of the Oak!"

As several others took up the call, I caught Connor's eye and shook my head. I mouthed, *"Not here."*

Connor displayed the mark of a true leader. He set his ego aside and nodded at Barnaby, the founder of Shevington, a man with whom no one in the community would argue.

Barnaby's steady gaze moved over the crowd. He spoke with authority in phrases that brooked no opposition.

"Good people," he said, "go home. There is nothing you can do here. We will tend to this matter, and see that justice is done for the Witch of the Oak. Hold her and Glory Green in your meditations."

If any of the townspeople thought to argue, their resolve melted away. One by one the citizens of Shevington left the square.

Releasing the breath I didn't realize I'd been holding, I went to Connor. "That was close," I said.

"It was," he agreed. "We'll keep Grayson out of sight. Are you coming with us?"

My eyes drifted to Kelly Hamilton who stood between my mother and Aunt Fiona. Bronwyn Sinclair and the Roanoke Witches along with the Women of the Craobhan had assembled behind them as if awaiting orders.

Connor followed my gaze. "Ah," he said. "You belong over there with them."

"Yeah," I said. "I do. If I know Myrtle, she'll have a plan that doesn't involve your mother turning Morris Grayson into a lower life form."

Widening his eyes slightly, Connor said, "You don't think Mom would do that, do you?"

"Look at her," I said. "What do you think?"

"I think," he said, "we need to keep her away from Grayson until she's calmed down a little."

"On it," I replied, giving him a quick kiss. "See you later. Okay?"

"Okay."

When Connor walked away, Moira and Greer joined me. Together we approached the assembled witches. As we drew closer, I saw Myrtle touch Kelly's shoulder.

"We cannot recklessly open a portal and attempt to follow them," the aos sí said. "With no landmark by which to plot our passage, we could become lost as well. We must speak with the Mother Tree."

"Listen to Myrtle," Fiona said. "She knows best about these things."

A looming shadow appeared behind Fiona. Her neighbor, a gentle giant of a Sasquatch named Stan, said, "Pardon me for interrupting, but the children who saw the explosion are afraid. I think we should try to help them as a group."

"Of course," Fiona said briskly. "We'll take them and their parents to my house." Then, remembering herself, she looked at her sister. "Can you manage without me?"

Kelly nodded tightly. "Take care of those babies, Fi. Jinx wouldn't want them to be afraid."

"No she wouldn't," Fiona said. "You send somebody for me if there's anything I can do. Promise?"

"Promise," Kelly assured her. Then, looking at Myrtle, she said, "Okay, let's do this."

Linking arms, the two women strode toward the Mother Tree. Brenna, Bronwyn, Moira, Laurie Proctor, Mom, and I followed.

Greer held back, but Myrtle beckoned to her. "We have need of thee, baobhan sith."

The few stragglers lingering on the sidewalks watched us. When we first began to visit The Valley, I assumed the stability of the community rested with Barnaby. I was wrong.

The beating heart of The Valley resides with the Mother Tree and her chosen witch. With Jinx gone, the people felt the foundation of their world shift.

My world felt shattered. But I refused to let my mind go there. Something deep inside told me that Jinx was alive. Yes, that sounds like I was grasping at straws, but all I can tell you is that if Jinx had been dead, I would have known.

Entertaining the possibility that she might not come back to us — even for a second — was not an option.

3

Shevington, Tori

We formed the ring around the Mother Oak. A few hours earlier, Jinx and Lucas wed in the same spot. I imagined the joy of their union lingering in the atmosphere and prayed for that energy to be a positive omen.

Myrtle brought a curtain of privacy and silence down around us. The Women of the Craobhan joined hands and bowed their heads in reverence for the Oak.

"Stay strong," Mom whispered to me. "The Mother Tree will tell us what to do."

The voice of the Oak entered my mind before I could reply. The force of the Tree's presence drove away all random thought.

More than once I'd ask Jinx to describe for me the sensation of communing with the Mother Tree.

"You have to be there, Tori," she'd say. "The Mother Tree . . . infuses your consciousness. I hate to use a worn-out word, but the experience is amazing."

I don't know if the experience is the same for everyone, but the Oak brought to me the awareness of a deeply rooted stability I sorely needed. The ageless calm of her presence made me yearn to rush forward and sling my arms around her trunk.

"Fear not. The Witch of the Oak and her companion live."

The connection felt so personal, I thought at first the Tree had spoken only to me. Relief and elation washed over me. I only realized the Oak had spoken to us all when I heard similar reactions from the other women.

When the Tree spoke again, however, her words sent a cold shiver through my body.

"They live, but not in the Three Realms as we know them."

Myrtle addressed the Oak. "They have gone into the rivers of time?"

"Yes, but with no anchor to secure their passage, they have drifted away on its currents."

"Can you track their movement?" Moira asked.

"I cannot. They made landfall far from this place. Jinx's thoughts come to me as but a distant echo. The words blur beyond meaning, but they are there."

Myrtle beckoned to Lauren who stepped forward hesitantly. "This woman admits to involvement with Morris Grayson in a plot to disrupt the wedding of the Witch of the Oak. She claims to have played no part in the action that caused the portal accident."

"Would your brother judge the actions you have taken to be worthy of your heart?" the Tree asked.

That left Lauren no place to run; the Oak cut to the heart of her motivation with a single question.

"No," Lauren said. "He would not."

"In your desire to regain your brother's company you have erred greatly," the Mother Tree said at last, "but now that your eyes have been opened to Morsyn Grysundl's true motives, I sense your earnest desire to make amends and be of assistance. Take care to earn the trust of the women who surround you."

In my mind, I finished the mini-lecture with, "Or we'll eat you alive."

The Mother Tree heard the words and scolded me privately. "Anger and fear will not bring Jinx home. Be guided only by the love you hold for your friend."

Like a petulant child caught in a bad moment, I mumbled a mental, "Sorry."

"You are afraid," the Oak said. "The way may be long and filled with doubt, but you have not lost Jinx."

I won't tell you that the Tree's words erased my fears. They didn't. But the Oak did assure me that I wasn't deluding myself.

Somewhere, though she might be very far away, my best friend was alive. My job was to help find her.

When the group emerged from beneath the shelter of the Oak, Kelly spoke to the Women of the Craobhan. "Go home to your Mother Trees," she ordered. "Be prepared to face any threat to the Grid that may arise."

Kelly looked at me next. "Come here," she said softly.

We embraced, and she rubbed soothing circles on my back. "We'll bring her home, honey." I felt her head lift. "We will bring them both home, won't we?" she asked someone standing behind us.

Myrtle answered. "Yes. Let us go to the Lord High Mayor's house and plan our next actions. I am inclined to leave Morris Grayson to the men while we adjourn to Moira's workshop to further question Lauren Frazier and to explore the metaphysical options at our disposal."

"Agreed," Kelly said, "but I need a minute with Jeff in private before we go inside. I'll be right back."

She crossed the street and went to her husband who was

standing with Festus and Jilly Pepperdine. The two of them discreetly moved away to give Kelly and Jeff some privacy.

Jeff has always been like a second father to me, but now that my dad is dead, we've grown even closer. I read equal parts anger and terror in the man's body language.

Jeff greeted his wife with a helpless, frustrated gesture. I wasn't sure if he wanted to hit something or break down and cry. Kelly pulled him into a kiss, wrapping him into a long, tight embrace.

Since his daughter's powers awakened, and his wife reclaimed her magic, Jeff has become comfortable in the complex world we inhabit. That speaks volumes for a man who possesses only rudimentary abilities of his own.

In the situation we now faced, Jeff was completely out of his element, but that didn't stop him from being a typical Southern father who wanted to protect his baby girl. Unfortunately, taking a 12-gauge to Morris Grayson might make Jeff feel better, but it wouldn't do anything to bring Jinx and Glory home.

Feeling like a voyeur, I looked away toward the bay window at the front of the mayor's house. Two figures stood silhouetted against the light. Lucas gesticulating wildly while Connor talked to him in what I knew would be calm, reasoned tones.

I dreaded going inside. At the moment I had nothing better to offer the man than some silly, empty platitude like, "Everything will be alright."

People don't say things like that because they know that everything will be alright, they say them because they can't stand not to say something even if that something is in no way useful or comforting.

A polite cough at my elbow brought my attention back to my immediate surroundings. Beau Longworth stood next to me with Rodney tucked under the collar of his suit jacket. The rat's eyes instantly filled with tears.

"Don't," I said urgently. "Don't cry, Rodney. Please. If you cry, I'll cry and I can't. Not yet."

Wiping at his eyes with one pink paw, Rodney nodded.

"What may we do to help, Miss Tori?" Beau asked. "We await your orders."

My orders?

Regardless of what century he finds himself in, Beau remains a military man to his core. Intellectually, I understood his choice of words, but I saw myself as Jinx's sidekick, not her second in command.

I stalled with a question of my own. "Where's Darby?"

"He and Miss Amity are with Madam Kaveh," Beau said. "They are all inclined to channel their anxiety into productive labor."

"What are they doing?"

"Marshalling the efforts of volunteers to package and distribute the food and drink from the reception so that it does not go to waste."

"Good idea," I said, "Jinx would . . . will . . . like that."

"I, too, wish to contribute in a meaningful way," Beau said. "Pray give me a task."

Myrtle must have seen me struggling to come up with an answer.

"Go back to the fairy mound," she said. "Take Amity and Darby with you. We don't know how long Jinx and Glory will be gone. We must prepare to disguise their absence from the townspeople of Briar Hollow."

Thank God her mind was working in the long term because mine wasn't.

To cover the wedding and honeymoon, we'd floated the story that Jinx would be away at a small business convention for a week.

When she and Lucas returned, they would announce their

marriage and invite everyone to a big party.

If we couldn't get Jinx and Glory back in a week's time, we'd need a longer-term solution.

With a direction at which to point his proverbial guns, Beau instantly took charge.

"Fear not," he said. "I will ensure the business operates as normal. For the time being, I will explain your absence, Miss Tori, by indicating you chose at the last moment to accompany Miss Jinx."

Rodney wormed out from under Beau's collar to stand erect on his shoulder. The rat pointed at his chest and raised his eyewhiskers questioningly.

"I know you want to help, little dude," I said, "but I don't know what we're going to do or where we'll have to go to do it. Beau and Darby need you. Go with them, okay?"

The rat mimed drawing a sword from an imaginary scabbard and striking a combative pose.

"We'll call on the Knights of the Rodere if we need you guys. I promise."

Valor comes in all shapes and sizes. Rodney may be the smallest member of our Scooby gang, but his bravery knows no bounds. He wanted to be on the front lines, but he also understood when not to argue. He did, however, have another idea.

Rodney mimed typing on a keyboard.

I frowned. "Huh? I'm not following."

The rat mimicked opening and reading a letter.

"Oh!" I said. "Glory's column! When is it due?"

Beau said, "*The Briar Hollow Banner* appears on newsstands each Tuesday. Miss Glory must submit her material 24 hours in advance."

Rodney nodded, pointing emphatically at his chest.

"You're sure you can answer the letters?" I asked.

The rat bobbed his head up and down.

"Okay," I said. "It's all yours. Ask Beau and Darby if you need help, and be sure to take good care of Jinksy's cats."

Clasping his paws over his heart, Rodney puckered his tiny lips and gave me an air smooch.

"I love you, too," I said, choking on the words. "I'll see you soon."

Note to Future Self. Get all agreements from super-intelligent rodents in writing.

Beau walked away to find Amity and Darby. Across the street, Kelly, who had now been joined by Bronwyn, beckoned to us.

When Myrtle and I went over, Kelly said, "Laurie volunteered to take Lauren ahead to the university. I didn't think it would be productive to have her in the room with Lucas. He's already agitated enough."

Glancing up at the window, I said, "It looks like Connor has at least gotten him to sit down. That's a start."

"A small one," Kelly said, taking Jeff's hand and climbing the front steps.

When we went inside the first thing I saw was Greer handing Lucas a glass of whisky.

I'd lost track of the baobhan sith when we'd all dispersed at the base of the Mother Tree, but I wasn't surprised she'd gone to be with her partner.

The pair work seamlessly as DGI agents, but Greer, from the perspective of her greater age, thinks of Lucas in protective terms as her "laddie."

Lucas thanked her for the drink and asked, "Why aren't they back? How long can it take to ask the Mother Tree a question?"

"Longer than you might expect," Myrtle said, entering the room with the rest of us trailing behind.

The aos sí moved to the hearth. "The Oak believes that Jinx

and Glory live, but their life force cannot be found in the Three Realms as we know them."

Lucas looked hopeful but confused. "What does that mean? How can they not be in the Three Realms?"

Moira sat down beside her nephew. "The Oak questioned Lauren, who believes she has evidence that her brother is alive in an alternate time stream. Lauren wanted the Copernican Astrolabe as a tool in her search for him. If Morris sent Axe into a variant reality, he likely sent Jinx and Glory to the same place. We are about to adjourn to the University to speak with Lauren at greater length."

"Fine," Lucas said, jumping to his feet. "Tell me where Jinx and Glory are, and I'll go after them myself."

Rube waddled in from the foyer. "It don't work like that, Hat Man," he said. "Alternate time is hinky business."

"What do you know about it?" Lucas demanded.

"Not enough," the raccoon admitted, "but the Pretty People deal in this stuff. You know how they are. It's all more, more, more with them. They pay guys to roam around in alternate time and get stuff for them. Lauren works for the Sídhe. I'm guessing that's how she got mixed up in this business."

Moira nodded. "Rube is correct. In acquiring alternate time stream antiquities for the Fae, Lauren discovered a sketch from some version of Elizabethan Londinium. This is the image. Adeline extracted it from Lauren's phone."

She handed Lucas a computer tablet. "Oh my God," he said, sinking back into his seat. "That is Axe. What are we going to do?"

"We will pool our talents and find a way to locate Jinx and Glory no matter where they are," Moira said. "I believe that Festus and Jilly can help us gain access to the Copernican Astrolabe."

Chase looked at his father in confusion. "How can you help with a Blacklist item?"

Festus, who had stolen a moment to shift into feline form, scratched at his whiskers, "There are some things you don't know about me, boy. I work with the Bureau of Enchanted Artifacts and Relics. Or I *did* work for them. I've been offered a promotion to Blacklist Agent."

"You have?" Jilly said. "When did that happen?"

"Last week, in relation to that thing we worked on."

Greer arched an eyebrow. "Would that 'thing' possibly have occurred on the Isle of Wight?"

"Possibly," Festus replied, "but the point is that I've been given latitude to form my team as I please. Lucas, we won't rest until we find the girls."

Turning haunted eyes on the werecat, Lucas said, "How long do you think it will take?"

"I don't know son," Festus said, "I honestly don't know."

4

The Druid Forests of Kent, 1590, Jinx

T he next morning I woke up staring at a stacked rock wall. Briefly confused, I rolled over only to find myself face to face with Orion. The wolf's penetrating gaze quickly snapped me back to the reality of my circumstances.

All the details flooded back in at once: my wedding, the portal accident, and our forest encounter with alternate time Moira.

A sound from the hearth drew my attention to the center of the room where the alchemist worked by the fireside preparing what appeared to be breakfast.

Although I hadn't spoken, she knew I was awake.

"Your companion still sleeps," she said quietly. "I have acquired additional clothing for you. Change now, so there is no risk anyone will see you and become suspicious."

Carefully throwing back the blankets to avoid startling Orion, I sorted through the pile of items lying on the low table beside my sleeping ledge.

I found a rough tunic, a belt, and shoes. The garments were

similar to Moira's. I guessed Druids didn't waste much time worrying about fashion.

When I glanced around for a place to change, my cheeks flushed with sudden embarrassment at the thought of disrobing in the open.

Moira must have sensed my discomfort. She spoke a few words in Latin and brushed her fingers toward a blank stretch of wall.

As I watched, a branch smaller than my arm emerged from between the stones. The wood grew outward 4 or 5 feet before it circled back on itself and re-entered the wall.

A long sheet of fabric materialized over the impromptu rack and dropped toward the floor. Leaves sprouted along the top of the curtain, lacing themselves through the fabric to hold it in place.

"Thank you," I said. "In my world most people don't do everything in one room."

"I understand," Moira said. "Forgive me for not considering that. I have lived alone for many years. Matters of privacy do not readily occur to me. Tonight I will create similar curtains around your beds."

For someone who wasn't used to having roommates, Moira proved to be a thoughtful and flexible hostess. Exactly what I would have expected from the woman I knew and loved, which made it all the harder to remember this Moira was not my Moira.

Both versions of the alchemist also possessed a keen sense of strategy. Addressing the issue of our clothing was definitely a high priority item.

Glory and I arrived in the 16th century dressed for a 21st century summer wedding. Everything about us screamed, "we're not from around here." That red flag we didn't need.

Before I stepped behind the drape, Moira handed me a soft leather pouch and a small role of linen.

"Hang this from your belt," she said. "Hide your rings securely in the linen then place the bundle at the bottom of the pocket."

Not understanding the reference, I said, "Which pocket?"

Moira pointed to the pouch. "There."

"Oh, sorry," I said. "To me a pocket is a piece of material sewn into the seam of a pair of pants or a dress."

"A cumbersome solution," Moira said. "Why resort to moving your possessions with each change of clothing?"

I will admit to wasting time in my life putting mental energy into topics not worthy of the effort, but reengineering the common pocket wasn't one of them. I did, however, have to concede that Moira had a point.

Leaving matters of clothing design aside, I said, "Why do you want me to hide my wedding rings?"

"My people are not given to ornamentation," Moira said. "Only a noble would wear such stones, and yours glitter with unusual brightness. Are they enchanted?"

"No," I explained. "In the future, people who make jewelry have learned to leave a hole at the bottom of the setting to let light pass through the stone."

"Fascinating," Moira said. "Such a simple thing to create so large a difference."

For some reason that observation stuck in my mind, and would come back to me in a powerful way before Glory and I found our way home.

When I went behind the curtain, I stared at my engagement ring, and the gold band Lucas had put on my finger beneath the spreading branches of the Mother Tree.

My throat knotted with pain when I slipped them off, carefully rolling the jewelry in the linen and placing the ball in the bottom corner of the pouch. At least there, I could touch the bag's exterior and know what lay hidden beneath my fingers.

Next, I pulled the mystery object out of my jacket and examined it. The thing looked like a brass bar with a circle in the center and some kind of hardware on the end.

I debated about showing it to Moira and then changed my mind. My Dad always says never show all the cards in your hand until you have to. The object went into the bottom of the bag with my rings.

Donning the tunic, I cinched the waist with the length of leather that served as a belt. The shoes puzzled me. There didn't seem to be a left or right.

After I crammed my feet into the uncomfortable monstrosities, I used magic to conform the shoes to the shape of my feet. Satisfied that I would be able to survive walking in them, I tied the pocket on the belt and stepped back into the room.

Moira looked up from the fire where she was dishing thick porridge into a bowl. "You use your magic without thinking," she cautioned. "Here among my people magic infuses our existence, but beyond the confines of the village, do not so casually lean on your powers."

Accepting the food, I sat down on a stool near the fire and began to eat. Traveling through time can leave a person hungry enough to eat a horse. I've never been a fan of oatmeal, but I finished the first helping in record time and asked for a second, dousing the mixture with a liberal portion of honey.

"Why shouldn't I use magic?" I asked between bites. "Last night you told us that the Fae are an integral part of this world."

"We are," Moira said, "but strange currents blow across the Channel from the Continent. Religious ideas that seek to portray our people as instruments of the Christian devil proliferate. So long as Brenna Sinclair holds power as the Ruling Elder, and maintains her alliance with Queen Elizabeth, we enjoy a measure of safety. There are, however, growing acts of violence in the countryside. Regrettably, most are perpetrated against women believed to be witches."

Movie-inspired images of prisoners tied to stakes atop blazing pyres flashed across my mind. "Got it," I said. "I'll be more careful. Are the women who are being victimized actual witches?"

Sympathetic pain filled Moira's eyes. "Not in all instances," she said. "Innocent humans are dying under accusation of the practice of black magic. In a few cases, the Fae have been able to intervene and stop the imprisonments and executions, but the incidents are spreading. Many Fae now fear to become involved lest they too become targets."

"Are your people in danger?" I asked.

Moira shook her head. "Our association with the humans in the countryside stretches into the time before time. They trust us as wise counselors and guardians of the Natural Order. Besides, we can always disappear into the forest veil."

"You can't seriously believe that an angry mob couldn't find you in the trees?" I said incredulously.

"The Veil is an enchantment," Moira replied. "One into which we can disappear for centuries if we so choose. The most virulent incidents have occurred far from here in small, isolated localities."

An infection always starts in a small wound. Untreated, it goes on to ravage, and even kill the body.

When I pointed that out, Moira said, "You speak a greater truth than you may realize. If we are to be honest with one another, the only place where the Fae and humans still mingle freely is in Londinium itself."

"In our world we call the city London for the human realm, Londinium in the Otherworld, and Lundenwic for the Middle Realm."

"Here we use the historic name Londinium," she said, "although many have begun to shorten it to London."

Our conversation awakened Glory, who ducked behind the curtain and changed into her new clothes. She emerged with such explosive excitement even Orion moved back a step.

"Jinx! I don't think I'm shrinking and greening anymore!"

For Moira's benefit, I offered a trimmed down explanation of what Festus refers to as "The Ballad of Glory Green."

"An evil sorcerer victimized Glory with magic that altered her size and skin tone. She managed to lift the spell, but the results have been unpredictable, especially when she's upset about something."

With disarming honesty, Glory said, "I go green sometimes. It's hard to hide."

Moira couldn't keep from smiling. "Undoubtedly," she said. "I have not noticed any alteration in your size or complexion since last evening."

Almost jumping up and down with excitement, Glory said, "Me either! I was really scared when you showed up in the clearing last night. And oh my goodness gracious, I thought Orion was going to eat us, but he's just the sweetest puppy dog ever, even if he is a wolf. Then last night, I had dreams about everybody back home, but when I woke up, I was still normal sized and everything. That's good, right?"

I assured her that it was, indeed, good. Not having Glory turning chartreuse in front of people already on the lookout for witches was a definite plus.

Remembering her manners, Glory thanked Moira for the clothes. "How do your shoes fit?" I asked.

"Okay, I guess," Glory said. "I couldn't figure out which one was right and which one was left."

Laughing, I said, "Let me help you with that."

After I spoke the simple incantation, Glory bobbed up and

down on her toes a few times. "Oh!" she said. "That's so much better. What's for breakfast?"

While Glory ate her porridge, I enjoyed another cup of the hot, strong tea Moira brewed for us. The liquid wasn't as dark as coffee, but it had a similar rejuvenating effect. Tori would've said the stuff made my brain cells kick into gear.

The idea touched off an instant wave of homesickness. Under normal circumstances, Tori and I would have been enjoying a breakfast of coffee and bear claws in the espresso bar and planning our day.

Outside, I heard the sounds of the village waking up. We couldn't stay inside Moira's hut forever. Sooner or later, we had to go out and interact with the Druids.

Honestly, I was curious to see their everyday world and to learn more about them. If we were here, we might as well look for a positive take away from the situation.

"Moira," I said, "do you mind if I ask a few questions?"

Filling her own mug with tea, she said, "Please do. The more knowledge you have of our world, the more successfully you will negotiate the ruse we have constructed to explain your presence here."

There it was again. Something I would've expected my Moira to say. Knowing that I could still count on the alchemist's quick and all-encompassing thought processes made me feel much more secure in this alien place.

"Last night you told us that Brenna Sinclair serves as Ruling Elder," I said. "In our time stream, becoming Creavit was considered heresy. Is the transformation acceptable here?"

Moira studied the flames in the grate, seeming to gather her thoughts. "Do you know the Greek root of the word 'heresy?'"

I shook my head.

"Originally, the word meant choice," she said. "The fathers of the Christian church maintain that women are more prone to heresy."

Getting into a discussion about feminism through the realms might've been interesting, but I forced myself to stay on point.

"Are most of the Creavit here women?"

"They are," Moira said. "By design. The originators of *Proditor Magicae* were two men, Irenaeus Chesterfield and Reynold Isherwood. They preyed upon innocent children, stealing their magic to fuel the transformation. For their crimes, the Queen ordered them drawn and quartered."

The Fae are difficult to kill, but an execution that involves hanging, being disemboweled while still alive, and then being ripped into four pieces would do anyone in.

"What happened to the Creavit who had already been made?"

"You must remember that Her Majesty is a halfling," Moira replied. "She has scant tolerance for the misappropriation of magic. Her father, King Henry, beheaded her mother for charges of having abused her Fae powers to bewitch him. In truth, no magic beyond that of a comely face and rounded breast were ever needed for Good King Hal to take notice of a wench."

I've seen pictures of Henry VIII. The fact that he got six women to marry him still amazes me.

"So how did Elizabeth deal with the existing made practitioners?" I asked.

Still staring into the fire, Moira said, "I cannot say Her Majesty acted with fairness. Many of the men were charged with having been in league with Chesterfield and Isherwood. They were punished accordingly. Thanks to Her Majesty's relationship with Brenna Sinclair, however, the women enjoyed much greater protection."

Our Brenna overcame the excesses of her past to become a new person. Still, those excesses are the stuff of legend.

"How did Brenna and the Queen become friends?"

"Following the execution of Chesterfield and Isherwood, the capital suffered a virulent outbreak of the pox. The superstitious claimed it was God's punishment for the Creavit heresy. Brenna protected Her Majesty from contracting the illness. Their friendship was formed first on a foundation of gratitude. Then they found common purpose."

So much for the slender hope that alternate Brenna might still wind up conveniently imprisoned in a cave on the Orkney Islands.

Moira went on to describe a radically different version of Elizabethan England, one in which two powerful women seized control of the government, the intellectual life of the realm, and the fruits of its commerce.

The partnership created a vibrant and cosmopolitan city, one in which people from all the realms interacted openly. As head of the Church of England, Elizabeth successfully shielded the Creavit women from charges of heresy by the rising forces of Reformation Christianity.

Glory, who had been listening to Moira speak with rapt attention, asked, "What's happened to change that? I heard you warn Jinx about using her magic. In our time stream, witch hunting in England didn't pick up momentum until after Elizabeth's death. What's different here?"

The intellectual tone of the questions startled me. Even though I knew Glory had earned one or more college degrees, it startled me to hear her talking like an academic, and not an airhead.

Moira hesitated. "I confess I find it difficult not to probe your knowledge of potential events in my world," she said. "There is great controversy about who will follow Elizabeth on the throne. Many fear that it will be Brenna herself."

When Glory looked at me, not knowing what to say, I

jumped in. "That doesn't happen in our time stream," I said. "We have no way of predicting what might happen here."

"Your caution is commendable," Moira said. She looked at Glory. "To answer your question, many of the common people believe that Elizabeth angered God when she shielded the Creavit. Forces of the Spanish government seek to restore the old faith to this land. Those who hunt witches are in sympathy with that goal."

I was beginning to put the pieces together. "You're worried for us on two fronts," I said. "In the wrong place at the wrong time we could be taken as Creavit heretics, but we could also be mistaken for foreign agents."

"Yes," Moira said. "I do not wish to give you false hope, but there is a man living in Londinium. He is part of the Lime Street community of botanists. There has been great speculation about his true origins. His experimentation with radical ideas has made him an object of interest to the Ruling Elder, and to the forces that seek to root out heresy in the land."

My heart skipped a beat. "Do you think he could be someone lost in time as well?"

"In truth, I cannot say. But the thought that he might be, occupied my mind deep into the night."

"What is this man's name?" I asked.

"He is called Alex Farnsworth."

I was certain Morris Grayson threw the flat, brass bar into the portal. Lucas had been involved in a portal accident that resulted in Axe Frazier's death. Those two things didn't add up to a coincidence in my book.

Could Alex Farnsworth be Axe Frazier? With Grayson as the common denominator, it might be possible.

5

Shevington, Tori

Greer joined our silent group as we walked from the Lord High Mayor's house to the University under a night sky ablaze with stars. Crossing the quadrangle, we passed clumps of students who tried not to stare.

Our footsteps echoed in the hallways of the alchemy building and on the stairs to Moira's workshop on the top floor. Her assistant, Dewey, had a fire lit. An odd assortment of chairs ringed the hearth, two of them occupied by Laurie Proctor and Lauren Frazier.

A nearby table held trays with mug. I sank into one of the seats nearest the fireplace and accepted a hot cup of tea from my mother.

"You keeping it together?" she asked quietly.

"I am," I replied, sounding stronger than I felt, "but Beau's right; it would help if I had something to do."

Myrtle overheard the conversation. "Positive action would be a comfort to each of us, but first we must take stock of the

current situation. Issues involving time offer unique complications."

Kelly sat down on the hearth with her back to the flames.
The night was warm, but I saw her shiver.

"Explain what you mean by 'complications,'" she said. "Back
at the Mother Tree, you referred to the 'rivers' of time. Plural."

Myrtle joined her and motioned for the remaining women to
claim chairs.

Looking at Greer, the aos sí said, "Baobhan sith, what do you
experience when you suspend time?"

"The force of a surging tide," Greer replied. "The intensity
increases with each moment."

Nodding, Myrtle said, "That is what you feel when standing
in a single time stream. There are, however, many such temporal
channels. Their combined force and weight, none of us can
imagine."

Dozens of sci-fi references sprang to mind; all useless in
present company. I may have spent two years learning magic
and alchemy, but apart from our experiences with Irenaeus
Chesterfield, all my time travel knowledge I owed to *Star Trek*.

"You're saying Jinx and Glory have gone to an alternate
version of our reality?" I asked.

Myrtle shook her head. "That," she said, "would be the most
favorable of outcomes. In truth, the landscape of time offers
many directions and possibilities."

Rubbing a hand across my eyes to keep from crying in frustration, I said, "Could we maybe get a visual aid on that?"

"Allow me," Bronwyn offered, leaning forward and using her
index fingers to trace shimmering lines in the air.

She interlaced blue verticals and green horizontals to craft a
square. The result could have been a complicated board game,
or one of those plastic mini looms we used at summer camp.

But then Bronwyn began to snap her fingers. The square

duplicated with each ringing *thwump* until a cube floated suspended over the hearth rug.

My heart sank. "How many dimensions are we talking about here?" I asked.

"That number," Bronwyn replied, "cannot be quantified. At any moment a single choice or even the consideration of a choice can, under the right conditions, create another avenue in the complete construct."

No one spoke until Greer observed quietly, "Even the most difficult of puzzles can be solved. Where do we begin?"

"We begin," Brenna replied, "with things long hidden in the darkest corners of Fae history."

"Not again," I groaned. "Why is it that every time something goes wrong around here one of you tell us there's *another* something you've been hiding?"

"We have hidden nothing," Myrtle assured me. "Brenna speaks of an old heresy long abandoned, of reckless knowledge set aside in favor of living life according to the natural order of our world."

Lifting my head, I said, "Exactly when have the bad guys in our world *ever* abided by the natural order and common sense?"

Regret washed over me the instant Brenna replied to my cutting observation.

"Tori is correct," she said. "I have made a life of uncovering the forbidden secrets of magic and bending them to my self-interest with no regard to the tenets of Fae law."

"I shouldn't have said that, Brenna," I apologized. "I'm tired and scared. I didn't mean you. You're one of the good guys."

The sorceress smiled. "Now I am among the virtuous," she said, "but if I possess insight into the darker underside of the magical world, is it not to our advantage?"

That got my attention. "Do you know what Grayson did?"

"No," Brenna said, "but I think I know what he was *trying* to do. I believe the implement he threw into the portal matrix to have been an instrument of temporal navigation."

Lauren Frazier spoke for the first time. "As the director of the DGI, Morris has access to the Blacklist vaults. The Copernican Astrolabe is considered to be the greatest of the time relics held there."

When everyone's gaze shifted in her direction, the woman paled, but Lauren met our suspicious eyes without flinching.

"Were you telling the truth when you said you didn't know what Grayson intended to do to my daughter?" Kelly asked.

"Yes," Lauren said. "I had no idea he planned to trigger that portal explosion, but I did agree to try to get between Lucas and Jinx in exchange for the Astrolabe. I was still angry about my brother. I didn't care about Lucas' happiness or Chase's either for that matter."

I could tell from the expression on my mother's face that she didn't intend to believe one word out of Lauren's mouth regardless of what the Mother Oak said. Lauren was an interloper, one who faced a steep uphill climb to redemption.

"The Copernican Astrolabe," Mom snapped, "is a registered Blacklist item stuck so far back in a containment vault it will never see the light of day again."

"That would be true if all the rules were obeyed," Lauren said. "Morris doesn't think rules apply to him. He had access to the Astrolabe, and he agreed to give it to me."

Before Mom could fire off another question, Myrtle took charge. "What led you to seek the Astrolabe as the correct tool for your search?"

"That's a long story," Lauren said, "which I will tell you, but please believe me. I would never have agreed to help Grayson trap Jinx and Glory in time the way he trapped Axe."

"Why should we believe you?" Kelly asked. "You've already

admitted you came to Shevington to sabotage my daughter's wedding."

"I agreed to *try* to sabotage it," Lauren said. "The instant I saw Lucas and Jinx together, I knew there was no point."

"Yet you came to the ceremony on Morris Grayson's arm," Greer said. "That behavior alone calls into questions your assertions of innocence."

Lauren nodded. "That's fair," she said. "Morris threatened to frame me for the theft of the Astrolabe and to expose my involvement with the Sídhe antiquities pirates. It didn't make sense to me at the time, but now I think I understand."

"What do you understand?" Greer asked.

"Morris intended to frame me for the portal accident, too," Lauren replied. "It would seem to be working."

No one rushed to assure her to the contrary until Myrtle spoke.

"Our judgment of your motives remains an open question. Tell us your story; then we will decide."

I don't know if I'm a good judge of character or not, but when Lauren began with, "I've loved Chase and Lucas like brothers my whole life," I heard truth in the statement.

You can't fake a lifetime of friendship, even when it's been derailed by the kind of tragedy that drove Chase, Lucas, and Lauren apart.

Thanks to his werecat blood, Chase is in his mid-80s but doesn't look a day over 35. Lucas and Lauren enjoy the same agelessness thanks to their Fae heritage, a mix of Welsh water elf and Druid in his case, and pure Seonaidh in hers.

Pronounced "sho-na," the obscure water spirits are distantly related to Lucas' ancestors, the Gwragedd Annwn and are now so rare, they are typically lumped in with that race. A fact that allowed Morris Grayson to claim that Lauren was a Gwragedd

Annwn noblewoman and thus a more suitable match for his nephew.

Brodie Frazier, raised and educated Lauren and her brother, Axe, in the human realm, in Raleigh.

"That's where my father met Festus McGregor," Lauren said. "The Fae community rallied around Festus after his wife's death. That group included Lestyn and Arianwen Grysundl. After they were killed, Morris took Lucas to Londinium, but we stayed close. Morris was different then. We all looked forward to holidays at his country home. He was everyone's favorite uncle."

I couldn't keep the sarcasm out of my voice. "From everything Jinx has told me, *Uncle* Morris slipped a major screw somewhere along the way."

"He did," Lauren said. "Morris had ambitions for his nephew that Lucas didn't embrace. If Lucas married the Witch of the Oak, he would be required to pledge his allegiance to the Mother Tree. Once he did that, Morris would lose all hope of ever getting Lucas on the Grysundl throne."

To say that Lucas didn't "embrace" his uncle's plans was at best a polite deflection. Lucas wanted *nothing* to do with his royal heritage. Zero. Nada. Zip.

He only wore the uniform at the wedding to make Jinx happy — well, that, and everyone wanted to see Rube decked out in the best man's miniature version of the finery.

Smiling inwardly at the memory of the regimental raccoon in all his sartorial spiffiness, I turned my attention back to Lauren. She described the ambitions she, Chase, Lucas, and Axe had nursed to become DGI agents in their younger days.

"Our test scores were good enough to get us into the academy on our own," Lauren said, "but having Morris on our side helped. We didn't understand that Morris thought Lucas was only going through a phase before he took up the Grysundl throne."

Grayson also didn't count on his nephew showing an unusual aptitude for DGI work. By the second year of his training, Lucas seemed destined for a brilliant career, a fact that appealed to his uncle's ego.

"Morris got behind Lucas then," Lauren said, "but when it became obvious Axe would graduate first in our class ahead of his nephew, Morris couldn't stand it. I believe that's when he decided to get rid of my brother."

"Tell us again what happened the day of the accident," Myrtle said.

"All DGI agents are schooled in portal mechanics," Lauren said. "The four of us typically worked as a team. The day Axe disappeared, we had a simple assignment to repair a Class I malfunction."

I interrupted. "What type of malfunction is that, exactly?"

"Frequency fluctuations in the portal matrix," Lauren replied. "There are a series of stabilizing incantations that don't require advanced magical prowess to execute."

She explained the spells in mechanical terms; word sequences to access and retune the energy field's modulations. Straightforward recitation magic.

"Lucas and Chase ran the standard sequence," Lauren said. "The test portal stabilized. Axe stepped inside to verify the repair. When he did, the opening exploded. What happened to Jinx and Glory was identical to what I saw that day."

A thorough search and rescue operation followed the incident, but after two weeks, the DGI had no choice. They declared Axe Frazier dead.

"The higher-ups, Morris included, made it sound like my brother died in the line of duty rather than falling victim to what I then believed to be a careless accident caused by Lucas and Chase," Lauren said bitterly. "Putting Axe's name on a plaque at headquarters was supposed to help. It didn't. Everyone went on with their lives, including the two men who were supposed to be my best friends. The fancy memorial didn't work for me. I didn't accept that the DGI's inability to find Axe meant he was gone for good."

Within the year, Lauren left the DGI. She did a short stint with IBIS and then took up private "security" work. She candidly admitted that her activities increasingly skirted the edge of legality, especially when she became an exclusive consultant with the High Sídhe.

"The elves enjoy their prominence in human society," Lauren said. "They pioneered the art of being famous for no reason. Between plastic surgery and glamour, it didn't take them long to become *the* 'A' list celebrities. To them, money is a toy. They're willing to pay high prices, and I'm willing to collect the fees."

Like most rich people, Fae or human, the Sídhe ultimately struggled with high-living boredom.

"I'm not sure how or when the bands of temporal pirates got started," Lauren said. "The crews hold their secrets close, but over the last three to four years, high dollar black markets in alternate time antiquities have started to thrive in Vegas and Los Angeles."

Wealthy Sídhe collectors went wild over variations of famous works of art, first editions of best sellers with radically different endings, and mystical objects "lost" in our timestream, but available in others.

"The Pretty People prefer to work through a go-between to avoid the appearance of anything tawdry," Lauren said. "I culti-vated connections with the most reliable pirate crews and brokered deals with the Sídhe. Before long the best customers began to make special requests. The rarer the item, the greater the danger, the higher the price."

Kelly didn't disguise her disgust. "You played with the fabric of time for profit," she said flatly.

"I did," Lauren said, "but my bill came due. One of my top operatives came back from a version of Elizabethan England with a journal kept by Dr. Roderigo Lopez, the queen's physician."

Moira frowned. "Elizabeth executed Dr. Lopez for supposed treason in 1594," she said. "I remember the case well. When it was found that the Earl of Essex wrongly accused the doctor of an attempted poison plot, the Queen made restitution to the widow. I have no memory of any journal circulating in London."

"You wouldn't," Lauren said, "because in our timeline there was no journal. The pirates, however, went to a London where Lopez was never executed. He remained Elizabeth's respected physician and astrologer until he died peacefully of old age."

"Would that the Lopez I knew had been granted such mercy," Moira said. "The journal you described contained the sketch you have shared with us?"

"Yes," Lauren said. "Lopez describes the man in the drawing as a 'foreigner' at court, a botanist from the continent prominent in the Lime Street naturalist community. That man is my brother, imprisoned in time by Morris Grayson the same way Jinx and Glory are now trapped. I'm certain of it."

"You planned to use the Copernican Astrolabe to locate and rescue your brother," Myrtle said. "Do you know how to wield the instrument or did you intend to turn a dangerous Blacklist item over to one of these temporal brigands whose exploits have lined your pockets?"

Lauren reddened. "I wouldn't have let the pirates keep the artifact," she said, "but I know nothing about temporal navigation. I needed them, and they said they needed the Astrolabe, so I went after it. I'll use my contacts to help get your friends back, but I want my brother back as well."

Even though I believed most of what Lauren said, I couldn't ignore the glaring hole in her story. "These pirate friends of yours have been jumping around timestreams without the astrolabe," I said. "How have they been doing that?"

"These aren't people who like to be questioned," Lauren replied.

Greer, who had listened to the entire recitation of facts without comment, smiled in that feral way of hers that will turn your blood to ice if you're not one hundred percent certain the redhead is on your side.

"*That*," she said, "depends entirely on who asks the questions."

Lauren's eyes widened. "Okay," she said, drawing the word out, "let me rephrase that. *I'm* not the one to ask the questions. I place orders. They fill them. Beyond that, I know what they do is dangerous. Nothing more."

Greer stood up. "Then let that be the first answer we seek," she said. "With your permission, aos sí, I will escort Miss Frazier to Las Vegas and meet with her temporal associates."

Lauren didn't look happy about the baobhan sith's plans, but she got to her feet. "With all due respect," she said, "I don't think they'll talk to you."

"Perhaps not," Greer said, "but when I drag them in front of Fer Dorich, I suspect they will become more loquacious."

Something akin to fear now registered in Lauren's eyes. "You know the Dark Druid?"

"I do," Greer said, "and he is not nearly so impressive as he would have you believe. Take my hand."

"Why?"

The redhead's smile returned. "Because you will find the flight of the baobhan sith most unsettling otherwise."

6

Shevington

Connor tracked Lucas' restless course back and forth across the parlor rug until he couldn't stand the pacing another minute. "Would you *please* sit down? I don't want to have to explain to Jinx why I let her husband drop dead of a heart attack."

Lucas, now out of uniform and back in his usual clothes, shoved his hands in his pockets and kept walking. "Let me talk to my uncle, and I'll sit down."

"We have to wait until Barnaby finishes his mirror call with the Ruling Elder," Connor said. "Until then, we don't know how much authority we have to detain Director Grayson."

Turning sharply on his heel, Lucas said, "I have all the *authority* I need to do whatever I like with the man. He's been trying to get me to take the Grysundl throne for years. Fine. I'm willing for my first royal action to be a public hanging."

"You don't mean that," Connor said. "Try to stay calm."

Chase jumped up from his chair and joined Lucas. "How are we supposed to stay *calm*?" he asked. "Jinx and Glory are drifting farther away from us every second while we waste time on Fae politics and etiquette."

Festus, who had been watching the scene from the hearth, flicked his tail in consternation. "Both of you sit down. *Now.* You're acting like a couple of hot-headed idiots."

They exchanged a sullen glance, but Lucas and Chase did as they were told.

"Nobody is going off half-cocked," Festus continued. "You know the plan. Myrtle and the others explore the metaphysics of this mess. We talk to Morris and get what we can out of him. Everybody meets back here in the morning to compare notes."

Across the room, Jeff stared at his watch. "I think it's morning already," he observed randomly. "Or at least it's morning in Briar Hollow. I have never been able to figure out how to keep time in both places at once."

Jilly looked up from the computer tablet where she'd been working with Adeline Shevington researching the alternate antiquities trade. She smiled at Jeff, "It's past midnight," she said. "Are you sure you don't want to lie down for a while?"

Jeff shook his head. "I'm with Lucas and Chase. I'm not going anywhere until we talk to Grayson *and* I don't give a rat's happy backside whether we have the *authority* to talk to the guy or not."

Festus sighed. "You'll all give a rat's backside if we do anything that lets Grayson get off scot-free for this stunt."

"Are you deaf, McGregor?" Jeff asked. "While we waste time the girls are getting farther and farther away."

"Vet cleaned my ears out last week," Festus said cheerfully. "You guys are the ones who can't hear. The Mother Tree said Jinx and Glory have made *landfall.* That means they've stopped somewhere. They're not drifting. Besides, making Morris wait works to our advantage."

Chase stopped and looked down at his father. "How do you figure that?"

"Morris Grayson is the kind of guy who thinks his litter box doesn't stink," Festus said. "He's pinning back the triplets' ears right now going on and on about how we'll all be working as garbage collectors when he's done with us. Rube's driving the guy nuts asking how much trash he'd be allowed to skim off the top."

"And your point is what, Dad?"

"My point, boy, is that the longer we outrage Grayson's delicate ego, the more likely he'll be to run his mouth when we finally give him the chance."

Lucas laughed in spite of himself. "You've got Uncle Morris nailed. He does like to be the most important person in the room."

"A personality flaw we will exploit to its maximum potential," Barnaby said, coming out of the study. "Hilton Barnstable has given his consent for Director Grayson to be detained in 'protective custody' for the immediate future."

Connor nodded. "I've already spoken with Mrs. McElroy at the Inn. She's preparing a special room for our guest."

Jeff frowned. "*Hester* McElroy? The one who fights Fiona for the Shevington Rose Cup every year? You're trusting Grayson's detention to her?"

"Mrs. McElroy had a previous career," Connor said evasively.

"Doing what?" Lucas asked.

Festus yawned. "Hester was a CARHOP. Retired when she put in her 150 years."

"So she waited tables a long time," Jeff said. "How does that make her qualified to sit on Grayson?"

Jilly laughed. "Allow me to translate," she said. "CARHOP stands for 'Carnivorous Horticultural Operative.' Hester McElroy is a legend in the field. She single-handedly wrestled down a *Dionaea muscipula giganticus*. The incident is in all the textbooks."

Taking in Jeff's uncomprehending stare, Jilly added, "That's a Venus flytrap roughly the size of a wooly mammoth. I assure you Mrs. McElroy is more than equal to containing Morris Grayson."

"Any chance we can get her to feed him to one of those big fly eater thingies?" Jeff asked hopefully.

Smothering a smile, Barnaby said, "I suggest we treat Morris with at least a modicum of courtesy but accede to none of his demands. I concur with Festus that in a state of self-righteous agitation, Grayson will likely tell us far more than he would were we to allow him to feel that he controls his fate. Festus, I trust you can assist us in keeping the Director . . . off balance?"

"Rube's already on it," the werecat said. "That trash panda is as off balance as they come."

"Good. Then we are all in agreement?"

Jeff grumbled his assent while Lucas and Chase gave grudging nods.

Jilly remained seated when the men stood to leave.

"Aren't you coming?" Festus asked.

"No," she said. "Adeline has put together a fascinating body of material on the antiquities trade. I'll get up to speed on the topic while you talk with Grayson."

"Great," Festus said. "Would you mind dropping a dime on Stank Preston?

Tell him we'll be in Londinium sometime tomorrow."

"Of course," Jilly said. "My pleasure."

In the hallway, Chase said, "You're going to Londinium *now*?"

"For Bastet's sake, boy, I'm not going for a pub crawl," Festus growled. "Stank Preston is a Blacklist containment specialist. Get your mind in the game."

When the group entered the dining room, Rube called out

cheerfully, "Hat Man! Uncle Mo here says he can get us a gig working the trash wagons. That's like my dream career, bro."

Almost purple with rage, Morris said, "I have made it quite clear that you are to address me as 'Director Grayson.'"

"Aw, Mo, you wound me," Rube said. "Here I thought we was getting close."

Grayson turned to his nephew. "How in the name of Merlin's beard do you work with this insufferable vermin?"

"If I were you, Uncle Morris," Lucas said, pulling back a chair and sitting down, "I wouldn't be insulting vermin. Rube has never lied to me. You don't even understand the *concept* of truth."

Laying his hands flat on the table and affecting a pained expression, Morris said, "This is what comes of your preference for mingling with commoners. When you embrace your heritage and assume the Grysundl throne, you will see that all I have ever done is to work in your best interest."

Barnaby sat with Lucas on his right. Chase took the next chair down, but Jeff and Connor chose to stand. Festus sprang onto the table top, puffed out his fur for a vigorous shake, and then stretched languidly staring at Grayson without blinking.

The director recoiled from the cloud of yellow fur floating in the air, hastily covering his coffee cup and glaring in distaste at the hairs adhering to his lapels.

"You are being unnecessarily uncouth, Festus," he said.

"Morris," Festus said pleasantly, "you haven't seen me be uncouth."

"Nor do I intend to be here long enough to experience that spectacle," the Director snapped. "I demand to be released immediately."

Steepling his fingers, Barnaby said, "With clearance from the Ruling Elder, you will remain in Shevington under protective custody for the immediate future."

"For what cause?" Grayson said.

Lucas leaned toward his uncle. "For what *cause*? You've been accused of triggering a portal incident that resulted in the disappearance of the Witch of the Oak and an innocent bystander."

"Surely you have no intention of listening to the demented ramblings of a known criminal whose mind broke years ago," Grayson said. "Nothing in Lauren Frazier's profile suggests her to be a credible witness."

When Lucas didn't answer, the Director attempted a more sympathetic angle. "Lucas, I know you have a lingering childhood fondness for Lauren, but that does not alter the lurid facts of her career with the High Sídhe."

"Miss Frazier will speak for herself," Barnaby said, "and we will examine her role in the events leading up to this evening. However, there is one fact you cannot deny, Director. You were standing adjacent to the portal. She was not."

Morris shrugged. "My geographic location in relation to the portal is hardly proof of anything. I wished to say goodbye to my nephew and to magnanimously wish him well as he began what would have undoubtedly been an ill-fated marriage."

"Did you or did you not throw something into that portal?" Lucas asked tightly. "If you're so hell-bent on my being the Grysundl heir, I'm ordering you, as your King, to tell me the truth."

Triumph glinted in Morris' eyes. "Now you are beginning to understand," he said. "Your royal blood gives you power. Relish it, nephew. Power will keep you warmer than any woman could."

Lucas stood up, shoving his chair back with such force it would have struck the wall if Connor had not stopped it.

"The triplets will escort you next door to the Inn," Barnaby said. "We will resume our discussion in the morning. Good evening, Director."

Connor caught hold of Lucas' elbow and steered him

outside. The others followed with Festus and Rube bringing up the rear. Lucas took three quick steps across the hall and rammed his fist into the plaster before stalking back to the parlor.

Rube shook his head. "Sorry, Connor. He ain't exactly at his best right now."

Barnaby moved his hand over the dust and broken plaster, which smoothly mended itself. "Do not leave him alone for the remainder of the night. I will return in the morning with Moira."

Festus looked at Chase. "You planning on putting your fist through any walls?"

Chase shook his head. "No," he said. "I'm saving my knuckles for that arrogant ass, Morris Grayson."

"Get in line," Jeff said, stomping back toward the parlor. "Father of the bride calls first dibs."

7

Shevington, Tori

Lauren gulped, but she took Greer's hand. The Scottish vampire addressed Myrtle. "We will return as quickly as possible."

"Fare thee well," the aos sí replied serenely.

The air around Greer swirled, stirring the papers on Moira's desk and making the flames in the wall sconces flare. When the wind died away, a collective wave of exhaustion washed over the group.

"There is nothing more we can do tonight," Myrtle said. "Let us rest and resume our labors at first light. We will convene at the Lord High Mayor's house for breakfast."

When I headed straight for the door, Mom called my name, hurrying to catch up with me. "Where are you going?"

"There's something I have to do before I can try to sleep," I said. "Don't worry. I'm okay."

With that, I turned on my heel and made straight for Horatio Pagecliffe's shop.

At first, I knocked with respectful discretion, but the gentle taps still sounded unnaturally loud on the deserted High Street. A werecat I didn't recognize emerged from between the buildings smelling strongly of Litterbox Lager.

"Nothing's open at this hour," the stranger slurred. "You're gonna wake the town."

I silenced him with a murderous glance. The shifter's bleary eyes widened in the dim light.

"Suit yourself, lady," he said, flicking me the tail as he stumbled away. "Get yourself arrested for all I care."

Stinging pain shot across my knuckles. I began to pour my fear and frustration into the blows, each landing harder than the last. A light came on in an upper window across the street. I ignored it.

Finally, after an eternity, Pagecliffe emerged from the rear of the building. In the glow of the brass candlestick floating beside the elderly proprietor, I made out a long striped nightshirt and cap straight out of Dickens.

He peered at me through the glass. "Miss Andrews, do I need to inform you I do not transact business at three in the morning?"

"Mr. Pagecliffe, you were at the wedding. Please let me in."

The words came out hoarse and strained, thick with unshed tears. Sympathy replaced irritation on the man's hawk-like features. The key turned in the lock.

"I was there," Pagecliffe said, standing aside to let me enter. "Do you have news of the Witch of the Oak?"

Swallowing against the aching lump in my throat, I said, "The Mother Oak says Jinx is alive. I need a pen and a journal."

The storekeeper frowned. "Of course, but why do you require these items in the dark of the night? Will they in some way help to bring your friend home?"

That did it. Hot rivulets coursed down my cheeks.

"No . . . I mean . . . I don't think so," I stammered. "Jinx writes everything down in her grimoire. All the stuff that happens in her life. I have to do that for her while she's . . . not here. I have to start now before I forget anything. I can't risk falling asleep before I write everything down that I remember about the wedding and . . . and . . . after."

The torrent of words petered out. The candle wick flared and hissed sympathetically. Pagecliffe turned, his slippers squeaking as he shuffled to a shelf filled with elegantly bound books.

Running his index finger along the inventory, he stopped and tapped a thick spine before removing the volume. Silver stars studded the cover. When Pagecliffe gave the book to me, the burnished leather felt buttery soft.

Holding one slender hand over the journal, he murmured, "*Conscius occursum tuum.*"

Meet thy confidant.

Next, he opened a glass case and selected a matching steel blue fountain pen. "*Audi er tu vocem recordarentur.*"

Hear the voice you will record.

"What do I owe you?" I asked.

"Nothing but the return of the Witch of the Oak to those who love her," Pagecliffe replied. "Have faith, Mistress Victoria. Believe the Mother Tree."

He wrapped the writing supplies in brown paper, resting his bony fingers on my shoulder in an attempt to offer comfort when the bundle passed between us.

Alone again on the empty street, I started back to the Lord High Mayor's house to see Connor and check in on Lucas. I clutched the parcel tightly, thinking about the things I needed to record.

I jumped when the package vibrated. "Are you listening to me?" I asked softly.

The word "yes" formed in my mind.

"You'll help me?"

"Yes."

The assurance steadied me until I turned onto the square and saw that same restless shadow moving back and forth across the drawn curtains of the parlor. Lucas was back on his feet.

With my emotions barely under control, I couldn't help him in that state — and honestly, I was too tired to try. Changing course, I took the alley and entered the residence through the kitchen door.

Connor sat at the plank table under the watchful eye of his brownie housekeeper, Innis, dutifully working through a plate of food.

The Elven Gray Loris wrapped around his neck locked eyes with me. "Connor's sister gone," the creature said mournfully. "Ailish sad."

"I know, sweetie," I said, holding out my hand. "I'm sad, too."

The Loris untangled herself from her master and came to me. "Too much sad," she said, her voice muffled against my hair. "Ailish want Jinx back."

"We're going to get Jinksy back," I said, hugging her tightly.

Innis scrutinized my appearance and clearly didn't like what she saw. "Sit down before you drop," she ordered. "You need food."

Reaching for another slice of bread, Connor said, "Don't bother arguing. She won't take no for an answer."

I mutely dropped into the empty chair across from him and put my package on the table.

"What's that?" Connor asked, nodding at the parcel.

While Innis filled my plate, I told Connor where I'd been. As I talked, he reached across the table and intertwined our fingers, giving me the full attention of his eyes. When my words petered out, he gave me a reassuring squeeze, "That's a great idea, honey."

"You can hold hands later," Innis said, the words kinder than you might imagine. "Eat."

I didn't think I was hungry until I took the first bite. When my stomach rumbled loudly, Innis gave me an "I told you so" look and stared at me until I began to eat steadily.

"Why didn't you come through the front door?" Connor asked.

"Because I'm a coward," I admitted guiltily. "I saw Lucas wearing a hole in the carpet through the front window."

Connor sighed, and absent-mindedly brushed back his already tousled hair. "He's been at it again since we had our first talk with his uncle. Lucas came out of the room and put his fist through the wall."

"I'm sure he would rather have put it through Grayson's face. Did the guy come clean?"

"No. He insulted everyone in the room and told Lucas he'd be better off when he embraces his royal prerogatives."

"Great," I said. "Where's Grayson now?"

"On ice at the Inn. The triplets have Registry guards outside his door."

I bristled. "Why the hell isn't he in jail?"

"Because he's the director of the DGI," Connor replied. "Barnaby spoke with the Ruling Elder. We're holding Grayson in 'protective custody.'"

Grudgingly, I acceded to the wisdom of the plan and filled Connor in on what happened at the University. "Greer took Lauren to Las Vegas. We expect them back sometime tomorrow with information on the time pirates."

We ate in silence after that, simply taking comfort in one another's company until I began to nod off in my plate.

"Why don't you try to get some sleep?" Connor suggested. "Innis lit fires in all the guest rooms. Take whichever one you like."

The offer tempted me, but I was almost afraid to close my eyes for fear of what I might learn when I opened them again.

"I don't think I can sleep," I said. "Too keyed up."

Connor didn't buy it. "Lie down and rest," he insisted gently. "You want to be fresh for the breakfast meeting, don't you?"

He clicked open his pocket watch. "You can get at least four hours. Go on. I'll wake you if anything happens."

"Promise?"

"Of course," he said, gesturing to Ailish who clambered over the table and back onto his shoulder.

When Connor and I kissed goodnight, I stroked the loris' soft fur. "Take care of him, for me, okay?"

"Ailish take care of Connor," she said, placing a protective paw on his cheek. "Ailish love Connor."

"Tori loves Connor, too," I said, touching his other cheek before gathering up the package from Pagecliffe's and going upstairs.

I picked a room with windows overlooking the square. The sight of the Mother Tree, strong and tall in the moonlight made me feel less alone. Changing out of my bridesmaid dress and into the pajamas Innis had laid out, I climbed into bed, unwrapped the journal and opened it across my lap.

Staring at the empty pages, I said, "Okay. Here we are. How does this work?"

On the bedside table, the pen's cap rotated and slid free. The barrel levitated and floated over the paper. Operating on instinct, I closed my eyes and concentrated. When the nib began to scratch against the page, I opened them again.

The pen executed a series of detailed line drawings. Jinx and me in the dressing room before the ceremony as I tucked a stray lock of her hair back in place. The calling of the quarters. The moment when Jeff walked his daughter down the aisle. The first dance. Cutting the cake. Throwing the bouquet — and finally,

Barnaby stepping forward to open the special "going away" portal.

The images unfolded page by page calming my mind. As it depicted the final pivotal moments of the evening, the pen extracted details from memories I didn't know existed. I saw Morris Grayson's act of sabotage without realizing what I was watching — a small object turning end over end as it sailed toward the portal.

"Can you make that bigger?" I asked the pen.

Turning to a fresh page, the nib sketched a bar made of dull gold metal. Brass, maybe? Each end slanted in opposing directions and seemed to be outfitted with hardware for attaching the piece to a larger device.

A center circle divided the object into equal halves, one higher than the other. The whole thing couldn't have been more than four or five inches long.

I had no name for the thing. I didn't understand how it interacted with the portal, but could this be why Jinx had reached out before the explosion? Could she have caught the bar?

Regardless, we had our first clue.

Sleep would have to wait.

8

Las Vegas

Before leaving Shevington, Greer asked Lauren to visualize their destination. The baobhan sith set them down in a deserted parking lot in an industrial part of Las Vegas.

As the cloud of dust settled around them, Lauren let go of Greer's hand. "That's not like passing through a portal," she said. "How do you do that?"

Greer shrugged. "For me to dissect the flight of the baobhan sith would be like asking a hummingbird to explain how it hovers above a flower. I am what nature has made me."

In the shadowed places at the edge of the asphalt, a vagrant scurried into the desert night.

"He saw us land," Lauren said. "Do you need to go after him and erase the memory?" Lauren asked.

Greer sniffed the night air. "Not given the amount of cheap vodka in his system. By dawn, I suspect he will be telling his compatriots that he witnessed the landing of space aliens."

"We get a lot of that in Vegas," Lauren said as they crossed the street toward a boxy building. Rows of blank windows marched up the facade, each one reflecting a perfect imitation of the full moon.

Lauren produced a key that unlocked the steel door. Inside, they boarded a service elevator and ascended ten floors.

"What was the original design of this building?" Greer asked. "There are more floors than I would expect in a factory."

"It was supposed to be a high-end storage facility," Lauren replied. "The company ran out of funding before they could rent any of the spaces."

The elevator doors opened onto a carpeted waiting room filled with orchids encased in climate-controlled growth chambers. A deserted receptionist's desk guarded an inner entrance secured by a touchscreen security system.

Lauren laid her hand against the glass plate. A blue light passed from the tips of her fingers down over her palm followed by the flashing words "Identity Confirmed."

"Elaborate technology," Greer observed, following Lauren through the passageway, "but Sídhe magic can easily defeat electronics."

Motion-controlled lights flicked on as Lauren approached a sleek, modern desk.

"The scanner accesses my aura," she said. "Any attempt to tamper with the mechanism initiates a cascade of interlocking spells, wards, and incantations. The idea is to slow down a Sídhe intruder, not stop them."

"Which," the baobhan sith said, "means you have a second means of exit. Difficult to achieve on the upper floors of a structure with no ledges."

"Not for someone with a fat checkbook and an understanding of portal mechanics," Lauren replied, using a combination to access one of the desk drawers. She pulled out a slender laptop. "There's a single-use portal behind that bookshelf. Don't worry. I have no intention of trying to bolt through it."

"And I," Greer said, taking a seat across from Lauren, "have no concern that you might try."

Lauren studied the vampire. "It must be wonderful to live with powers that give you such self-confidence."

"My sense of self-possession does not derive from my powers," Greer replied. "I have negotiated both successes and failures through the centuries. Every living creature makes mistakes, Miss Frazier. I have found that with time, atonement can be made for all but the most heinous of transgressions."

The other woman's face registered surprise. "Are you saying you believe me?"

"I believe you did not foresee the outcome of your association with Morris Grayson," Greer said. "I also believe your desire to assist our efforts to recover Jinx and Glory to be genuine."

"What changed your mind?"

Greer flicked a bit of dust away from the ebony cuff of her jacket with one crimson nail. "The thoughts of those who fly with the baobhan sith are subject to my access."

Lauren blinked. "You wanted to bring me here so you could read my mind?"

"In part."

"It's not ethical to probe another's thoughts without fore-warning and their express permission."

Lacing elegant fingers across her knee, Greer said, "Normally I would agree with you, but Jinx and Glory are missing. I have no time for ethical considerations."

"And if I had been lying?"

"We would not be enjoying nearly so pleasant a conversation."

Lauren took a moment to absorb the vaguely murderous

undercurrent of Greer's statement. Then, picking up the laptop, she said, "I assume you drink whisky?"

"Like a suckling babe," Greer smiled. "I apologize for being blunt, but I think you will agree that the more honest our dealings from this point forward the greater our chance of retrieving Jinx, Glory . . . and your brother."

Tears welled in Lauren's eyes. "Thank you," she said. "That's all I've wanted from the beginning — someone to help me find Axe."

"Do not mistake the distrust of the others in Shevington for an absence of sympathy," Greer said. "The intensity of your distress over your brother's disappearance struck a deep chord with all those assembled in Moira's workshop. His fate will not be left to the uncertainties of time."

Struggling to regain her composure, Lauren said, "Let's go into my apartment. I can project the pirate profiles onto the big screen TV while we have a drink."

Greer rose from her chair with fluid grace. "I do not see a door."

"That's the idea," Lauren said, approaching a floor-to-ceiling modern painting. "The sorcerer who made this for me is a mediocre artist, but a superb magical architect. He pioneered the engineering of impressionist incantations."

As the baobhan sith watched, Lauren touched a magenta L-shaped fragment in the swirl of color splashed over the canvas.

When she dragged the piece into an upper corner, other lines moved with it to create the outline of a door. A vibrant chartreuse circle moved off the surface of the painting to form a handle, which Lauren grasped and pulled.

The painted door swung open revealing a short foyer. Greer followed her hostess inside. When the canvas closed behind them, Lauren used a second touchscreen to activate a solid steel sheet that whisked out of sight with a brisk *whoosh*.

The second opening revealed a warm, cozy living room with paneled walls and a vaulted ceiling accented with exposed beams. The fireplace sprang to life and with it a series of sconces mounted around the room. On their left, a glass wall looked out over the lights of Las Vegas in the distance.

"Holographic glass," Lauren explained as Greer moved to take in the view. "On the outside, the wall shows rows of industrial windows like every other floor in the building."

"You own the entire floor?"

"I own the building," Lauren said, moving behind a well-stocked bar, "and the properties on either side. I believe in the power of income diversification. If my dealings with the Sídhe collapse or become too dangerous for my tastes, I can live nicely on the rental income. My clientele are business people who require nondescript facilities and guaranteed privacy."

Lauren poured them each a glass of single malt and joined Greer at the massive window. *"Slàinte."*

"Do dheagh shlàinte," Greer replied as they touched glasses.

"You've done well for yourself here," the baobhan sith said after a moment. "Yet you risked all that you have built to deal with Morris Grayson."

"I'd risk this and more to get Axe back," Lauren said. "I want you to know I didn't set out to become a criminal. After we lost Axe, my father went to pieces. His business dealings in the human world collapsed, ending in bankruptcy. I started working with the Sídhe to get the money to pay his debts."

Greer frowned. "It would have been a small matter to make his human creditors forget the indebtedness."

"Maybe," Lauren said, "but I wanted his legacy to count for more than that. There are fewer than a hundred surviving Seonaidh in the realms. My father made his life among the humans. He lies buried in one of their cemeteries. His memory in their world mattered to me."

"May his spirit dwell in perfect peace across all the realms," Greer said.

"Thank you," Lauren said, pausing to take a mouthful of Scotch before adding, "He killed himself."

"Suicide does not come easily for the Fae," Greer said carefully. "Are the Seonaidh burdened by beliefs of punishment for such an act in the nether realms?"

"No," Lauren said. "Our belief is that all living energy returns to its source, but I've spent a great deal of my life in the human realm. Suicide leaves a shadow that's hard to move beyond. My father died a hard death. All I could do for him was to honor his obligations. That goal left me with an established business and few concerns about my personal reputation. I don't blame the women in Shevington for distrusting me."

The words carried the unmistakable note of resigned bitterness.

"Do not be so quick to assume the finality of their judgment," Greer said. "Given time, your actions will speak louder than your attempted assurances. Begin now by showing me the temporal bandits with whom we will be dealing."

Moving to the sofa, Lauren touched a hidden control that lowered a TV from the ceiling. Her fingers flew over the laptop's keyboard, and the face of a saturnine man appeared on the screen. He stood next to a lithe woman with sparkling blue eyes and long blond hair braided in a thick plait hanging over one shoulder.

"They are a study in opposites," Greer said, taking a seat on the sofa as well. "Who are they?"

"The woman," Lauren said, "is Miranda Winter. The man is her partner, Drake Lobranche."

"Translated Elvish names?"

"Yes. Miranda captains a crew of temporal pirates she calls

the Hourglass Men. Drake is her first mate and current companion."

"Current?" Greer asked, sipping her whisky.

"She slit the last one's throat for making a move on her crew," Lauren said. "That was before she cut his body in pieces and scattered him in dumpsters all over town. The LVPD still has the killing listed as a cold case on their files."

"Cold being an apt term for so efficient an execution," Greer observed wryly. "This is the woman who sent you in search of the Copernican Astrolabe?"

"The Hourglass Men are the best in the business," Lauren said. "Miranda's crew brought back Dr. Lopez's diary. She was with me when I found the sketch. Seeing Axe's face again after so many years hit me hard. I couldn't hide my reaction. When I told Miranda I thought the man in the drawing was my brother, she offered to go after him."

The baobhan sith swirled her whisky contemplatively. "If the Hourglass Men accessed Dr. Lopez' timestream once without the astrolabe what was Miranda's rationale for requiring so esoteric a tool to retrieve your brother?"

"She told me that bringing back 'loot' is easy. People are harder."

"Not an entirely unreasonable assertion."

"Do you want me to contact her?"

Greer downed the last of her whisky in a single shot. "No. I think we shall call on Ms. Winter unannounced. I assume you know their base of operations."

"I do," Lauren said, "but they're not going to just let us walk through the front door."

The baobhan sith smiled. "Who said we were going to walk?"

9

The Druid Forests of Kent, 1590, Jinx

My preference would have been to go to Londinium immediately, look for Alex Farnsworth, and show him the brass bar. Unfortunately, the Druid social schedule superseded that idea. We arrived a week before the Winter Solstice and Yule.

A trip to Londinium couldn't happen without Moira; she couldn't leave the village for any length of time until after the celebrations.

Which is why, on our first morning in the past, Glory and I walked behind Moira through the center of the encampment on our way to meet the Elder.

We passed a plump woman with red cheeks milking a complacent cow. Sometimes the maid squeezed the warm liquid into the bucket at her feet, other times she aimed for the mouths of the cats sitting to either side of her stool waiting for their treat.

The blacksmith, sweat streaming down his face from the

heat of the forge, called a greeting to Moira. "Your new bellows make a proper hot fire, Mistress."

A woman in a flour-dusted tunic came out of her home to press a loaf of fresh bread wrapped in cloth into the alchemist's hands.

"The poultice worked on young Cedric's cough," she said. "Bless you, alchemist."

Keeping my voice low, I said, "What exactly is your job description around here?"

"To use my talents and skills for the greater good," Moira replied. "We each have parts to play in the larger whole."

Ahead, I made out a structure nearly identical to Moira's hut. In the doorway, a gray-bearded man leaning on a staff waited for us. He wore a white tunic covered by a gray hooded cloak.

As we neared, Moira said, "Merry meet, Newlyn. These women are novices sent to me from the continent."

Newlyn bowed slightly. "How are thee called?" he asked formally.

The question caught me off guard, but Glory picked up the ball.

"Genevieve and Jeane," she said, bobbing a kind of curtsy in his direction. "Merry meet, Elder Newlyn."

"Merry meet, Mistress Genevieve," he said, "and to you Mistress Jeane. Moira tells me you have journeyed long to find us."

"Merry meet," I said. "Thank you for sheltering us. We have indeed followed a long path."

Smiling broadly, Newlyn said, "The gods have blessed the timing of your arrival. In mere days we travel to Coldrum Long Barrow for the celebration of the Winter Solstice followed by the Festival of Yule. A most auspicious time for you to begin your studies."

Moira started to answer for me, but I had this one covered.

"We look forward to the lengthening of the days and the returning sun," I said. "As nature is reborn, so we hope to awaken to our future in the days that lay ahead."

At our feet, Orion made a sound in the back of his throat that I took to mean, "Nice save, lady."

Newlyn fairly beamed. "Well spoken, Mistress Jeane. Fare thee well in thy studies."

On the way back to Moira's hut, Glory said, "Good job."

"If, by 'good job' you mean a commendable performance," Moira said, "I agree. You know more of our ways than you have let on."

"Not really," I said, "but I do know the significance of the solstice. We don't celebrate Yule where we're from. We call the holiday Christmas. You're going to have to help us, so we know what to do."

"Fear not," Moira assured me, "we have several days to prepare for the journey. We shall use them well."

Someone told me once that if you want to learn a new language, you have to put yourself in a situation where English is not an option.

Glory and I were in for the immersion experience of a lifetime. Starting to feel less optimistic and more overwhelmed as the day wore on, I asked Moira for pen and paper.

I assumed as an alchemical scientist that she kept notes about her observations and experiments. Instead, her reply offered yet another lesson into the Druid way of being in the world.

"Though we are skilled in the arts of literacy, we do not commit our knowledge or thoughts to paper," she said. "Ours is an oral tradition. I can produce the materials you request, but if you are to appear to be a proper novice, use them only in private."

That night, behind the drawn curtain of my sleeping berth

under the glow of a floating lamp, I wrapped my fingers around a sharpened goose quill and tentatively dunked the tip in a pot of magenta ink.

A small blank book lay open before me. I used the empty pages to test the strange implement in my hand. The experience felt like learning to write all over again.

I produced blotches and smears instead of handwriting, repeatedly snapping the ink off my fingers and wiping the pages clean with an irritated sweep of my hand.

Half an hour later, I finally found the rhythm of the exercise. How many words I could produce before I needed more ink. When to wipe the quill's tip free of excess liquid. How to blot the wet lines before turning the page.

That left me staring at the expectant sheets at a loss for a starting place. I was used to sharing my ideas and recollections with a sentient grimoire and pen. The prospect of doing things the old-fashioned way left me temporarily stumped.

On the other side of the curtain, I heard Glory cooing to Orion. "Who's a good boy? You like your cheese, don't you, good boy?"

After our first night in the hut, the bedtime snack became a routine for Glory and the wolf. The well-muscled brute nursed a puppy-ish soft spot for my companion, resting his head on her knee, and listening to her rambling recitations with patient, good humor.

Moira may have assigned the wolf to follow our every step, or the creature may have taken on the chore himself. Regardless, Orion never left us. He catered to Glory, playing the part of a pet, but when my eyes met his, I saw an intelligent, formidable ally looking back at me.

Wetting the quill, I wrote, "We've been here only 24 hours and already we're looking for the comfort of routine. That's why I asked Moira for this book."

In the coming days, as I mastered the quill, the journal became my private place, the space where I could vent my fears and try to come to grips with the events that had upended my world.

In the space of 36 hours, I married the man I love, fell through a time-warping portal, and woke up in an alternate version of the 16th century. Maybe Druids didn't commit their thoughts to paper, but I needed a place to vent.

There's an inherent contradiction in the emotion we label "loneliness." The condition doesn't require solitude. I wasn't alone. Far from it.

I was surrounded by people in a strange and interesting place. So long as I thought about our situation that way, the hours passed quickly. But in moments of stillness, desolation stalked me followed by oppressive worry.

Questions swirled in my brain. What did Lucas think? Did he and the others believe Glory and I were dead? Or worse yet, was he hatching some foolish, reckless plan to come after us?

That thought twisted at my insides. I know the man I married. I imagined him pacing the front room of the Lord High Mayor's house, growling at anyone who suggested he sit, actively hatching a dangerous rescue.

On our second day, sleep deprived and trying to disguise my fear, my temper grew short. Glory, caught up in her fascination with the living history surrounding us, didn't seem worried at all, which frankly irritated the hell out of me.

When Moira left us alone for a few minutes, I came right out and put the sharp question to my companion, "You're having such a good time with all this, are you even thinking about Chase?"

Poor Glory looked like I'd slapped her. "Of course I think about Chase," she said in a small, wounded voice, "but he knows that as long as I'm with you, everything will be okay. If I make myself have a good time, I don't have to think about how awful this is, especially for you."

Talk about making a person feel small.

I apologized, ashamed of myself, and glad I hadn't given voice to what I'd been secretly thinking since the moment I came to in the forest clearing.

Of all the people who could have fallen through that portal with me, why in the name of Merlin's beard did it have to be Glory?

Back in Shevington, Lucas had Rube, Greer, Festus — everyone in our world armed to the teeth with their overlapping powers and areas of competence. With all that combined metaphysical might, someone would come up with a way to get us home.

Until then, I told myself bitterly, I was stranded in time with a woman whose biggest life ambition was to discover her inner Elvis.

On our third evening, when we sat around the communal bonfire and listened to the village bard tell tales of Roman Britain, I forced myself to set aside my negative judgment about Glory. Festus was right. There was another side to what he called the woman's "insufferable nonsense."

Glory could have posed her questions with far fewer words, but active curiosity informed the inquiries. She instantly won the love of the children by joining in their games and sat listening to the bard holding a cherubic, blue-eyed girl of three nestled on her lap.

To my surprise, Glory remembered the names of all the Druids to whom she'd been introduced, as well as their role in the community. Certainly, I watched and listened. I interacted and tried to learn, but whereas Glory held herself open, I might as well have been crouched defensively in a corner.

Like Robinson Crusoe, I felt hopelessly marooned on an island in time.

Tori and I read the book in high school, spending hours at lunch talking about how we would cope as castaways. It didn't occur to either of us that we could wind up on a deserted island with anyone but one another.

Years later, when Tom Hanks made the movie Castaway, we picked the debate up again, arguing about which one of us would be Wilson, the mute, companionable, oddly helpful volleyball.

My volleyball was named Glory. She was anything but mute, but grudgingly I had to admit she could be good company. It's almost impossible to spend more than five minutes with Glory and not laugh, even if you're laughing at some absurdity that's spilling out of her mouth.

One thing I can confirm with certainty; Glory always wants to help even if she doesn't know how.

In the journal, I interspersed such observations with vignettes from our days.

Awakening in the predawn light to the sight of Moira cooking breakfast over the open fire.

The animated give-and-take of Glory's endless questions.

The silent, solid presence that was Orion.

I dedicated several entries to Moira alone. The woman sheltering us crafted a more utilitarian relationship with her magic than the Moira who married my grandfather.

This Moira actively engaged the world with her powers. She conducted action driven experiments and explorations. Her connection to the natural world felt palpable as evidenced by her telepathic communications with Orion.

As if taking a cue from Moira's practicality, I made a list at the back of my book with running additions of her instructions on proper manners, minute details of Elizabethan life, and the highlights of our cover story.

When all else failed, we were to fall back on the idea of a language barrier. Our strange, modern accents and inability to understand common words of the day were attributed to our supposed origins in an obscure region of Europe.

In this way, we managed to settle in as best we could. The welcoming Druids accepted rather than questioned our eccentricities. We picked up on the infectious excitement that preceded the Solstice and Yule, and began to look forward to the celebration.

Then we made our first mistake. We went to town.

10

Shevington, Tori

Throwing on a robe I found in the closet, I asked the journal to detach the page from its spine. Magical writing supplies have a major advantage for obsessive-compulsive types — no ragged or fringy torn edges. Plus, I could (and did) ask the book to reattach the page later to keep my record of events complete.

Clutching the drawing of the mystery object, I went downstairs and headed for the front parlor.

Festus, Rube, Chase, and Jilly all looked up at the sound of my footsteps. I started to tell them about my discovery, but Festus raised a paw to stop me. He shook his head, jumped down from the window seat, and padded across the carpet.

When he reached me, the werecat jerked his head indicating I should follow him. We went to the dining room; Festus whispered, "Close the door."

Confident that we wouldn't be overheard, he explained why he'd wanted us to relocate. "Lucas finally fell asleep on the couch after we went through round one with his uncle. I didn't want him to wake up. Watching that boy pace is worse than having a case of spring fleas."

"You haven't had a flea in all the time I've known you," I said.

"You only have to have them once," he assured me, "before you get serious about taking your seasonal anti-pest potion. Stuff may taste like last year's sardine juice, but it's a lifesaver."

The curious alchemist in me wouldn't have minded discussing shifter maintenance potions, but I filed that conversation away for a future date.

"Connor told me you confronted Morris. What's your read on what he had to say?"

Festus made that cat face. The one that looks like he smelled the foulest substance on earth right under his nose.

"It was a load of self-serving crap about how he wants Lucas to get a feel for royal power. That went over so well Lucas came out of the room and promptly punched a hole in the wall."

Even though Connor had already told me about the incident, I still winced at the visual. "How's Chase holding up?"

"Better than Lucas," Festus said. "He's taking the attitude that as long as Glory is with Jinx, she'll be okay."

A wave of guilt assailed me. "I hate to admit this, but I can't get on board with that interpretation. If Jinx had to get tossed through the wrong side of a portal, Glory wouldn't be my first choice for wingman."

Festus surprised me with his reply. We all knew he'd been warming up to Glory, but I didn't realize his confidence in her abilities had also increased.

"Don't sell the Pickle short," he said. "Under all that silliness, she's smart. She loves Jinx. They'll take care of each other."

Then, switching gears, he asked, "What are you doing down here? You're supposed to be upstairs getting some sleep."

For a fleeting second, I felt like a kid who had been caught wandering around the house after being sent to bed. "Who told you that?"

"Innis," he said. "She brought us a plate of sandwiches about an hour ago — and tried to get all of us to call it a night. Woman's a pint-sized drill sergeant at heart."

"She made me eat, too," I said, "but when I got in bed I couldn't fall asleep." I launched into an explanation about my earlier errand to Pagecliffe's, ending by laying the drawing on the table.

Festus, who had been sitting on one of the chairs, jumped up for a better look. "Can you get me some light?" he asked.

Snapping my fingers, I ignited a glowing energy ball.

"Nice," he said, glancing up, "you're getting better at that. Caught anything on fire recently?"

His whiskers twitched when he asked the question, suppressing a Cheshire cat grin.

"One time," I muttered, "one time I *barely* ignite a tablecloth, and you're never going to let me live it down."

Chuckling under his breath, Festus studied the sketch. "What the heck is this thing?"

"It's what Grayson threw into the portal," I said. "The journal extracted the image from my subconscious memory. I can't be certain, but I think Jinx may have caught this thing right before the explosion."

Festus looked up sharply. "You saw that?"

"I saw her hand move. That's all I can say for sure. But if she did catch this object, maybe that's what triggered the accident."

The werecat nodded approvingly. "Nice. Now we have something concrete to shove in Uncle Mo's face in the morning."

I raised my eyebrows. "Uncle *Mo?*"

"Yeah," Festus laughed. "Rube started calling him that to get *Herr Direktor* riled up enough to run his mouth without thinking. Drives the guy bat crap crazy."

Good. Anything that made life uncomfortable for Morris Grayson had instant approval in my book. I made a mental note to buy Rube a party-sized bag of cheese puffs as soon as our lives got back to normal.

Returning to the sketch, I said, "Are you sure you don't want to show this drawing to Lucas now?"

"Positive," the werecat replied. "The others will be here in two or three hours. I swear Innis put something in that sandwich she fed Lucas because he barely finished swallowing the last bite before he was out for the count. Even a couple hours of sleep will do him good — and maybe keep him from punching any more walls."

Festus had a point, but I couldn't keep the irritation out of my voice when I answered. "This waiting isn't doing my nerves much good either. I'm scared to death Jinx and Glory are moving farther away from us by the minute."

Shaking his head, the werecat said, "Now you sound like Lucas and Chase. The Mother Tree said Jinx and Glory aren't adrift. Believe the old girl. She's more connected to the greater matrix of creation than any of us. Did Greer stay at the university with Moira?"

"Sorry," I said, "I forgot to tell you. Greer took Lauren to Las Vegas."

Festus' eyewhiskers went up. "Kinda not the time for a girls' trip to hit the slots. What's Red up to?"

Beginning from the moment we'd left the mayor's house for the university, I broke down the evening's events. Since we were alone, I also seized the opportunity to clear up a few inconsistencies that bothered me.

"Lauren said you've known her since she was a child. Do you believe her when she said she didn't know about Grayson's real plan?"

Festus scratched at his left ear. "The girl I knew wouldn't

have been involved with a caper like this in the first place, but I haven't seen Lauren in years. After Axe died she lost her way. She cut ties with everyone who reminded her of her brother."

"I'm confused," I said. "When Chase and Lucas were clashing over Jinx, you said you didn't know what happened to screw up their friendship."

Festus shrugged. "That wasn't a lie. Those boys were close as brothers growing up. When Axe died, they supported one another at first, but then the questions started. I think it was easier for them to blame each other for the accident, plus they were both half in love with Lauren, and she wouldn't have anything to do with either one of them. The next thing I know, nobody's speaking. Chase erupted every time I'd try to ask. I decided to let it alone since the only possible fix couldn't happen; resurrecting a dead man."

"Lauren thinks her brother is alive," I said. "You saw the image from Dr. Lopez's journal. Is that man Axe Frazier?"

"The drawing looks like him," Festus admitted, "and Lucas is certain."

"But you're not?"

Festus blew out a sigh that made his whiskers ripple. "I'm not sure I want to throw false hope about Axe into an already complicated situation."

The words "false hope" made me go cold inside. "But if Axe is alive," I said, "that means Jinx and Glory are alive too. Right?"

Festus laid a soft paw on the back of my hand. "Tough night, huh, kid?"

"Yeah," I replied, slumping in my chair. "I wish I could be as calm about all this as you seem to be."

The werecat chuckled again. "*Looking* calm and *being* calm are two different things," he said. "Smoke and mirrors. The skill gets better with age."

"But you think we're going to get them back, don't you?"

"I think," Festus said, "that for once I've got the right ace up my sleeve, and I intend to play it for everything it's worth."

"The Blacklist job?"

He nodded.

"Tell me about it," I said, hoping the intricacies of overlapping Fae agencies would distract me from the worry gnawing at my gut.

Festus seemed to understand what I was trying to do. He launched into a florid description of his covert career with the Bureau of Enchanted Artifacts and Relics.

The longer he talked, the happier I was to be sitting down. Unbeknownst to any of us, the werecat, Rube, and the raccoon Wrecking Crew had taken some wild rides in the name of magical object recovery.

Festus supplied only a sketchy account of their most recent escapade that resulted in this promotion to Blacklist agent, but that status gave him a considerable advantage in our current dilemma.

"If Grayson was screwing around with the Copernican Astrolabe and other artifacts involved in temporal navigation," Festus said, "I have clearance to look at the stuff. None of the usual red tape. I also have access to Blacklist containment specialists. As soon as we take another run at Grayson, Jilly and I are heading to Londinium to talk with a guy named Stank Preston."

"*Stank?*" I said. "Pardon me for saying so, but it's hard to have confidence in someone named 'Stank.'"

"You ever smell a ferret up close and personal?" Festus asked. "Stench aside, the guy's brilliant. He'll give us something we can use."

Before I could squelch it, my body let out with a massive yawn.

"Go back to bed," Festus said. "You're about to drop."

"Okay," I mumbled, getting to my feet and shuffling toward

the door. I paused with my hand on the knob and looked back. "All this time we thought you were staying drunk at The Dirty Claw you've been gallivanting around the realms recovering objects for BEAR?"

"Well," Festus said giving me a disarming, furry grin, "there was plenty of Dirty Claw drunkenness in between missions, but yeah, I've been playing secret agent cat."

"Why didn't you tell us?"

"Look up the word 'secret,'" he said. "Now, *scat*. Go to bed."

This time I started to drift off the instant my head hit the pillow. Hazy, half-awake dreams took me back to the wedding — specifically to the moment when Jinx and I said good-bye.

"Don't you worry about anything," I told her again. *"I've got this. Concentrate on having an amazing honeymoon."*

The Jinksy in my dreamscape gave me a different answer than the one I'd heard in real life. *"It's not your fault, Tori. Remember, everything happens according to the Natural Order."*

Wherever Jinx was, had she heard my worry transmitted along the fine filament of our mental connection? I couldn't be sure, but the next day the journal and pen came through a second time.

Before I went downstairs for the group meeting, I would discover a new drawing — a woodland village filled with strange stone huts that looked like beehives.

Our second clue.

11

Las Vegas

A hot desert wind rippled across the empty parking lot. Bedraggled clumps of grass pushing through the crumbling asphalt swayed under its force. Off to the right, modern Las Vegas glowed in the night. The lurid prosperity of the casinos and hotels set a sharp contrast to the collection of abandoned signage displayed across the street.

Greer studied the swooping concrete arches overhanging the glass doors and windows of the Neon Museum.

"This is where your pirates choose to make their home base?" she asked.

"Not in the museum," Lauren said, "underneath it."

The baobhan sith's eyes flickered as she scanned the darkness. "I do not feel the presence of a fairy mound, but the warding magic tastes familiar."

"Miranda hired a sorcerer to cloak the base. The barrier magic is similar to what you'd find surrounding a fairy mound."

Still studying the museum, Greer asked, "Why go to such

elaborate measures with the protective incantations only to call attention to the location with a flamboyant surface structure?"

Lauren laughed. "Miranda has a good side hustle going with the museum. Originally the building served as the La Concha Motel lobby. It dates from 1961. The humans consider it to be one of the finest surviving examples of Googie architecture."

"Granted, my tastes tend to differ dramatically from modern humans, but the overall effect strikes me as cartoonish."

The two women continued to talk as they crossed the roadway. "You're right on the money with the reference to cartoons," Lauren said. "The Googie aesthetic developed from a restaurant mascot with fried eggs for eyes."

Greer paused on the meridian. "A droll image to be sure. Why do you know so much about the history of this museum?"

Shrugging, Lauren said, "I guess you could call it a hobby. I've always been interested in old Las Vegas and the Sixties in general. That's something that Miranda and I share. After all, she is an elf, and they do love shiny objects. The museum may not look like much now, but when the signs are lit, they're impressive. This place rakes in the tourist dollars."

"You are closely related to the Elvish peoples," Greer pointed out. "Do you share their affection for shiny objects?"

"I guess it takes one, to know one," Lauren laughed. "Miranda is one of the most dangerous women I know, but she's interesting and quite likable."

Without looking toward the museum, the baobhan sith said, "We are being watched."

"I see him," Lauren said. "Miranda keeps guards posted day and night. They've had a lot of problems with unauthorized humans trying to get in after hours."

"Let us find out how the guard feels about unauthorized Fae."

The instant they stepped onto the property, a swarthy man

melted out of the shadows. "We're closed," he said sharply. "No after hours photography."

"Do I look like paparazzi, Trippin?" Lauren asked.

The guard stepped closer and peered at her in the dim light. "Oh, Ms. Frazier," he said. "I didn't recognize you. Your name isn't on the approved visitor list for tonight."

Lauren made a self-deprecating gesture. "My bad," she said. "This is a spur of the moment visit."

Trippin looked at Greer suspiciously. "Who's your friend?"

Filling her smile with a glimmer of her true self, the baobhan sith said, "Greer MacVicar. A business associate."

Trippin's nostrils flared as if he sniffed the vampire's energy on the wind. "Let's try this again," he said. "*What* are you?"

This time, Greer made no effort to tamp down the fire in her eyes. "That," she said, "is an exceptionally rude question."

The guard shifted uneasily on his feet, but he held his ground. "Give me a break, lady. I'm not looking to insult you. I've got a job to do here."

"Then," Greer said, "let us say simply that I am far more than you can imagine and considerably more than you wish to confront."

A woman's laugh crackled over a loudspeaker from somewhere farther inside the grounds.

"She's a baobhan sith, you idiot. Let them in before Ms. MacVicar decides she's in the mood to make you a midnight snack."

Raising her voice slightly, Lauren said, "Hi, Miranda. Sorry to show up unannounced. I should've called in advance, but we're dealing with a situation. We'd like to come down and discuss it with you."

"Would this situation have anything to do with a missing Tree Witch?"

"It might," Lauren said, "but I suspect you can understand

why we're not anxious to have that discussion out here in the open where anyone might be listening."

Over the loudspeaker, they heard a man's low voice in the background. The words were unintelligible, but decidedly disapproving in tone.

Miranda replied with a rapid-fire burst of Elvish. Trippin ducked his head to keep from laughing; Greer showed no such restraint.

After a pause, Miranda asked, *"You speak Elvish?"*

"Several dialects," Greer replied dryly. "I must say that I do not believe your suggestion regarding your colleague's cautious opinion can be anatomically accomplished."

Miranda's hearty guffaw touched off a squeal of feedback over the electronics. *"Oh, I have to meet you in person, Ms. MacVicar. Bring them down Trippin."*

"Aye, Cap'n."

The guard motioned for Greer and Lauren to follow him along a dirt path that wound through the maze of vintage advertising. After several turns, a faded yellow and red arch came into view. The letters formed the name "Sassy Sally's." A second sign resting on the ground proclaimed, "Binion's."

"Step between the 'N' and the 'I,'" Trippin instructed. "You'll feel a jolt. Mind your step."

Lauren went first, followed by Greer, with the guard last. As they passed through the letters, the air thickened and grew sticky. When they broke through the resistance, the women found themselves at the top of a flight of stone steps.

Beneath them, in the blackness, a salty dampness filtered toward the surface bringing with it the smell of the ocean.

"We have entered the In Between," Greer said.

"Yeah," Trippin said, "we have. Thanks to the Ruling Elders lifting The Agreement that's legal again. Watch your step, the stairs can be slick."

Darkness surrounded them until they reached the third bend in the descent. Then, wavering light from the cavern began to illuminate the passage.

When the stairs cut through the cave's stalactite-studded roof, Greer paused to stare at the pirate base below.

A busy port sprawled over an island resting in the underground sea. Three-masted schooners sat tied up on the wharves where gangs of workmen transferred cargo from the ships' holds to storage areas in the cavern walls.

In the center of the community vendors hawked food and drink in a thriving market. Their voices echoed in the cave, joining the aroma of roasting meat and pungent sea brine to create an exotic and oddly tropical ambiance.

"Remarkable," Greer murmured.

"Be sure to tell the Captain that," Trippin suggested. "Isla de Chronos is her baby."

Five minutes later the trio stepped onto a causeway that ran from the base of the stairs to the front porch of a rambling, two-story colonial bungalow.

There, standing on the top step with fists planted on her leather-clad hips, a blonde woman waited. Next to her, a tall man leaned arrogantly against one of the columns. His right hand rested on the hilt of the dagger tucked into his belt.

"I gotta get topside," Trippin said. Then, under his breath, he added, "Don't turn your back on Drake. Bastard would knife his own grandma."

As he started back up the steps, the woman called out, "Welcome to Isla de Chronos. Captain Miranda Winter at your service. Tall, dark, and suspicious here is my first mate, Drake Lobranche."

Crossing the causeway, Lauren greeted Miranda and then glanced at her companion. "Hey, Drake. Slit anyone's throat lately?"

The question won her a bark of laughter from the pirate. "To my disappointment, no. It's been a slow day."

"Miranda," Lauren said, "allow me to introduce Greer MacVicar. Greer, Miranda Winter."

Ascending the steps, the baobhan sith offered her hand. Miranda accepted, locking their fingers in a firm grip. Pale iridescence flowed from beneath the pirate's shirt cuff, answered by crimson power from the vampire. The magicks danced warily, encircling the women's wrists like glowing bracelets before smoothly retreating.

Without breaking their gaze, Miranda said, "You're going to fit in fine around here. How do you feel about rum?"

"Not as favorably as I regard scotch," Greer replied, "but I won't turn it down."

Releasing their hands, Miranda clasped the baobhan sith on the shoulder. "That's the spirit! Come inside by the fire. The air over the water gets cold down here."

The pirate captain led the group into a long foyer running the width of the building interrupted only by stairs leading to the second floor. A fire burned merrily in the parlor's oversized fireplace.

Without being asked, Drake drew flagons of rum from a tapped cask resting on the sideboard and passed them around.

Raising her drink, Miranda said, "May your anchor be tight."

"And your cork loose," Greer replied.

Miranda eyed her appraisingly. "That's a proper pirate toast. Where did you pick that up?"

Greer answered with a wry smile. "They that go down to the sea in ships do business in great waters."

Knocking back her rum, Miranda said, "a vampire who quotes Holy Scripture. Unusual."

"Almost as unusual as a pirate captain who recognizes the verse," Greer replied.

"Ah," Miranda said raising one finger, "let us not forget that I was not always a pirate captain; I am a woman of rich and varied interests."

She waved them toward the chairs facing the hearth. "So, baobhan sith, have you brought me something interesting to consider this fine night?"

Taking one of the offered chairs, Greer said, "Perhaps I have. Lauren has explained to me the nature of your shared business association. I find myself in need of a temporal expert."

Sitting on the raised brick hearth, Miranda leaned forward and rested her arms on her knees. "Then the rumors are true," she said. "The Witch of the Oak did disappear on her wedding night."

Greer arched an eyebrow. "As usual," she said, "the efficiency of the Fae gossip mill does not disappoint."

"Would that I could get messages through to my men as quickly as a rumor circulates through the three realms," Miranda said. "But you have to admit, this is the kind of news that can't be suppressed. From what I hear, old Barnaby Shevington has Morris Grayson on ice under suspicion of tampering with the portal matrix."

She turned her attention toward Lauren. "And, *you* are reputed to have had something to do with it."

Lauren held up her hands defensively. "Not intentionally," she said. "I'm here now trying to help."

Drake spoke for the first time, "What is it that little green guy says in the movies? Do or do not, there is no try?"

"An apt observation," Greer said. "But Lauren speaks the truth. By facilitating our meeting, she is attempting to aid in the return of the Witch of the Oak."

"What is it you think we can do for you?" Miranda asked.

"In the interest of full disclosure," Greer said, "I will share with you that the Mother Oak has told us that Jinx Hamilton and her companion, Glory Green, have been sent to an alternate time stream. These are waters so to speak that you make it your business to know."

"We don't rent out pleasure craft," Drake said. "We're business people."

Greer nodded in his direction. "You would, of course, be compensated for your services."

The pirate's thin lips curved into a smile. "We would be *well* compensated."

Miranda cut him off with a wave of her hand. "You're not the one who does the negotiating around here," she said. "You would do well to remember that. For your insolence, you can wait here with Lauren while the baobhan sith and I take a walk."

Rising smoothly, Greer followed her outside. Strolling toward the harbor, Miranda said, "So far, Drake amuses me. One day, he will go too far."

"What is it the humans say?" Greer asked. "Good help is hard to find?"

The pirate laughed. "Good help is especially hard to find for a woman in my line of work. I have found ruthlessness to be the best way to manage ambitious first mates."

"So I have been told," Greer said.

"That's why I wanted us to have this discussion in private," Miranda said. "Woman to woman."

Greer inclined her head in acknowledgment. "I will be direct," she said. "The Witch of the Oak and her husband are dear personal friends. I will be indebted to anyone who facilitates her return."

"You want us to go after the Hamilton woman."

"Lauren has told me you are the most successful of all the time pirates," Greer said. "I did not expect to discover that you use actual ships of sail to ply your trade."

The women paused to watch a work crew lower a bulging

cargo net onto the dock. "Isla de Chronos is not our homeport," Miranda said quietly. "We relocated here when the Dark Druid set up shop in Las Vegas. We honed our craft in the Middle Realm when the Ruling Elders passed The Agreement and confined us there."

"I do not understand," Greer said. "You are not *nonconformi*."

"No," Miranda said, "I'm a garden-variety elf. But I'm also a temporal mariner. We felt the heavy hand of The Agreement same as the *nonconformi*. The decree outlawed our way of life."

"I know of no such stipulation in The Agreement."

Miranda made a harsh sound in the back of her throat. "You wouldn't," she said. "Do you think the high and mighty Ruling Elders would admit they shut down the third *and* fourth realms?"

"I am afraid you have lost me," Greer said. "There is no fourth realm."

"Oh, but there is," Miranda said. "Time is the fourth realm, and the vessels that lie at anchor in this port have plied the temporal waters for centuries. My ships have sailed out of Cibolita and explored the great uncharted variations of alternate realities. Here, in this timestream, we have the reputation of being pirates and brigands, but among own kind, we're explorers."

"Why are you telling me all of this?" Greer asked.

"When our magics touched," Miranda said, "I knew we were kindred spirits. You came here with no concern about working with criminals. How do you feel about working with members of the temporal resistance?"

"I will work with anyone who can return the Witch of the Oak to those who love her."

Miranda gazed out over the port. "These ships are insulated against the buffeting waves of time. Even lacking the great tools of temporal navigation, we can sight a line on a distant star and

find our way through the darkest night. If I help you baobhan
sith, my price will be steep."

"Name it," Greer said flatly.

"If we go after the Witch of the Oak, I want the Copernican
Astrolabe in return. It's the pivotal implement of temporal navigation, the one to which all others are drawn. We've waited
centuries for an opportunity to reclaim our rightful place in the
realms. With the astrolabe in hand, we can begin the work of
freeing the Fourth Realm from the secret restraints that still
hold it captive."

"It is not within my authority to give you the Copernican
Astrolabe," Greer said honestly, "but if what you say is true, and
the entirety of The Agreement has not been lifted, I will not rest
until your case is put before the proper authorities."

Miranda considered the offer. "Do you know what caused
the portal to throw the Witch of the Oak back into time?"

"No," Greer said, "unless that discovery has been made in my
absence from Shevington, we have only the suspicion that
Morris Grayson tampered with the portal in some fashion."

"All right then," Miranda said. "Let's start by finding the
answer to that question. Take me to Shevington with you, and
then I'll tell you if I'm in a position to help you."

12

The Druid Forests of Kent, 1590, Jinx

Two days before the procession to celebrate the Winter Solstice, Moira told us she needed to go into a neighboring village to visit the local apothecary.

The shop Gemma runs in Briar Hollow combines the modern ideas of the corner pharmacy, health food store, and gift shop. Sixteenth-century apothecaries, however, played a vital role in public health, practicing folk medicine and offering "safe haven" with in-house hospitals.

Such healers relied on herbal medicine, but with a more flexible philosophy than modern physicians. They tested their recipes one patient at a time, working on the holistic belief that one cure doesn't necessarily apply to all patients.

We listened as Moira described how her friend, Patience, crafted general "cures" for specific ailments, which she then custom formulated for the patient on hand. Several times a month, Moira went into the village to share supplies, discuss formulations, and enjoy a working friendship with another well-respected woman.

As she filled her basket for the walk, Moira told us that the most common ingredients with which Patience worked included lily root, garlic, mint, vinegar, and roses.

"I share lesser-known plants with her," Moira said, "those that grow in the deepest regions of our forest and those we acquire from Druid brethren who pass through our community on their travels."

Even with two powerful women in charge of the human and Fae realms at the national level, women in general, had few opportunities to excel in the Elizabethan world in independent professions. Over the years, however, Patience cultivated a regional reputation for the effectiveness of her treatments.

The longer Moira talked, the more I wanted to see this woman's shop so I could tell Tori and Gemma about the experience when we returned to Briar Hollow.

Glory couldn't contain her enthusiasm and curiosity over the chance to witness the day-to-day life of a rural 16th-century community. She begged, in only the way Glory can beg, a mixture of persuasive plaintiveness and irritating persistence.

I have no doubt Moira could have told her no and gotten the message across, but since I quietly supported the idea of organizing a "ride along" on this excursion, the alchemist wavered.

"You truly wish to see the village and meet Patience?" she asked me.

"I do," I said. "In our world, I have a friend who is like a sister to me. Her mother has a shop similar to the one your friend runs. I'd like to be able to share my observations with them both."

Covering the contents of her basket with a cloth, Moira picked up her cloak. "You may come," she said, "but there are rules you must follow."

Glory was already pulling on her outerwear. "We'll do anything you want us to do, Moira, honest we will. Just tell us your rules, and we'll be good. I swear on Elvis and the Baby Jesus."

The alchemist looked to me for a translation. "She really means it," I said. "What are the rules?"

The list amounted to: follow Moira's lead at all times, no unsupervised interactions with villagers, and when in doubt, use the language-barrier excuse.

We stepped out of the hut into a cold, but clear winter day. Passing through the deep forest, with Orion protectively shadowing our journey, we emerged onto a dirt track that showed the passage of wagon wheels.

When the wolf didn't follow us out of the trees, Glory said, "Doesn't Orion get to come, too?"

"He will wait for us here," Moira said. "Many humans are afraid of wolves."

Orion looked at Glory and wagged his tail as if to say, "Don't worry. I'll be here when you get back."

After 30 minutes or so, we came into a collection of half-timbered buildings with thatched roofs. The villagers knew Moira and greeted her by name, but stared at us.

In an insular, self-sufficient community of only two or three hundred people, strangers presented a curiosity. In warmer weather, there would have been more activity in the mud streets, but we still saw women tending poultry and milking cows.

On the way into town, Moira had answered our questions about daily life in the village. We learned that many of the people arose as early as 3 o'clock. We'd be arriving mid-morning when the women would already be preparing the noon meal.

Patience Arnold's apothecary shop sat in the center of town facing the village green. I envisioned a quaint shop with fragrant bundles of herbs dangling from hooks set in exposed beams.

Instead, shelves and cabinets lined the walls of the well-ordered establishment. There was a work table littered with a variety of mortar and pestle sets, but neat labels identified the contents of the jars and bottles in the inventory.

A red-faced woman came out of the back when the bell on the front door jangled to announce our arrival.

"Mistress Moira!" she cried happily, wiping her hands on her apron. "The cayenne cut Master Tom's cough right in half and brought all the phlegm up from his chest. Can you get more of the plant?"

Smiling at the woman's enthusiasm, Moira said, "Cayenne comes from far to the south. It grows in warmer climes, but I will attempt to replenish your store."

Ignoring us, the woman said, "Could we not raise the plants ourselves? I have heard tales of the botanists in London cultivating delicate vines indoors during the winter months. Would that not be possible?"

"I shall try to acquire seeds," Moira assured her, "and we shall find out. Allow me to introduce two young women come from France to study with me. Jeane and Genevieve, meet Mistress Patience Arnold."

When we exchange greetings, the woman frowned at the inflection of our speech. "You are surely from away," she said. "You speak strangely. Where did you learn English?"

"From books," Glory/Genevieve said. "We had little opportunity to practice our pronunciation."

I still wasn't used to Glory coming out with appropriately couched comments, but in historian mode, she seemed to easily nail the fine points of our cover story.

"Well," Patience said, "you'll learn quick enough living among us." Then, turning her full attention back to Moira, she asked brightly, "What have you brought me today?"

The two women moved off to discuss the contents of Moira's basket. Glory and I amused ourselves by looking around the shop and watching activity on the village green through the latticed front window.

Three roads converged onto the green, which I guessed was the site of community gardens during the summer months. In the center, next to a well and a small raised platform, three sets of wooden stocks sat empty.

Keeping my voice low, I asked Glory, "Are those what I think they are?"

"Yes," she whispered. "Stocks were used for centuries to punish people for crimes, even in the American colonies."

"Well," I said, "they certainly look like they would be uncomfortable, but not lethal."

Glory shook her head and cast a hasty glance over her shoulder to make sure we weren't being overheard. "That's not true at all," she said. "People died from being locked in the stocks."

Studying the devices, I said, "Did they suffocate or something?"

"Oh no," Glory said. "People would gather around and throw things at the prisoners being punished. If they were lucky, it would just be rotten vegetables and cow dung, but sometimes if the crowd got really angry, they threw rocks."

Mob justice. Ugly in any century.

Looking back now, it's ironic that Glory and I stood at the window discussing community punishment. No sooner had she told me about the potential for a rock-throwing mob, than the sound of agitated voices rose up in one of the side streets.

As we watched, two men dragged a third forward in chains. The prisoner wore no coat. I could see him shivering in his thin linen shirt — probably because he sweated profusely and bargained non-stop with his captors. Long, straggly black hair clung to his forehead and cheeks; I think he was crying.

The spectators trailing behind shouted encouragingly. Some

gestured wildly with the farm implements and tools they carried.

My mind immediately went to the classic torch carrying mob at the base of Frankenstein's castle. If you haven't seen one of the variations of the movie, or better yet read the book, let me cut to the chase.

Crowds with torches and pitchforks are not an indicator of good things to come.

I expected the guards to slam the prisoner into one of the stocks; instead, they led him to the rough woodblock. A sick feeling snaked through the pit of my stomach.

"What are they going to do to him?" I asked.

Preoccupied with the drama outside the window, I hadn't thought to lower my voice. The apothecary came forward with Moira following behind so the four of us stood at the window watching the mob scene.

"They're going to give the thief what he deserves," Patience said scornfully. "He took old Joshua Wyndham's oxen by dark of night and should hang for the crime, but he claimed benefit of clergy so it's the brand for him. He'll carry the scar for life as a sign to all of his crime."

As we watched, a burly man in a leather apron emerged from what I took to be a blacksmith shop. In his gloved hand, he carried an iron with a red hot tip.

Glory gasped. "They're going to brand him like an animal?"

Patience stared at her curiously. "How do they deal with thieves in France?" she asked.

Beside her, Moira said grimly, "They cut off their hands."

The blood drained from my face. "Are you ill, Mistress Jeane?" Patience asked.

"No," I stammered. "I'm just . . . upset by the prospect of the branding."

Patience frowned. "Is it not better for a man to endure a few moments of pain and carry a scar than to lose a hand for life?"

When she put it that way, I had no choice but to agree. Actually, I agreed, because over the woman's shoulder Moira's eyes signaled the importance of giving the correct answer.

"It is," I said. "We come from a . . . remote region of France with few criminals. I am not accustomed to witnessing public punishments."

"You are fortunate," Patience said, folding her arms over her chest. She kept her eyes on the village green the way we would have watched a football game on TV.

A man I assumed to be some kind of official read from a piece of paper before the guards held the thief down. The blacksmith lowered the brand onto the man's hand, aiming for the fold of flesh between the thumb and forefinger. Even now when I describe the scene, I can hear the thief screaming in pain.

But for as horrible as it was to helplessly witness the man's searing punishment, the enthusiasm of the crowd frightened me more.

In the 21st century, we're intellectually aware that the mood of a large group can turn ugly — often with little provocation. We've seen the images on the news. A protest gone bad. A stampede at a concert. Even Christmas shoppers trampling one another to get to a sale.

Typically, in those situations, however, there are no cheerleaders. This crowd was different. They regarded the branding as an entertainment spectacle. I can say without question the people would have been totally onboard for a second act involving harsher measures.

It took no leap of the imagination to understand how a community could turn on a woman suspected of eccentric or suspicious behavior that some pious official labeled "witchcraft." I didn't want to be that woman; neither did Glory.

In the aftermath of the branding, we kept our eyes averted. Groups of people lingered around the green laughing and discussing what they had seen. I lost sight of the thief in the crowd. I devoutly hoped someone would take pity on him and do something to treat his wound.

We followed Moira out of the apothecary with ducked heads. I couldn't get out of that town fast enough. When we were clear of the village and alone on the open road, Moira asked, "Are legal punishments meted out in a different fashion in your world?"

"They are in America," I said. "Torture is still used in some countries, but we have a legal system that emphasizes trial and incarceration. In some parts of our country the death penalty is used, but only after a lengthy appeal process in the courts."

"I regret you had to witness events that have disturbed you so deeply," the alchemist said. "Perhaps you can now understand more clearly why it is necessary that your behavior not call attention to itself."

We understood all right.

The remainder of the trip back to the Druid encampment passed in silence. When we entered the woods, I was aware of The Veil. It descended around me with soothing security. Orion trotted out of the trees and approached Glory with an inquisitive whine.

Going down on her knees, Glory buried her face in the wolf's fur. "It's okay boy," she said, her voice breaking. "We just saw something that wasn't very nice."

Orion raised one massive paw and pulled Glory into the canine version of a hug. We let her cry into the wolf's fur until she was able to regain her composure.

Back at Moira's hut, I excused myself to write in my journal and disappeared behind the thin curtain surrounding the sleeping pallet. With that scant privacy hiding me, I opened my clenched fists for the first time since we'd left the village. My hands still trembled uncontrollably.

I began to record the day's events in shaky, uneven lines.

Glory and I had treated the preceding days like a temporal field trip. Fascinated by the Druid way of life, and insulated from the mainstream of Elizabethan society, we had avoided confronting the difference of the larger world beyond the trees.

Held back by fear and a raw need for self-preservation, I had stood aside and watched an act of brutality — one I could have stopped with a single blast of kinetic energy.

But if I'd done that, I could have consigned myself, Glory, and maybe even Moira to a burning pyre.

The words of the Wiccan Rede are one of the codes that govern the use of our native powers. "An' ye harm none, do what ye will."

That day in the village I could do nothing that would not potentially harm others, including the innocents in the Druid village. I made the right choice, but I still felt like a coward.

The experience drove home what Moira had been saying to us for days using different words — we weren't in Kansas anymore.

If we attracted the wrong kind of attention in Londinium, we could die.

Moira described the city as alive with vibrant scientific inquiry and experimentation. If Alex Farnsworth was Axe Frazier he may have believed he could hide there in plain sight while looking for a way to return to our time stream.

Could we pull off the same trick?

The safest thing we could do was to stay in the woods with the Druids and wait for Lucas and the others to find us.

Or, we could spend years in the past while life back home went on without us.

The tip of my quill hovered over the journal entry where I

tried to hash out my conflicting emotions over what to do next. I made my decision at the same time I wrote the final two sentences.

"As soon as the Solstice is over, I'm going to ask Moira to take us to Londinium. We can't stay here; we have to find our way home."

13

Shevington

W hen Tori disappeared into the darkness at the top
of the stairs, Festus returned to the parlor. He
found Chase stretched out on the remaining sofa.
Jilly dozed by the fire, while Rube snored in one of the wingback
chairs.

"I picked a hell of a time to explore being nocturnal," the
werecat muttered. He returned to the window seat, closed his
eyes, and fell into a half-awake meditative state.

Lost in thought, hours or minutes could have passed before a
sound on the square made him open his eyes. Peering out the
window, Festus watched the figure of a woman who crossed the
Common and sank onto the stone bench at the base of the
Mother Tree.

Swearing under his breath, the werecat stood up and
stretched. He jumped down and limped toward the front door.
From the looks of things, he wasn't the only one who couldn't
sleep in Shevington that night.

Letting himself out, Festus crossed the street and

approached the silent figure. As he drew closer to the Oak, Kelly said, "Your stealth skills are rusty. I heard you when you came out of the mayor's house."

Festus sprang onto the bench and sat down beside her. "I wasn't trying to be stealthy," he said. "Why do I keep finding women wandering around in the night when they should be sleeping?"

Kelly looked down at him. "Who else is awake?"

"Tori," he said. "When she left your hen party at the University she bounced old Pagecliffe out of bed to get a journal and pen."

"You're trying to get a rise out of me," she said. "I dare you to call any of the women who met at the University a hen to her face."

Festus held up a paw. "No thank you," he laughed. "I have no desire to spend the remainder of my life as a toad."

"Why did Tori go to the bookbinders?"

"The kid's got it in her head she needs to write everything down so she can tell Jinx exactly what happened when we get her back."

"Poor thing. She must be beside herself with worry."

"She is," Festus agreed, "but she's also damn smart. The pen extracted a memory Tori didn't even know she had. She saw Morris Grayson throw something into the portal, something she thinks Jinx caught."

Kelly's head jerked up. "Does she know what it was?"

"The drawing looks like some kind of a metal bar," the werecat said. "I think it's a machine part of some kind. The bar has a circle in the center with a hole in it, and there are fasteners on either end."

"Did you confront Grayson with the drawing?"

Festus shook his head. "No," he said. "Tori didn't come downstairs and tell me about it until we had already finished round one of questioning the Director. He's on ice at the Inn. Hester McElroy and the triplets are watching him. Lucas is finally getting some sleep. I figured we could all look at the sketch over breakfast."

Kelly looked around the area where they were sitting. "It's hard to believe that a few hours ago Lucas married my daughter on this very spot," she said. "I can't imagine what that poor boy is going through."

"He's blaming himself," Festus said. "No matter how many times we tell him the accident wasn't his fault, he just keeps asking why he wasn't in the portal with her."

Kelly passed a tired hand over her eyes. "Bless him," she said. "That's one of the things I love about Lucas. He never thinks twice about putting himself between Jinx and danger. But thinking this is his fault won't do anything to help."

"Every one of us has told him that a dozen times," the werecat assured her. "Let's face it, there's nothing we can say that won't sound empty."

Looking up into the Tree's branches, Kelly said, "If the Oak hadn't told us that the girls are alive, I wouldn't be much better off than Lucas. I'm supposed to be one of the most powerful witches in the realms, and everyone around me keeps saying all I can do is wait. "

"The waiting has nothing to do with how much power anyone does or doesn't have," Festus said. "We have to be careful. I can't tell you how many times I've said as much to those two boys tonight. Having them or anyone else lost in time right along with Jinx and the Pickle would only make a bad situation worse."

"I know you're right," Kelly said, "but that doesn't make the situation any easier. Especially since it feels so familiar."

"You're thinking about when you had to give Connor away, aren't you?"

Kelly nodded. "After we sent him here to Shevington to be raised, we were always able to keep Jinx safe."

The werecat laid a paw on her knee. "That's a fiction we parents tell ourselves to feel better," he said. "As long as we think we have our children wrapped up in a protective bubble, we don't have to face how dangerous the world can be."

"Lucas wonders why he wasn't in the portal with Jinx," Kelly said. "I wonder why I deprived her of the knowledge of her true heritage that might have protected her tonight."

"You don't get to do that to yourself this time," Festus said. "We were knee-deep in magical practitioners within spitting distance of that portal. Nobody knew what was coming."

"At least if I could blame myself," Kelly said, "I could make some sense of this. Why would Morris Grayson send Jinx and Glory into alternate time? Did he say anything?"

"He's playing his cards close to his vest," the werecat said. "Try not to worry about Jinx. Maybe she didn't study magic for years, but when it landed in her lap, she learned fast. She can take care of herself."

"That doesn't stop me from wanting to find my daughter and protect her," Kelly said. "It's a mother thing."

Festus sighed. "It's a father thing too."

Kelly looked ashamed of herself. "I've been sitting here going on and on about Jinx, and I haven't asked about Chase. He must be crazy with worry about Glory."

"Well," Festus said, "for a minute there I thought he was gonna get furry and rip Morris Grayson's head off, but we got through it."

"Maybe you should've let him do it," Kelly replied darkly. "As far as I'm concerned Grayson deserves whatever he gets."

"You're not gonna get any argument from me," the werecat said. "But right now we need the Director in one piece to get information out of him."

"That's what I told Jeff when he wanted to go back to Briar Hollow and get his shotgun."

"This can't be easy for Jeff."

"It's not," Kelly said. "He feels powerless. He's beating himself up for not having sufficient mastery of his magic to have done something to protect Jinx."

"The events around the accident happened too fast," Festus said. "Besides, if Tori is right, Jinx's reflexes may have worked against her."

"What do you mean?"

"Well," Festus said, "I've been thinking about the way portal mechanics work. It wasn't my best subject when I went through The Registry Academy, but if I remember correctly, an artifact passing through a portal matrix is in an inert state..."

"... unless it's carried through the matrix by a living being," Kelly finished.

"Right," the werecat said. "Which would mean that if Grayson did have something to do with Axe Frazier's disappearance the way Lauren thinks he did, there's another artifact or another piece of this artifact involved in the story."

"How are you going to figure that out?"

"Well," Festus said, "after we all meet at breakfast, I suggest we take another run at Grayson. If he still won't talk, I'll round up Jilly, Rube, and Greer, if she's back, and head to Londinium."

"To use your new contacts with the Blacklist," Kelly said. "That makes sense, but how are we going to handle Chase and Lucas? I know those two. They're not going to react well to being made to sit still while everyone else springs into action."

"I'm still working on that part," Festus said. "As much as I don't want them going off half-cocked, it is good to see them getting along. They were thick as thieves growing up. Axe's disappearance drove a wedge between them. I hated to see that happen. There have been lots of times through the years when Chase could've used a buddy."

The glow from the streetlights glinted off the tears in Kelly's eyes. "Jinx and Tori have never really been separated," she said. "One summer we tried to send them to different camps. They didn't make it a week before we brought them home."

"I remember," he said. "Kathleen and I shared a good laugh about it."

"I never told you how much it meant to me to know that you were looking after Mama," Kelly said. "I saw you in the window watching over her casket in the parlor the night she died."

"Some of that," Festus said, "was watching over you, Fiona, and the girls. You're all Daughters of Knasgowa."

Kelly shook her head. "You don't get to write that kind of friendship off as duty, Festus. You've been through a lot for us. I'm glad you're here now."

Staring up into the Oak's branches, Festus said suddenly, "I've always regretted that Chase doesn't have a brother or sister. The way you and Gemma raised Jinx and Tori? That's the best gift you could have given them."

"Gemma and I wanted them to have the same kind of friendship she and I have."

"You raised them like sisters. They know how to help each other. That's why I . . . I like Glory. She knows how to help Chase."

They sat in silence for several seconds before Kelly observed mildly. "That had to hurt."

"You have no idea."

In spite of themselves, the two old friends laughed. "Glory can be a trial," Kelly said, "but she has a heart of gold."

"And sometimes a brain of Spam," Festus growled, "but she gets that boy of mine out of his head. Chase thinks too much."

"He gets that from you," Kelly said, "even if you don't want anyone to know it."

"True," Festus said, "but my thinking generally has a purpose. Chase turns things over and over in his mind until they get all confused and twisted up. I've been watching the Pickle. When she sees him start to do that, she does something to make him laugh. The twit has people smarts, it just takes some digging to find them."

"I'm glad you see that," Kelly said. "She wants so much for you to like her. When you started letting her call you Dad, she looked like she'd won the lottery."

Festus made a scoffing sound in the back of his throat.

"*That*," Kelly accused, "was a fake hairball. How is Chase doing now?"

"Calmer after he blew off some steam," Festus said. "Before I came over here he was stretched out on the other couch. He has total faith that as long as Pickle and Jinx are together, they'll be okay. How's your faith holding up?"

"Shaky," she admitted. "But I can't let Jeff see that. I gave him something to help him sleep. I need to get back before he wakes up."

"Do you want me to walk you to Barnaby and Moira's?"

"No," she said. "I . . . I want to take the time to pray."

Festus looked at her, his amber eyes bright in the dim light. "I promised you a long time ago that I would never let anything happen to Jinx. I meant that, Kelly."

"I know you did," she said, her hand hovering over his head hesitantly before coming to rest between his ears. "Thank you for caring about my girl."

The werecat stilled under the weight of her touch as a soft, rumbling purr rose in his throat. "We're family," he said finally. "Family looks after family. I'll see you in a few hours."

Festus watched until Kelly was out of sight, then he crossed the street to the Mayor's house where Jilly sat waiting for him on the front steps.

"How long have you been in love with her?" the wereparrot asked.

"A long time," Festus said, "but it wasn't to be."

Jilly shifted over so the werecat could sit down beside her. "That's good," she said, "because I don't move in on another woman's territory."

"You're not moving in on anybody's territory but mine," Festus said. "That is if you want to."

"I want to."

From the darkness behind them, Rube said, "Me, too."

Without looking over his shoulder, Festus warned, "Do not make me turn you into a coonskin cap."

The raccoon snickered. "Now is that any way for the leader of a Blacklist team to talk to one of his most valuable operatives?"

"So you're both in on this Blacklist thing?" Festus asked.

"Dang straight," Rube said. "You ain't taking a suh-wheet job like that without old Stripedtail here."

Jilly smiled. "I don't think you boys should be left unattended. I'm in, and I'd like to bring Lucy along."

"Absolutely," Festus said. "Birds of a feather, and all that."

After a silent beat he added, "Even for a Fae outfit, we're a strange crew."

"That we are," Rube agreed, "which is what makes us so *freaking* awesome."

14

The Druid Forests of Kent, 1590, Jinx

We awakened early on the morning of the Winter Solstice. Infectious enthusiasm filled the village. I asked Moira how far we'd have to walk to reach Coldrum Long Barrow. She told me distance didn't matter.

"Today we travel in The Veil," the alchemist said. "To you, it will seem like a sojourn in the forest, but the enchantment will carry us to the Barrow and back again in the perfect space of time."

By mid-morning everyone had assembled in the center of the village talking in small groups. When Newlyn raised his staff to signal the beginning of the procession, the people immediately fell in place behind him and moved toward the trees.

The Elder motioned for Glory and me to walk with him. "You are our guests," he said. "I would be honored by thy company as we journey to the Barrow."

Moira, ever watchful, took her place behind us with Orion close by. Since our return from the village the day before, I had become more aware of the continuous presence of The Veil. Like the magic of the fairy mound in Briar Hollow, the enchantment created a sense of secure enclosure.

The sensation grew stronger as we followed Newlyn into the sheltering woods. The wind disappeared. The snow glittered in the light of the morning sun, but we felt no bite of cold.

"Will other villages join us at the Long Barrow?" I asked the Elder.

Striding along with his staff, Newlyn looked like a character straight out of some epic fantasy. Tori would be green with envy when she learned I spent the Winter Solstice with the living equivalent of Gandalf.

"In the days of old," the Elder said, "we would have gone to the great standing stones in Wiltshire for the Solstice. There, Druids from as far north as the land of the Scots gathered in a temporary village to travel as one people to the henge."

It took my mind a minute to put the pieces together, but I realized he was talking about Stonehenge. "But that no longer happens?" I asked.

"Alas, no," Newlyn said. "Although we still inhabit the human realm, the world is not as it once was. Since religious controversy began to rend the fabric of human society, the Druid bands have kept more to our isolated woods. We celebrate the Solstices at Coldrum because the ashes of our ancestors lie in that place."

Glory nudged me. "Look," she said, jerking her head toward the woods.

All around us men and women in forest garb materialized out of the shadows. They wore bows slung over their shoulders. With their long hair tied away from their elongated faces, I saw that the woodsman had the slanting eyes and pointed ears of elves. They were, however, the most elvin looking elves I'd ever seen.

Moira followed Glory's gaze and smiled. "They are my brethren from the forest," she explained. "They come to celebrate the Solstice in our company."

Don't think multiple viewings or readings of *Lord of the Rings* gives you a complete understanding of elves. Not even the most learned Fae anthropologists can accurately sort out the intertwining Elvish tribes. They all claim kinship and use words like "brothers" and "sisters" to refer to one another.

Since *my* Moira is Lucas' aunt, I assumed *this* Moira was also half water elf. Not certain how to pose a question about ethnicity, however, without saying too much or being offensive, I went with, "Are you related to them?"

"The Elvish tribes form one great, dispersed nation," she said. "The forest elves live entirely in The Veil. They began to hide themselves from humankind in the last century."

Given their looks, the woodsmen certainly couldn't disguise their identity from humans without a healthy dose of glamour. "Why did they retreat from the world?" I asked.

"Out of concern for the direction in which they believe humankind to be evolving," Moira said. "They preferred to seek the safety of The Otherworld at a time of their choosing rather than be driven there by dire circumstances."

The day before Glory and I witnessed humankind's current "direction." The experience left us both sleepless in the middle of the night.

Without a clock, I didn't know what time it was when Glory whispered, "Jinx are you asleep?"

"No."

"Can I come over there so we can talk?"

"Sure."

When she scooted under the curtain and climbed up to sit cross-legged on my pallet, I peeked out into the main room.

Moira lay sleeping on her bed of animal furs by the fire. Orion looked straight at me, ears alert.

I put a finger against my lips to signal quiet. When the wolf rested his head on his paws, I cast a light privacy spell over the curtain.

"Okay," I told Glory, "we won't wake Moira up now."

"I just can't stop thinking about that poor man in the village," she said. "Everytime I close my eyes I see everything that happened all over again in the most awful detail. I mean, I know he was a thief and everything, because they said he took that ox, which was wrong. I'm not saying he shouldn't have been punished, but couldn't they have given him community service or something?"

Leave it to Glory to inadvertently interject humor into a situation that was in no way even vaguely funny. I told her as gently as I could manage that it didn't seem to me Elizabethan justice included any humanitarian options.

Glory looked at me with watery eyes and a quivering lower lip.

"I want to go home," she said. "I wasn't scared when we first got here because everyone in the village is so nice, and Orion wouldn't let anyone hurt us, but now I miss Chase, and Rodney, and Beau, and . . . and . . . Dad."

An image of Festus' yellow-striped face, luxurious whiskers, and sardonic expression filled my mind. The visualization shot me a cocked eyewhisker and said, *Do not wimp out on me here, Jinx.*

"I miss everyone, too," I admitted. "I can't decide what's worse, being away from Lucas, or knowing my parents must be climbing the walls. Tori has probably got it in her head that somehow she should have done something to prevent the accident."

Glory nodded. "I know," she said. "I bet they're all blaming themselves. Well, not Dad, but all the rest of them."

That did it. I laughed, and after a beat, Glory giggled.

"Dad doesn't have a lot of confidence issues," she said.

"Hardly," I replied. "Festus wrote the book on self-esteem."

"Do you think they're trying to find us?"

Catching hold of her hand, I said, "I *know* they're trying to find us. We'll get home, Glory. I promise."

The late night conversation came back to me as we walked through the forest at the head of the Druid procession. In our timestream the Solstice and Christmas had already passed but caught up in the communal excitement of the village, I couldn't fight off aching loneliness for home.

I'd never celebrated any kind of major holiday with strangers. Memories of past happy times warred in my head with the hopes I cherished for the future — for that time when Lucas and I would start a family of our own.

The idea of my Dad teaching his grandchildren to fish or "Uncle" Festus corrupting my kids in endlessly creative ways brought a knot to my throat. I imagined introducing my son or daughter to the Mother Tree and picnicking with Lucas and our baby beneath her spreading branches.

By an act of supreme willpower, I forced myself to bury those thoughts and concentrate on being fully present with the Druids that day. Allowing myself to be overwhelmed by my emotions would do nothing but destroy my focus.

Any responsible wielding of magic requires focus. Although I abided by Moira's caution not to use my powers and thus call attention to myself, I held my abilities close at hand. My Southern outdoorsmen daddy would have described what I was doing by saying, "Keep one in the chamber, just in case."

That ballistic analogy makes it sound like I regard my magic as a weapon. I don't. But knowing that I could defend myself and

Glory if I needed gave me some measure of self-assurance, especially after the events of the previous day.

If someone had asked me to gauge how long we walked, I
would have said a couple of hours. When the procession
emerged from the trees, however, the sun sat low on the horizon.

In my imagination, I thought that Coldrum Long Barrow
would be a massive circle of standing stones like Stonehenge.
Instead, we stepped out onto a raised rectangle of earth
bordered by flat boulders.

A small, tight formation of upright stones stood at the far
end of the elevation. The overall effect was intimate but
impressive.

As the sun moved lower in the sky, the Druids and elves
arranged themselves in loose rows facing the stones. Newlyn
raised his staff and began to speak in a language I didn't understand. Moira whispered a translation for our benefit.

Druids don't have a holy text nor do they worship a single
deity. They live inclusively, taking their spiritual clues from the
natural world around them. Newlyn spoke of the coming long
night as a turning point in the year, the darkness that heralded
the coming light, the rebirth of spring, and the richness of
summer.

As he continued, first the elves and then the villagers began
a low rhythmic chant. Someone beat out a steady cadence on a
drum, and a lone flute played a haunting melody.

At the exact moment the sun touched the horizon, a single
beam shot through the circle, bathing Newlyn in its glow. He
stood framed in the light, chanting with his people until darkness fell.

Orion threw his head back and howled. I flinched when
the night erupted with answering cries so near to the circle we
must have stood at the center of a huge pack of the wild
beasts.

As the animals' voices faded, the Elder brought his staff down with a resounding blow.

"Educ nos illumina tenebras noctis."

Bring forth light to guide us in the darkness of this night.

The cold torches in the people's hands blazed to life. Men and women threw their arms around one another, greeting their friends and loved ones with wishes for happiness and good health.

"Happy Solstice," Moira said, hugging me and then Glory, "and a blessed new year."

When I first began to study with the elder practitioners in my life — first Myrtle, then Moira, and in time Brenna — they all impressed upon me the difference between a religious life and the spiritual life.

The kind of witchcraft we practice, unlike Wicca, is not a religion, but for a Fae witch to become truly in tune with her powers, she must cultivate a spiritual connection with Creation.

Brenna once told me, "The greatest heresy that lies at the heart of being Creavit is the severing of one's power from the True Source."

Until I stood at Coldrum with the Druids, I never understood what she meant. You see, we weren't alone that Solstice night among the stones.

The Ancestors didn't appear to us as corporeal spirits. They came bearing a deeper weight — the presence of a heritage so deeply connected with the existence of the Druids that to sever one would be to destroy the other.

For their part, the elves glowed with the borrowed energy of beings long since passed into the Higher Realms. With no need to conceal their glamour, the woodsmen radiated and reflected back the elemental joy of the first seed of awakening spring.

We returned to the village wrapped in the security of The Veil. We had no need of the torches to find our way through the trees. The elves guided us with the brightness of their existential radiance.

Animals watched from the surrounding darkness, their eyes bright at the spectacle. The ceremony at the stones and the return to the village filled me with the same sense of wonder I experience each Christmas Eve at the lighting of the Mother Tree on the square at Shevington.

We humans — and yes, there is a part of me that will always think of myself as human — miss so much with our science and our rationalism. We look at nature as a quantity to be measured rather than a magic to be experienced.

That Solstice night, I felt at one with the world. It made me realize that part of the solution to reaching home again lay not just in deciphering the mechanics of time but in seeking the source of wisdom that had never failed me.

Catching up to Moira, I touched her arm. When she bent to hear what I had to say, I asked, "Can you take me to the Mother Tree?"

Amid the singing and revelry around us, no one could hear what we were saying. The alchemist looked at me with empathy in her eyes.

"I know that in your time you are the chosen witch of the Tree," she said. "But here, there is no guarantee that the Oak will speak with you."

She was trying to protect me from what could've been a bitter disappointment, but I wasn't worried.

"The Oak will hear my voice and answer," I said. "Besides, if she does talk to me, then you'll know for certain that I am who I say I am."

The alchemist smiled. "You have not lied to me. When the Yule celebration is over, I will take you to the Mother Tree."

Glory, who was close enough to hear, said, "Doesn't Yule last twelve days? I'm not sure Jinx wants to wait that long, do you, Jinx?"

"Not really," I admitted. "Can't we go sooner?"

Moira considered the request. "When we reach the village there will be feasting and drinking until dawn," she said finally. "It is not unusual for many to need a period of . . . recovery. Perhaps that would be our best opportunity."

"Recovery." That was a nice way to say that in the morning, there would be a lot of hung over Druids and elves in the village.

15

Shevington, Tori

The smell of frying bacon woke me the next morning. Innis might not be able to bring Jinx and Glory home, but in the interim, none of us would starve.

Sometime in the night, my suitcase and clothes appeared in my room. A feat no doubt also accomplished by superior brownie efficiency. You know that old saying, "Familiarity breeds contempt?" Not in this case. Seeing familiar things instantly made me feel more secure.

I dressed in my favorite jeans and a soft, worn, work shirt that had belonged to my father. In the months since his death, I'd worked hard to remember the good things about the man.

Dad made a lot of mistakes, chief on the list cheating on my mother and leaving her for a younger woman. None of that, however, meant he deserved to die the victim of a pair of psychotic vampire sisters.

Forgiveness can take a long time, but I was working on it.

The sunlight streaming through the windows beckoned to me. I walked over and looked down at the town square. All traces of the wedding were gone. A brief surge of anger flooded through me at the idea that Shevington could so quickly return to at least the appearance of normal business. Then I realized none of us needed to look at the remnants of the celebration gone bad.

At the sound of voices downstairs, I ran a brush through my hair and started to walk out of the room. I almost made it to the door before an insistent tapping directed my attention toward the bed.

I saw the pen standing on end beating out a rhythm against the top of the nightstand. When I went over, the journal flipped open and detached a page, which floated toward my hand.

Staring at the sheet, I asked, "Did I dream this?"

The pen wobbled back and forth in the affirmative.

"I've never seen anything like this place," I said. "I think I'd remember a bunch of rock huts that look like beehives."

The pen cap rotated free and settled on the table. The barrel did a mid-air turn and descended toward the paper. As I watched, the nib wrote, *"Not everything that comes into your mind originates with you."*

Jinx tried to warn me that keeping a sentient journal meant dealing with a fair amount of attitude. She wasn't kidding.

"Are you trying to tell me this is a message?" I asked excitedly. "Is Jinx trying to tell me something?"

The pen wrote a second sentence. *"We cannot be sure."*

"That's okay," I said. "I'll take whatever I can get."

This time when I started to leave the room, a rustling in my suitcase stopped me. Eyeing the bag suspiciously, I backed away when the lid bobbed up and down a couple of times. If I had acquired an insect stowaway, the bug had to be enormous to pull off that stunt.

Looking around for something to extend my grasp, I spotted a coat hanger in the closet. Straining not to get any closer to the suitcase than necessary, I used the hanger to flip back the lid. Rodney's head popped up. One of my socks was stuck on his head.

"*Rodney!* You scared me half to death!" I said. "What are you doing here? You're supposed to be back in Briar Hollow."

Wriggling out from under the sock, the rat looked at me defiantly. He didn't need to mime what he wanted to say for me to get the message.

"I know you want to help," I said. "We went over this last night. You were supposed to go back with Beau and take care of Glory's column."

Diving head-first into the contents of the suitcase, Rodney came up with a rat-sized laptop.

Forgetting to be cross with him, I leaned in for a better look. "That's pretty cool," I said. "Where did you get it?"

After a complex series of gestures I couldn't possibly describe, the rat made me understand that Brenna miniaturized a MacBook for his use.

"Huh," I said. "Why didn't we ever think of that?"

Rodney struck a pose that clearly said, *"Yeah, why didn't you ever think of that?"*

"Okay," I said. "Sue us already. We're lousy friends. The general idea here is that you're planning to take care of Glory's column from Shevington?"

He nodded, fixing me with an expectant look.

What was I supposed to do? He'd gone to a lot of trouble to pull off this stunt and equip himself to work in the process.

"All right," I said. "Fine. You can stay. But don't go getting eaten by a stray werecat."

Grinning from ear-to-ear, Rodney crossed his heart, promising to stay out of the way of hungry shapeshifting felines. When I held out my hand, the rat scrambled up my arm and settled into his familiar spot on my shoulder.

Addressing the room in general, I said, "Any more surprises?"

When nothing responded, I took that as my cue to join the others for breakfast.

At the top of the stairs, I looked down into the foyer and saw my mother waiting for me. I resisted the urge to run into her arms, but I did take the last few steps quickly. She engulfed me in a welcoming hug that threatened to smother Rodney.

"Hey," I said, my voice coming out muffled against her shoulder. "Watch the rat. Where did you sleep last night?"

Mom leaned back and looked at Rodney. "Just couldn't take no for an answer, huh?"

He had the good grace to look sheepish when he nodded.

"To answer your question," Mom said to me. "I slept at Barnaby and Moira's house. Did you get any rest?"

"Not a lot," I said, knowing better than to lie. "Maybe three hours. What about you?"

"About the same," she replied. "When Connor sent word that Grayson was being held at the Inn, Barnaby had Jeff and Kelly's things moved down to the house. Kelly finally gave Jeff something to get him to calm down and go to sleep."

Over her shoulder, I saw Jinx's parents standing in the parlor talking with Festus and Jilly. "Jeff looks pretty good this morning," I said.

"He's keeping it together for Lucas."

On cue, I heard Lucas' voice from the front room. He sounded agitated. "*Can we* please *get this meeting started?*" he demanded. "*I'm sick and tired of wasting time.*"

To my surprise, I heard Innis answer sharply, "Crisis or not, Master Lucas, I'll thank you to mind your manners in the Lord High Mayor's house."

The rebuke must have startled Lucas into some awareness of

his behavior. He apologized, and when he stepped into the hallway and saw me, he came forward and hugged me.

"Hi, Tori," he said. " I guess you heard that?"

Hugging him back, I said, "Under the circumstances, you get a dispensation."

Jerking his head back toward the parlor, Lucas said, "Tell Innis that."

"She's just being protective of Connor," I said. "Everyone understands you're tired and worried."

"I don't do waiting well," he admitted.

"Nobody does," I assured him. "Just keep reminding yourself that everyone here has Jinx and Glory's best interests in mind."

From the doorway of the dining room, Connor said, "Listen to my girlfriend. She's pretty smart."

Giving him a good morning kiss, I said, with a hint of teasing in the words, "And don't you forget it."

Connor handed me a plate and gave one to Lucas. We made our way along the lavish breakfast buffet that Innis had laid out on the sideboard.

I don't know what I needed more, the food or the coffee, but I was grateful to see a self-refilling urn from Madame Kaveh's.

Everyone was seated when a knock sounded at the front door. A moment or two later, Greer walked into the room followed by Lauren Frazier and two newcomers.

Lucas instantly tensed. "You've got some nerve showing your face here, Lauren," he snapped. "If you'd told me the truth about Uncle Morris from the beginning, none of this would have happened."

Lauren didn't have time to attempt an answer. The blonde woman standing by Greer did it for her. "You must be the aggrieved bridegroom," she said pleasantly. "This time I'll cut you some slack. Next time you insult my friend like that, I'll cut your throat."

Starting out of his chair, Lucas snarled, "Who the hell are you to tell me what to do?"

At that, the swarthy man who accompanied the blonde stepped in. "Keep a civil tongue in your head when you're speaking to the Captain."

Before the war of words and egos could erupt in actual violence, Connor said firmly, "That will be enough out of all of you. Sit down, Lucas."

Frankly, that level of authority from Connor shocked us all. Lucas sat down, but he continued to glare at the strange woman who didn't care in the slightest.

From the look of her, I suspected she might indeed cut a man's throat for insolence. Dressed in a sleeveless leather jerkin belted at the waist, she sported a sheathed dagger on one side and a holstered pistol on the other.

The full sleeves of her white shirt tightened at the wrist, partially hidden by leather gauntlets. I'm pretty thin, but I'll never see the day I can pull off tight leather pants or thigh high boots the way she did.

The dark man beside her wore similar attire. Brass buttons decorated the lapels of his black frock coat, which hung open to reveal a flintlock pistol tucked into a wide belt.

If the pair hadn't moved with such casual, confident ease, I might have mistaken them for pirate movie extras Greer picked up by accident in Vegas.

From his seat at the end of the table, Rube waved a fork in the direction of the baobhan sith. "Nice entrance, Red," he said with his mouth full. "We ain't had a good fight at breakfast in a long time."

Greer regarded the raccoon with fond tolerance. "Good morning, Reuben. I see that both your droll humor and appetite are intact."

"There ain't much that can knock me off my chow," Rube

replied, going in for more eggs. "You gonna introduce your friends before Round Two?"

Staring pointedly at Lucas, the baobhan sith said, "I would prefer there be no Round Two. Allow me to present Captain Miranda Winter and her first mate, Drake Lobranche. They are experts in temporal navigation."

Miranda smiled disarmingly. "We're alternate time pirates."

I found myself immediately liking the woman. She made no bones about her occupation and saw no reason for others to gloss over the illegality of her work.

Connor extended his hand to both pirates in turn. "Welcome to my home," he said. "My name is Connor Hamilton. I'm the Lord High Mayor. This is my grandfather, the founder of our community, Barnaby Shevington and his wife, our alchemist, Moira."

"A pleasure," Miranda said. "Your reputation precedes you, Mr. Shevington."

Connor continued to make introductions around the table. When he reached Myrtle, Miranda's manner changed completely.

Bowing her head, she said, "I am deeply honored to stand in your presence, aos sí." Several sentences in Elvish followed that I didn't understand.

Myrtle acknowledged whatever Miranda said with a serene smile and one of her maddeningly cryptic statements. "The day will come, Captain Winter, when a fair wind will carry you to any port of call you desire."

"From your mouth, aos sí to the ears of the gods," Miranda replied.

Since no one knew what to say to that, Connor suggested the newcomers fill their plates and join us at the table.

"With pleasure," Miranda said. "You'll never meet a seafaring soul who will turn down good grub over hardtack."

Lucas, who was about to expire from impatience, said, "Can we at least eat and talk at the same time?"

With prompting from Festus, I shared both drawings produced by the journal. Miranda asked to see the mystery object, while Moira reached for the village scene.

"Do you recognize the place?" I asked her.

The Alchemist nodded. "This looks like the Druid village in Kent where I spent a portion of my girlhood."

"And this," Miranda said, "is the rule from an astrolabe."

The second announcement touched off a cacophony around the table until Barnaby called for order. "You are certain?" he asked.

"I am," Miranda said. "Now that I've seen it, I think I can explain what happened to your Witch of the Oak."

"Pray continue," Barnaby said.

Miranda leaned back in her chair and crossed her booted legs. "Don't you think we ought to lay all our cards on the table first Mr. Shevington?"

Barnaby blinked. "I do not take your meaning, madam."

"If I'm going to explain the great temporal artifacts to you, I think you should come clean about the captive nature of the Fourth Realm."

Honestly perplexed, Barnaby said, "There is no Fourth Realm."

Miranda started to push away from the table. "If that's the position you're going to take," she said. "We won't be able to conduct business together."

"Take your seat, Captain Winter," Myrtle said. "Barnaby is not lying to you." Then speaking to the room, she added, "The Fourth Realm of which the captain speaks is time itself."

"I appreciate your honesty, aos sí," Miranda said. "Since the passage of The Agreement, the Fourth Realm has been held captive by its terms. The Copernican Astrolabe was consigned to

The Blacklist vaults while the other great instruments of temporal navigation were scattered to the time streams."

Lucas erupted. "I hope you won't be offended when I tell you that I don't give a damn about Fae politics right now. I want my wife back. Either you can help make that happen, or you can't. Which is it?"

"I can make it happen," Miranda said. "But in return, I want the Copernican Astrolabe. All of it. Not just pieces."

Festus cleared his throat. "Let's take one thing at a time," he said. "You're telling us that this thing Grayson threw into the portal, which we think Jinx caught, is part of the astrolabe?"

"Show them, Drake," she ordered.

Her companion reached into a bag hanging from his belt and removed a strange object I first thought might be a pendant or maybe a pocket watch. Then he pointed to a smaller version of the metal bar my pen and journal had drawn hours earlier.

"This is a pocket-sized astrolabe," he said. "The rule rotates across the face to locate positions on the plate. Those positions are then related to the scale of hours marked here on the limb."

Festus, never one for social niceties, stepped onto the table-cloth and sauntered past everyone's breakfast coming to a stop in front of Drake. "Run through that for me again," he ordered.

Clearly amused by the werecat's brazenness, the pirate complied.

Turning his amber eyes toward Miranda, Festus said, "You know so much about this, what would happen if a piece of the Copernican Astrolabe got tossed into a portal and somebody caught it?"

"The piece would instantly seek out others of its kind in the streams of time," she said. "The astrolabe is enchanted with magnetic association."

Moira spoke. "The disparate parts seek one another out in an effort to reassemble themselves."

"Exactly," the pirate said. "You want to find your witch? Toss another piece of the astrolabe into a portal. You should get sucked straight to her. But if you want to get back, you need us. Or more specifically, you need our ships."

Miranda didn't give away any trade secrets, but she did reveal that the temporal vessels in her fleet are insulated against the buffeting action of a journey across the threads of time. She claimed that some unknown portion of the now-defunct Agreement outlawed her trade, turning her and her kind into pirates when once they had been great explorers.

"A piece of the astrolabe will get us where we're going," she assured those assembled, "and I'll get us home. That's assuming that you can get another piece of the astrolabe."

"Oh," Festus said, "we can get it. But before we do, I have a few more questions for Morris Grayson, and, no offense intended, I need to verify your story."

Miranda rose from her chair, which brought Drake instantly to his feet. "None taken," she said. "You know my price. The Copernican Astrolabe for your witch. We'll be in Vegas waiting to hear from you."

Greer exited with them to escort the pair to the portal. Lauren stayed in her chair but said nothing.

When the pirates were gone, Lucas jumped to his feet, "I want to talk to my uncle."

"Agreed," Barnaby said, also standing. "I am most curious about one aspect of Captain Winter's assertions."

"Which one?" Moira asked.

"If the separate parts of the astrolabe are drawn to reunite with one another — and if Grayson did maroon Miss Frazier's brother in time — how did he engineer the first accident?"

Rube burped and wiped at his whiskers with a napkin. "He pitched another part into the portal."

"If he did," Barnaby said, "to what was that part attracted?"

The raccoon shook his head. "Geez, it's always something, ain't it? Just one time I wish we didn't run into one connie-nun-drum after another."

Barnaby paused, uncertain what to say next.

"Conundrum," Festus translated.

"Ah," Barnaby said. "Colorfully expressed, Reuben, but quite correct."

"That," the raccoon said, biting into a cinnamon roll, "is why they pay me the big bucks."

Lucas slammed his hand on the table. "You people can theorize all you like. The solution sounds pretty damn simple to me. We get another piece of the Copernican Astrolabe from the Blacklist containment vaults, and *I* go after Jinx. We don't need to deal with common criminals. I'm perfectly capable of rescuing my wife."

Chase, who had been silent through the whole breakfast said quietly, "*We* go after Jinx *and Glory.*"

Festus curled his tail around his body, sat up straight, and said, "No."

Both Lucas and Chase erupted. Festus endured their heated protests with backed ears until he finally lost his temper.

"Bastet's whiskers!" he roared. "Both of you can it before I take you in for a worming or worse. When Greer gets back, I'm going to ask her to go to Londinium with me, Rube, and Jilly. We'll visit BEAR headquarters and have a talk with Stank Preston. He's a Blacklist containment specialist. If there's any truth to this Fourth Realm business, he'll know."

"I'm going with you," Lucas said.

"No," Festus replied, "you're not."

"Why not?"

"You," the werecat said pointedly, "aren't a member of my Blacklist team. You need to stay here and talk to your uncle. Get whatever you can out of him; I don't care how you do it."

"I don't work for you," Lucas said.

Rube tossed a grape in his mouth and said cheerfully, "Yeah, Hat Man, you kinda do. As a Blacklist agent, Festus outranks us all. Blacklist agents can pull rank on every other agency. I keep telling you, you gotta read the rule book otherwise how you gonna know which ones you can break and which ones you gotta keep?"

"I'll go over your head," Lucas sputtered.

"To who?" Festus asked. "You're holding the Director of the DGI under house arrest. IBIS won't touch this with a ten-foot pole. I've got seniority over you at The Registry and BEAR, and there's no way Hilton Barnstable is going to let you do anything until you quit acting like a hot-headed fool and remember you're a professional Fae agent. You need a piece of the Astrolabe. I'm the only person who can get it for you."

Deflated, Lucas sank into his chair. "Why are you doing this?"

Festus walked across the table, delicately missing the butter and sidestepping a gravy boat. "I'm doing this for Jinx," he said.

Lucas looked up, shocked. "What do you mean?"

"I'm not letting you or Chase hop into a portal with stray astrolabe bits until I'm damned sure you'll come back. If Jinx gets home and you don't, I'll be the one to have to deal with a pissed off witch for getting her husband killed, *and* I'm stuck with the Pickle for life. *Nobody* gets paid enough for that."

16

Shevington

As everyone filtered out of the dining room, Rube caught Festus' eye and nodded toward the back of the house. The werecat followed the raccoon to the darkened formal drawing room.

When they were inside, Rube said, "Hat Man's losing it."

"You just now catching on to that?" Festus asked, jumping onto the velvet settee and kneading the upholstery with his front paws. "Why don't we come in here more often? The furniture is nicer, and it's quiet."

Scrambling up beside him, Rube ran his hand speculatively over the material. "Hey, this stuff is *suh-wheet!* Comfy on the tootsies. So, like I was saying, Lucas ain't firing on all cylinders."

Festus sat down and tucked his paws under his chest. "I guess we can't blame the guy. His wife did get sucked into a portal before they even made it to the honeymoon. Still, we can't have him going rogue, especially around those time pirates."

Rube pulled one of the satin pillows onto his lap and started to bat a tassel back and forth. "That Dirk guy . . .

"Drake."

"Dirk, Drake, whatever. He's working too hard on the whole big bad pirate vibe. Now, the chick? She's legit dangerous."

From the doorway, Greer said, "You would be correct in that estimation, Reuben. Does Connor know the two of you are shedding all over the good furniture?"

"I don't *shed*," Festus said archly, ignoring the tufts of yellow fur that floated past his nose when he shifted his weight.

"Duly noted," Greer said drily, taking the chair across from them.

"Do you believe Captain Winter when she says she can navigate to wherever Jinx and the Pickle wound up?" Festus asked.

The baobhan sith steepled her fingers. "There were many things Miranda did not say at breakfast."

Festus arched an eyewhisker. "Such as?"

"To begin with," Greer replied, "she does not want the Copernican Astrolabe for profit-based motives."

Rube frowned. "Why would Pirate Lady sit on info like that? Saying she ain't in it for the dough woulda made everybody trust her more."

"It is my theory that Miranda has not imparted her true motives to her associate Mr. Lobranche," Greer said. "He does not strike me as the idealistic sort."

"Naw," Rube said. "Ya think? And here I was figuring him for doing charity work on the side."

Greer nodded approvingly. "Aptly sarcastic *and* droll, Reuben. I negotiated in private with Miranda to arrange her visit to the Valley. During our conversation, she described herself as part of a temporal resistance of mariners confined to the Middle Realm."

The raccoon shook his head vehemently. "That ain't good, Red. You don't never run a job in a job."

"The trash panda's right," Festus said. "We don't need to

bring anyone in with ulterior motives. Thanks to Grayson, we're up to our ears in double crosses already."

"According to Miranda, these mariners wish only to regain their status as legitimate time-faring explorers and navigators."

Rube's black mask crinkled. "You understand all this time travel business, Red?"

"Not enough to judge the veracity of Miranda's claims," the baobhan sith replied.

Twirling the pillow with his back feet, Rube said, "Too bad. Sure would be good to know if the dame's lying."

Greer smiled tolerantly; Festus closed his eyes and groaned.

"What?" Rube said. "Did I say something amusing like?"

"Not at all, Reuben," Greer replied. "We're simply delighting in the pleasure of your company."

The raccoon grinned. "I know. I got charm in spades."

Ignoring Rube, Festus looked at Greer. "Feel like taking a trip to Londinium with us?"

"Who is 'us?'" she asked.

"There's a spot on my Blacklist squad for you if you want it. I've asked Jilly and Lucy to come onboard, too."

Still twirling the pillow, Rube said, "I like them birds. Five's a good number, Red. You broads would have the upper hand over us guys."

"He means, you '*ladies*,'" Festus said.

Realizing his mistake, Rube froze, the fringe on the pillow dangling over his toes. "*Right*," he said hastily, "I totally meant to say *ladies*. 'Cause you ain't broad, Red, except for *being* a broad, by which I mean a female lady girl person."

The baobhan sith held up a hand to silence him. "Do not dig the proverbial hole deeper. I cannot speak to the long-term, Festus, but I will come with you to Londinium."

"*Suh-wheet!*" Rube said. "Check out the bennies before you say no on the Blacklist gig, Red. We score higher security clearances *and* bigger paychecks. With that last part, I got zero issue."

"You wouldn't," Festus said. "Your monthly grocery bill must be through the roof."

Patting his ample gut, the raccoon said proudly, "Fine tuned machine like me needs fuel, McGregor."

"Well, if you think you've eaten enough to survive the trip, let's round up Jilly and get to Londinium," Festus said, standing and stretching. "I have a few questions for a certain stinky scientist."

He started to jump down only to stop when he saw Rodney looking up at him from the floor. "Hey, Rat Boy. Something we can do for you?"

Rodney nodded. He stood on his hind legs and held up his clenched front paws. One at a time, he extended his toes to the count of six.

"Six what?" Festus asked.

Rodney pointed at the werecat, the raccoon, and the baobhan sith.

Festus looked blank. "I don't get it."

"I do," Rube said, "His Rodentialness wants to join the team."

At that, Rodney pretended to shoot and sink a basket, throwing his paws up in victory.

"See," the raccoon said. "Plain as the whiskers on your face."

Shaking his head, Festus said, "As much as I enjoy playing charades, the answer is no. Jinx and Tori would yank my whiskers out one at a time if I let anything happen to you."

Striking a gallant pose, Rodney pantomimed drawing his sword.

"Yeah, yeah, I know. Knight of the Rodere. You're still not going."

At that, the rat crossed his arms and stared defiantly at the werecat.

"*No*," Festus said, following the conversation now without visual cues, "you will *not* stowaway. That trick is getting old."

The rat's whiskers quivered indignantly.

"Do not take that tone with me," Festus warned. "It's been years since I've had a good mouse d'oeuvre."

Rodney stuck his tongue out, blew the werecat a raspberry, and shot him the tail.

"Hey!" Festus cried."Language!"

Holding up his tiny fists again, Rodney repeated his six-finger count.

"I said *no*."

Locked in a cross-species contest of wills, the rat and the werecat glared at each other across the rug.

When neither seemed inclined to budge, Greer played peacemaker, "As I have not officially accepted your invitation to become a member of the team, Festus, Rodney may come to Londinium as my personal guest."

"You're a lot of help," the werecat grumbled. "Fine. Rat Boy can ride along, but in no way Rodney does this mean you stand a rat's chance in Hades of becoming a Blacklist agent."

Turning his back on Festus, Rodney scaled Greer's chair, ran up her arm, and perched on her shoulder. He clasped his hands over his heart and bowed at the baobhan sith.

"You are most welcome," the vampire said. "It will be refreshing to travel in the company of so gallant a gentleman."

"McGregor," Rube said, "I think we was just insulted."

Stalking toward the door, Festus grumbled, "I'll give him something to be insulted about. Damned upstart cheese-eating pretentious . . . "

The string of insults trailed away as the werecat moved toward the front of the house.

"He's really quite sweet underneath that gruff exterior," Greer assured Rodney.

"No, he ain't," Rube said. "You land on your head or something when you blew in from Vegas, Red?"

FESTUS, Jilly, Rube, and Greer stepped out of the portal in Trafalgar Square. Rodney, riding on the vampire's shoulder, sat up eagerly, taking in his surroundings with twitching whiskers.

A raven fluttered down from Lord Nelson's head and landed at their feet. "I guess I won't ask how the wedding went," Lucy said.

"Good idea," Jilly replied. "You know Festus and Rube. Lucy meet Greer MacVicar. Greer, this is my associate, Lucy George. And this, Lucy, is Sir Rodney de Roquefort."

The rat waved a cheerful paw in the raven's direction.

"Pleased to meet you both," Lucy said. Then she tilted her head to one side and looked up at Jilly. "I assumed we were going in feathers. Do I need to get back in human form?"

"No," Jilly said. "I'll use one of the shifter changing rooms when we get to BEAR headquarters."

When Greer hailed a Hansom cab for the group, Rube insisted on riding in the box with the driver saying, "Wind in my fur feels good. So, what route you taking to BEAR HQ buddy, 'cause I know a shortcut."

Thirty minutes and four wrong turns later, Jilly doubled the driver's fare. "I'm sorry," she said, "Rube seriously exaggerates his sense of direction."

The driver tipped his hat. "No trouble, Missus. He's a good sort even if he couldn't find his arse with all four paws."

From the sidewalk Rube said, "You wanna talk about somebody's arse, buddy . . . " but stopped in mid-sentence when Greer picked him up by the scruff of the neck.

"Hey!" he roared. "Put me down, Red! You're gonna give me a case of the whipped lash."

Walking placidly toward the entrance dangling the struggling raccoon effortlessly with one arm, Greer said, "I'm sorry, Reuben. Did you say something?"

Inside the building, the group waited while Jilly used a free shifting room. Emerging as an elegant African Grey, she extended both wings and gave her feathers a vigorous shake,

"Feel better?" Festus asked.

"Much," Jilly said. "I've been longing to stretch my wings for hours."

Gliding in lazy circles, she and Lucy followed Festus and the others down a series of corridors leading to Stank Preston's lab. When Festus banged open the door, the ferret scientist looked up from his computer, eyes widening at the sight of the werecat's entourage.

"McGregor, what are you doing here?"

"I'm here," Festus said testily, "because you've been holding out on me. What's this BS about part of The Agreement not being lifted? And why did I have to hear about it from a pirate captain who makes her living pilfering temporal loot?"

Stank's eyewhiskers shot up. He turned to his assistants. "You guys take a break. Close the door behind you."

When the younger ferrets were gone, Stank said, "McGregor, you wouldn't know discretion if it walked up and smacked you in the snout."

"I don't have time for discretion," Festus shot back. "Have you stuck your head out of this damned lab long enough to know the Witch of the Oak is missing?"

The ferret's brow furrowed. "What do time pirates and the secret half of The Agreement have to do with Jinx Hamilton's disappearance?"

Smiling with lethal sweetness, Festus said, "Gee, Stank. I

don't know. That's what I was hoping you could tell me. Start with The Agreement."

Stank shifted his soggy cigar from one side of his mouth to the other. "You're not going to like it."

Festus answered with an irritated swish of his tail. "Color me shocked. Talk."

Pausing long enough to pick a fleck of tobacco off his whiskers, the ferret took a deep breath and said, "You are correct. There were two parts of The Agreement. The Conference of the Realms lifted one of them."

Lucy let out an annoyed squawk, extending her wings and ruffling her feathers. "This isn't going to be good."

"You're not wrong," Stank admitted. "The Agreement quarantined the Middle Realm *and* outlawed alternate time travel."

Rotating her head, Jilly fixed one golden eye on Stank. "How do you know all this?"

"I know," he said, "because the instruments that make accurate travel across the timestreams possible are the purview of the Blacklist."

Festus hopped on the table and nodded toward the computer. "Put your paws to work and tell me if Morris Grayson visited the containment vaults before he came to Briar Hollow for the wedding."

Chewing on his cigar, Stank tapped a few keys. "Yeah," he said. "The Director spent some time with the Copernican Astrolabe the day before he left Londinium."

"Do you have eyes on that thing?"

"Sure," Stank said, typing again. "We have cameras on each artifact. I haven't looked at the Astrolabe in years but . . . "

He enlarged the image on his screen, squinted at the display, and muttered, "This is highly irregular."

"What?" Festus asked.

"There are two pieces missing from the Astrolabe, the dial, and the rule."

Leaning over the table's edge, Festus said, "Rube, show him the drawing."

The raccoon reached into the pack at his waist and pulled out an iPhone. "What's your email, bro?" he asked Stank.

"Mustela46@FaeMail.com."

Rube's black fingers flew over the screen. "Okey dokey, take a look at that."

Stank opened the message and clicked on the attachment. The drawing from Tori's journal opened.

"Is that one of the Astrolabe parts?" Festus asked.

"I don't know if it's from *the* Astrolabe," Stank said, "but it is a rule from *an* astrolabe. Why?"

"We think Morris Grayson threw that thing into the portal and Jinx caught it before the explosion."

The ferret's eyes darted back and forth. "Not good," he mumbled. "Seriously not good. Let me check the logbook to see who's been signing off on the integrity of the artifact."

Rube, who was digging through the trash can said, "Bet you doughnuts to dollars it was Mo Grayson."

"Fortunately, I'm not a betting ferret," Stank said, "because you're right. Director Grayson has certified the Astrolabe's integrity for decades."

Festus let out a frustrated hiss. "So far I'm not impressed with Blacklist security protocols."

"Be glad I'm telling you any of this," Stank said. "If you hadn't pulled off that Merstone caper and snagged a promotion, this information would have been miles above your pay grade."

Narrowing his eyes, the werecat said, "Don't flatter yourself, Stank. Blacklist or not, if I thought you had information that would bring Jinx and Glory home, I'd get it out of you one way or the other."

The ferret curled his lips back and showed his teeth. "You couldn't get me to talk on your best day, McGregor."

Festus arched his back, but Jilly cut off whatever he intended to say next. "If you boys are done measuring your fangs, can we get back to business?"

Forcing his fur to lie flat, Festus nodded. "Fine. Let's hear the rest, Stank."

The ferret coiled his body and sprang across the distance from his desk to the tray of the wall-mounted whiteboard. Picking up a marker, he scrawled the words, "Temporal mechanics."

"Anybody know anything about how time travel works?" he asked, studying the group like a professor surveying a slow class.

With murder in his eyes, Festus said, "We don't have all day. Give us the short version."

Radiating aggravation the ferret said, "Do you have a single academic bone in your body?"

Greer smoothly interjected herself into the conversation. "As you know, my kind have minimal temporal abilities. I am able to halt the flow of time in a confined space as if routing a strong stream of water around a stone."

"Good," Stank said. "That's a good analogy. The powers of the baobhan sith are limited to a single strand of time, as are the course of our lives. We live in the warp of the temporal tapestry, but with the right tools, we can move across the weft."

"Nobody signed up for a damned weaving class, Stank," Festus growled. "Speed this up."

Jilly fluttered to the whiteboard tray and picked up a second marker in her beak. She used it to draw a series of parallel vertical lines.

"Those," she said, holding the pen in her claw, "are the threads in a tapestry that are called the warp. The lines that cross them are the weft. With a little poetic license, Dr. Preston is telling us that there are threads of time parallel to our own."

Rube reached in his pack and pulled out a bag of potato chips. "Hate to rain on your whiteboard parade, but we already figured that part out. And we been using watery terms 'cause you know, pirates and all? Could we pick a vocabulary sheet and stick with it?"

Gritting his teeth, Stank said, "Time forms the great body of reality. Whether you're talking about streams or threads, the point is that some are horizontal and some are vertical. If you travel up and down a vertical, you're going to the future or the past. Travel on a horizontal, and you're in the same time, but access different versions."

The raccoon munched contemplatively. "Can you mix it up and go like across and drop down?"

"As astonished as I am to say this," Stank replied, "you're correct. If Jinx and her companion were propelled into alternate time, they traveled across and were then pulled down."

"Why not up?" Lucy asked.

"Even time pirates tend to avoid future travel."

Jilly dropped the marker back into the tray. "What role does the Astrolabe play in all this?"

"Under the terms of The Agreement, the great tools of classical temporal navigation were scattered across the timestreams," Stank said, "never to be reunited. The Copernican Astrolabe is the cardinal object. The separate parts share essential magnetism. If Jinx carried the rule into the portal, the matrix would activate the magnetism."

Licking a candy bar wrapper clean, Rube said, "In English?"

"The rule pulled Jinx and Glory to a place in time where another fragment of the Copernican Astrolabe exists," Stank said. "Instead of passing straight through the portal, they were pulled to the left or right into the energy field that creates the opening between the realms. I've debriefed Sídhe pirates who have made the journey. They describe a tunnel with horizontal junctures that reveal glimpses of the passing timestream."

Jilly clacked her beak. "How do the pirates navigate the tunnel?"

"Every crew has their individual method," the ferret replied, "all developed after they were deprived of the temporal navigation artifacts. It's not just figuring out where to enter any given timestream. They also have to understand how to return to the correct horizontal to find their way back to their point of origin."

Rube rolled back onto his butt, propping his back against a file cabinet. "Gotta be the sugar rush. I heard you talking words but nothing made sense."

Festus, who sat staring at the drawing, contemplatively thumping the table with the tip of his tail, said, "Oh, he made sense. Jinx and Glory weren't the first people Grayson sent spinning off into wonky alternate time. There's only one other person connected to the Director and a portal accident — Axe Frazier."

17

The Druid Forests of Kent, 1590, Jinx

The lack of a written cultural record condemns the Druids to exist only in memory, and to be a subject of tremendous speculation. Let me clear up one point. Druids have serious party skills.

As soon as the procession returned from the Barrow, the men lit a large bonfire in the center of the community. Mountains of food appeared out of nowhere.

The rest of the night was given over to eating, drinking, singing, chanting, drumming, and dancing. Joy infused the celebration. It was the kind of party where the old folks sat at the edges of the revelry beaming their approval while the children galloped underfoot with happy abandon.

As embarrassed as I am to admit it, Glory and I didn't last as long as the kids. When my eyelids began to droop, I looked over and saw Glory snuggled against Orion sound asleep.

I gave up the ghost for both of us.

"Hey," I said giving Glory a gentle shake. "Bedtime. You'll be warmer inside."

Blinking in groggy confusion, she mumbled, "I'm warm now."

"I know," I said, going for the strategy I knew would work. "But Orion will be more comfortable in the hut."

Coming a little more awake, Glory said, "Oh my goodness gracious, what am I thinking? He can't be out here in this awful weather."

The wolf had a better winter coat than any of us, but to Glory, he was a puppy dog in danger of freezing to death without a proper bed.

I looked down at Orion who was grinning up at me as if to say, "Well played, lady."

Catching Moira's eye, I nodded toward the hut and mouthed, "We're going to bed."

The alchemist nodded back, signaling Orion to go with us. The wolf took up a position on Glory's other side. Between the two of us, we kept the half-awake woman from stumbling into anything.

For all the heat that came rippling off the bonfire outside, I welcomed the cozy interior of the hut. The banked coals and dim light invited snuggling under the blankets for a long winter sleep.

Once out of her cloak Glory fell onto the pallet. I slipped off her shoes and pulled the blanket up.

Orion gave me a questioning whine.

"Keep an eye on her, okay?" I said. "Big day tomorrow. I need some sleep."

To my shock, Orion nodded.

"You understand everything we say, don't you?"

Amusement danced in the wolf's eyes.

"Not gonna answer, huh? Okay. Keep your secrets for now, but there's more to your story than howling at the moon."

Giving me another toothy grin, Orion jumped onto the

pallet and settled down beside Glory. She immediately rolled into his thick coat with a deep, contented sigh.

Moira came home sometime before dawn. I didn't hear her, but the smell of breakfast cooking on the open fire awakened me as usual.

Shrugging into my cloak for extra warmth, I padded to the hearth and sat down close to the flames.

"Good dawning," the alchemist said, passing me a cup of the strong tea I'd grown to love.

"Hi," I said. "Is the sun even up?"

"Not for a few minutes longer," she said, spooning porridge into my bowl. "We will leave for the Mother Tree when the light grows stronger."

"I should get Glory up."

"Orion will do it," Moira said, looking toward the wolf who began softly nuzzling Glory's cheek.

When she fussed and tried to roll over, he stopped her with a heavy paw and began licking her face.

Glory came awake giggling. "Hiya boy," she said happily. "You're the best alarm clock ever."

We both ate hearty shares of porridge and drank two cups of strong tea before dressing with extra layers for the morning's journey.

No one moved in the village when we stepped outside. I saw a few slumbering lumps covered in animal skins near the smoldering bonfire, but otherwise the settlement could have been utterly deserted.

Moira led us back along the path we took the night of our arrival. I recognized the clearing where we landed, but we walked beyond it, shadowing the tree line until we reached a snow-covered meadow.

The Mother Tree, solitary and majestic, stood alone in the center of the pristine scene.

Breaking the smooth ivory surface seems sacrilegious. But when we started toward the Tree, I looked back only to discover that once again magic erased our tracks.

Erring on the side of caution even in the Druid woods, Moira used magic to hide our progress.

Within minutes, I met the woman who taught the alchemist that trick. As we approached the tree, a voice I recognized called out, "Merry meet, Moira, and happy Solstice."

When I asked to see the Mother Tree, it hadn't occurred to me we might run into Adeline Shevington there. I should've known better. The morning after the Solstice, I would have been with my Oak, too.

Moira and Adeline embraced, and then the alchemist started to introduce us with our cover story. I stopped her with a wave of my hand.

"It wouldn't be right for one Witch of the Oak to lie to another," I said. "Besides, I know we can trust Adeline."

The woman looked at me curiously. "Do I know thee?" she asked formally.

"Let us step under the shelter of the tree's branches and warm the air around us," Moira said. "The things about which we must speak are complicated and lengthy."

The alchemist told the outlines of our story with greater economy than I could have managed. Remaining silent, I let the alchemist talk, counting on the trust between the two women to work in our favor.

"Jinx wishes to speak with the Mother Tree," Moira finished. "She misses her communion with the Great Tree in her own time stream and seeks solace from the company of our Blessed Oak."

Adeline's eyes met mine. "In your world, are you my descendant?" She asked.

What was I going to say to that?

"No, you see, you were murdered by Brenna, but your essence got stuck in this crystal thingy that I opened by mistake. So then you wound up in my brain, and we shared mental space for a while before I stuck you in a computer — that's a thing in the future — and now you're like a Fae AI."

Opting for the more diplomatic answer, I said, "No. There was an interruption in the Tree Witch line, and the women in my family were chosen to take up the privilege."

Adeline accepted the news serenely. "So long as our Great Mother is never alone. You understand that in our time there is no guarantee this Oak will speak with you."

"I'm not worried," I said. "I believe the Tree will hear my voice."

Turning her eyes toward the branches of the Tree, Adeline said, "The bond runs strong. I believe it may well transcend all realities. I would never deny a fellow Tree Witch the company of her Guardian and Guide. We will move away and give you space to make the connection."

Being with the Tree in the glistening snowy place felt both strange and familiar. I knew the Oak as the gentle entity dwelling at the heart of Shevington.

In my world, the Mother Tree accomplished an impossible feat. Sinking into the earth, she moved through the land beneath the deepest oceans to rise again from the soil of The Valley.

Her decision to move to the New World with Barnaby Shevington and his Fae settlers redistributed the power of the Grid. Just as Barnaby changed the balance of Fae society, the Oak altered the framework that supports our reality.

Standing under the branches of the mighty Tree, I opened my mind and said, "Mother Oak, I come to you from another time and place, but I am a daughter of your branches. I need your help and the wisdom of your counsel. Will you speak with me?"

I felt her before she answered me. When the Great Tree opens the link that allows our communication it arrives on a warm summer breeze. I smelled wildflowers, a hint of damp earth, and the ineffable vibrance of growing things.

"You speak the truth Daughter," the familiar voice answered.

It's impossible to describe the source of that voice. Tori has asked me to put the experience in words many times, but no description equals the reality.

Sometimes I think the Tree enters my consciousness. At others, the resonant tones filled the air around me. The Oak is with me, and I am with her, but the bond between us encompasses everything.

"Thank you," I almost sobbed. "I've felt so alone since the accident."

"Tell me."

The simple response of a nurturing parent. The acknowledgment of hurt and the encouragement of confidence.

If I couldn't have my husband, and I couldn't have my mother, I blessed Creation for giving me the voice of the Tree.

I told her everything. The wedding. How my eyes filled with tears when Lucas spoke his vows and slipped the ring on my finger. The happiness of my reception. Dancing with our friends. Laughing and eating too much of Darby's wonderful food. And then the explosive moment when I caught a metallic object turning end over end in the air.

When I ran out of words, I waited for the tree to digest my account and recover from the torrent of words that spilled out of my mouth.

Even in this strange place with a different Mother Tree, I expected the Oak to tell me how to go home.

Would that the answer had been so easy.

"There is an imbalance in the Natural Order," the Tree said. "Of this, you are a victim. There is only one place where the channels of time should be opened to the passage of living beings. That place is the Middle Realm. The forces that brought you here tear at the fabric of the portal network. They are artificial in construction and detrimental in essence."

"Are you telling me that the portal network is broken?"

"Not broken," the Trees said, "but damaged. Part of your task in returning to those you love is to repair that which has been breached."

Remember that feeling when the teacher gave you homework on Friday, and you resented the intrusion on your weekend? That's kind of how I felt.

"I don't know how to do that," I said, trying hard not to whine and failing.

"Do not fear, my child, or give yourself over to doubt," the Tree said. "You will have a companion in this task."

"Are you talking about Glory?" I asked. "Because I don't think she's really up to this kind of job."

The Oak's laughter rippled past me on a puff of cool air.

"The one who travels with you does not trouble her mind with complications," the Tree said, "but she too has come here with a purpose. Do not fear that you must lead her in that way. Glory Green's destiny will unfold before her as yours will unfold before you."

"How do you know these things?" I asked. "Do you have the ability to look into my time stream?"

"I, like all the Mighty Trees, have awareness across the great tapestry of time," the Oak said. "Through the layers of your thoughts I see that you believe the Grid to encircle the world. In truth the grid forms a lattice work throughout Creation. We, the Trees, are the primary temporal constant. In each of the streams of time I stand. In each of the streams of time my Sister Trees stand. We are more than your ability to imagine and yet, the simplest of beings. For what living creature cannot understand that life springs from a common taproot and reaches its branches toward the warmth of the sun?"

One thing I can say with certainty. Regardless of the Oak to which I am speaking, the Mother Tree always leaves me with a feeling of utter peace even when I don't understand a darn thing she's just said.

The idea that the Mother Trees existed in all places, across all time streams, forming a constant in the fabric of Creation told me all that I needed to know. No matter where I might find myself, I would always be a Tree Witch, and the Oak would be my guide.

That relationship gave me the confidence I needed to dig deep and find the strength I would need to return to the places and people I love.

Still, a few specifics wouldn't hurt.

"Can you give me a hint where I should start?" I asked.

"You and your companion are not the only displaced travelers in this world," the Tree said. "Your plan to travel to Londinium to seek the company of the man who calls himself Alex Farnsworth will put you on the correct path."

When I came away from the Oak, Adeline smiled at me. "You heard the voice of the Great Mother," she said.

"I did," I said. "And she's just as awesome here as she is in my world."

The vernacular I used might have sounded odd to the 16th-century woman, but she understood what I meant all the same.

"My service to the Great Mother fills my life with purpose and joy," she said. "Is it the same for you?"

My answer came out thick with unshed tears. "Everything about my life changed the first time I heard the Mother Tree's voice."

"How I look forward to the day when I will introduce my daughter to the service of the Oak," Adeline said. "It pains me to learn that in your time my line did not survive."

To my surprise, Glory spoke up. "We know who you are," she said, "or who you were. Nobody forgot about you, and in a strange way, we kinda, uh, feel like you're a friend of ours."

"So long as the name of a person falls from the lips of the living," Adeline said, "a measure of immortality has been gifted to them."

Moira shifted the conversation to more practical matters. "Did the Oak suggest your next course of action?"

"She did," I said. "She says we're right about going to Londinium."

Adeline's face registered alarm. "Londinium under the control of Brenna presents danger for anyone or anything that can be perceived as a novelty. The Ruling Elder might fancy you to be a worthy addition to her collection."

"Her collection?" I said, horrified by the idea.

"Like many in our time Brenna maintains a cabinet of curiosities," Adeline explained. "Unfortunately she does not confine her interests to fossils and rare plants. She confines living creatures for her study and amusement. You must take great care not to fall into her hands."

No problem with that strategy. Living out my life as a Fae zoo animal didn't make the top 10,000 items on my Bucket List.

"My husband, Barnaby, will remain in Londinium for several weeks," Adeline said. "I will write to him that you are coming to the city, Moira. We have ways of communicating that cannot be deciphered by those who would seek to monitor our correspondence. Should you have need of his aid, Barnaby will understand your circumstances and stand at the ready."

When we said our goodbyes, Adeline embraced me. I started to return the gesture but stopped when her hands tightened on my upper arms. Looking into her face, I saw an opaque film covering her eyes.

"What's happening?" I asked Moira.

"Shh," the alchemist cautioned. "Listen. Adeline has the gift of the Sight."

Speaking as if she stood at a great distance, Adeline said, "A mirror cast into a tunnel of windows. Every reflection a choice. Every frame a constant truth. Look into the mirrors, Jinx Hamilton, and see that which is to come, that which will herald the next phase of thy life."

Adeline's eyes cleared, and she drew me into her arms. "Fare thee well, Sister Witch. Until we meet again."

Over her shoulder, I saw Moira shake her head.

"Until we meet again," I stammered, too stunned to say more.

After we'd walked a few paces, the alchemist said, "She does not remember the visions. The words are not hers to interpret. That task belongs only to you."

And here I'd been complaining about fortune cookies all my life!

At the edge of the woods, I looked back and saw Adeline standing at the base of the Mother Tree bathed in golden light.

Look into the mirrors Jinx Hamilton and see that which is to come.

I had no idea what Adeline's vision meant, but I felt no fear, only a frisson of excitement and expectation. My inner voice told me that whatever the vision described about my future, it would be good.

Before I looked away, I whispered a prayer of thanks to the Goddess. Meeting Adeline — even alternate time Adeline — made me truly understand what Barnaby lost in our timeline when she died.

What would my grandfather have been like had his wife lived? I was about to find out.

18

Londinium, 1590, Jinx

The visit to the Mother Tree allowed me to relax. I could enjoy the remainder of the Yule season with the Druids. Experiencing my familiar connection with the Oak and through her, the Grid grounded me — and gave me a lot to think about.

Cryptic or not, one theme ran through the Tree's words — we would find our way home.

Detailed instructions on how to get there would have been nice, but I believed the Oak when she said our current situation amounted to a detour.

Every time that thought crossed my mind, I heard my father warbling a few words from an old Patti Page song. We'd get lost during the annual family vacation, and he'd let out with, *"Detour, there's a muddy road ahead."*

The memory made me smile and comforted me with the camaraderie of my relationship with my father. He was with me in spirit, giving me something to laugh about while I confronted a different level of "lost."

Here's the thing. I never looked up the rest of the lyrics to the song — the ones that talked about the bitter events the singer experienced because she didn't pay attention to the sign's warning.

I can tell you that now through the lens of 20/20 hindsight. At the time, I put my fears and loneliness aside to relish every detail of the *good* experiences the "detour" afforded us.

Each day Glory and I made memories. We watched the bowyer run his file along a length of yew as he fashioned a six-foot English longbow. We drank the strong, dark forest tea while the women baked fragrant bread.

Slathering the hot slices with butter, we let Orion lick the excess off our fingers, giggling when his tongue tickled our skin.

At night around the communal campfire, the bard told stories of England's history back to the Norman Conquest and beyond. Some of the tales had been passed down since the days of the Saxon King Ecgherht in the 9th century.

Later, in the privacy of my sleeping cubicle, I recorded every detail I could remember in my journal, hoping that when we returned home, I would be able to bring the book with me.

I imagined being curled up on one end of my favorite sofa in the lair, reading fragments of the entries to my husband, our family, and friends. The future promise of their loving interest and laughter let me fall asleep free of tormenting worries.

More than a few pages of the journal held my speculations over the meaning of Adeline's vision.

For someone who has never been big on riddles, I live in a Fae world filled with word puzzles and hidden meanings.

Adeline spoke of mirrors and windows; neither existed in the beehive huts. Maybe when we reached Londinium and found Alex/Axe the answer would reveal itself to me.

Unfortunately, my familiarity with brain-teasing Fae prophecies warned me that those mirrors and windows could be metaphors.

I hoped not. Me and Metaphors? Not close friends.

The love/hate relationship developed in high school along with a 75 on a critical test that cost me my "A" for the semester. I blame Similes for causing the confusion. The three of us never sat down and worked it out.

Scribbled musings aside, the brief time I spent with Adeline left a lasting impression on me. I couldn't escape the feeling that she had given me an insight that, when I understood it fully, would be precious.

The night before our departure for Londinium, Glory posed a riddle of her own.

"Do you think we've been gone more than two weeks in Briar Hollow or is that just how we see it? I mean, if it has been that long back there, what are they telling people to explain where we are? The story about the small business conference would only work for a week, and I wasn't supposed to go on that trip anyway. Do you think someone is writing my column for me? I love my job so, *so* much. I would be just heartsick to lose it."

Wiping the excess ink off the point of the quill, I confessed I couldn't answer her question. "Time runs at a different pace in the Valley, but I don't know what happens in an alternate timestream. I *hope* our disappearance is shorter for them."

I didn't give voice to my secret fear that if Lucas had been forced to endure two weeks with no definitive answer about my fate, he might have given up on me. I didn't want to believe that, but the only event to which he could compare our "accident" was Axe's "death."

We let the subject drop when Moira gently suggested we retire early to be rested for the trip. Thankfully we would be traveling horseback, not walking.

When the subject of horses first came up, Glory assured us she "knew how to ride." I should have known better than to take that statement at face value. On further probing, I learned the entirety of her equine experience had been confined to merry-go-round horses.

Confronted with a saddled sorrel mare, Glory took a step back. "She's way bigger than the horses on the carousel. How do I get up there?"

Moira led the patient steed over to a stump and showed Glory how to put her foot in the stirrup and throw her leg over the saddle. Then, cupping the horse's ear in her hand, the alchemist whispered a set of instructions in Elvish.

Without a definitive translation, I can't be sure, but since the mare — Betsy — proved placid and tolerant, I assumed Moira asked her to go easy on the newbie.

My black gelding stood a hand or two higher than Glory's mount. "He's called Robin," Moira said. "You can give him his head. He's sure-footed and intelligent."

Laying my hand on the horse's muzzle, I stroked down toward the animal's soft nose. "Hi there," I said. "You're a handsome man, Robin."

The gelding nickered softly and laid his head on my shoulder. We were going to get along fine.

Once we were all in the saddle, Orion jumped onto the stump and laid a paw on Glory's knee.

"You're not coming, are you boy?" she asked. I heard the thin thread of hope in the question; Glory wanted the wolf to contradict her.

Orion shook his head.

"Will I ever see you again?"

He whined softly.

"What's he trying to tell me?" Glory asked Moira.

"He said you shouldn't worry about a thing in the future,"

the alchemist replied. "We all meet in the time and place Fate designs."

With her lower lip trembling, Glory said, "I'm going to take that as a yes. You be a good boy until we get back, okay?"

As we rode away, I caught Glory looking over her shoulder at the wolf who remained seated on the stump like a statue carved in black marble. I felt his eyes on us until we disappeared into the tree cover.

Irrepressible as always, Glory's good humor returned by the time we reached the road. She kept up a running stream of questions, which Moira answered patiently. Lost in my thoughts, I let Robin's steady rhythm lull me into a pleasant, contemplative trance.

At noon, Moira called a halt at a small copse of trees near a flowing stream. There, we ate a meal of apples, hard cheese, and bread. Since no one was around, the alchemist magically ignited a fire and brewed tea in a small kettle.

Rested and invigorated by the food and drink, the remainder of our day passed quickly. Moira judged we'd covered half the distance to Londinium by nightfall. Rather than risk igniting too much curiosity by taking a room at a village inn, we camped in a cluster of boulders about a hundred yards from the road.

Keeping the fire low, Moira cloaked the site to hide our presence from anyone wandering about in the night. We discussed the timing of the next day's travel, agreeing that we didn't want to arrive in Londinium at sunset.

Instead, we spent our second night on the road in the ruins of what had been a Catholic priory before the dissolution of the monasteries during the reign of Henry VIII.

The next morning, excited and apprehensive, we entered the city and discovered a teeming metropolis of crisscrossing, muddy streets filled with foul-smelling animal and human byproducts.

We hadn't gone two blocks before I witnessed a woman cheerfully fling the contents of her chamber pot out an upper window with no word of warning to the people below.

Holding her hand over her nose, Glory said, "Does it always smell like this?"

"Be thankful we are here in the winter," Moira said. "Summer can be all but unbearable."

Craning her neck to get a better view of the people in the streets, Glory said, "What are those strange shoes everybody's wearing? They look like stilts."

"Pattens," Moira said. "They elevate the wearer's regular shoes above the filth."

Speaking for myself, it would take more than the Elizabethan equivalent of platform shoes to get me out of the saddle and anywhere near the muck underfoot.

Robin must have felt the same way. The gelding nimbly picked his way through the crowd, steering clear of the open gutter running down the middle of the street.

I tried and failed to imagine being forced to adapt to life here full-time. Lucas had never said specifically when Axe Frazier's accident occurred, but I gathered he'd been missing for decades.

Thanks to his Fae heritage, Axe would appear younger than the humans around him, but he'd still experience the passage of the years and the gnawing separation from the people he loved.

After several minutes, we passed an area Moira identified as Leadenhall Market before turning into a neighborhood unlike any other we had traversed.

Well-appointed houses with walled gardens stood on either side of a clean, narrow lane. Free of the overpowering stench, Glory and I drew in deep breaths of the blessedly fresh air.

"What is this place?" I asked Moira.

"Lime Street," she replied. "The home of an international

community of physicians, merchants, and naturalists — and the beneficiary of healthy doses of hygienic magic."

In preparing us to experience the city, the alchemist told us that the Fae in Londinium practiced magic openly. Lime Street was one of several enclaves that functioned as oases of order thanks to cleansing enchantments.

"This is where we'll find Alex Farnsworth?" Glory asked.

"Yes," Moira said. "My sources tell me he married the daughter of a prominent Dutch botanist, Noah van Buskirk. Farnsworth lives in his father-in-law's home."

I considered our surroundings. The area was a good choice for a man lost in time. With so many foreign immigrants in close proximity, Axe could have easily hidden his modern speech and eccentric habits. A good cover story. Sufficient time. He could absolutely have learned to pass himself off as a 16th-century man of letters.

Reining her horse to a stop, Moira asked a passerby to point out the home of the naturalist Alex Farnsworth. We were directed to a three-story building. The bottom floor advertised itself as an herbal apothecary. I assumed the upper floors to be the residence.

Tying our mounts out front, we entered a more sophisticated version of the village apothecary where we witnessed the thief's punishment. A balding man with a florid complexion and the trailing scent of strong pipe tobacco greeted us.

"Welcome," he said. "How may I be of service?"

By tacit agreement, we let Moira take the lead.

"We come in search of a man called Alex Farnsworth," she said. "Is he here?"

Before the proprietor could answer, a child's voice asked, "Why do you want to see my Papa?"

The girl emerged from behind the counter, small and frail, pale of complexion, with large, luminous eyes.

"Forgive my granddaughter," the man said. "She has a milder version of her father's audacious curiosity."

Far from being a criticism, the words were spoken with eyes that glowed with pride.

"Alex Farnsworth is your son-in-law?" Moira asked.

"He is," the shopkeeper said. "I am Noah van Buskirk."

Without prompting, the child announced, "Mama went to heaven to be with the angels."

Sadness dimmed the light in Van Buskirk's eyes. "Naomi speaks the truth. My Esther died shortly after the birth of her daughter. May I ask what business you have with Alex?"

"We come from the Druid forests of Kent," the alchemist replied. "I am Moira, and these are my apprentices, Jeane and Genevieve. We wish to consult Mr. Farnsworth regarding a series of herbal remedies."

Van Buskirk nodded. "You are correct to seek the services of my son-in-law then. I am but a middling gardener compared to Alex's expertise with all things botanical. I will show you to his cabinet."

"I'll take you to where my Papa works," the child volunteered. "May I Grandpapa?"

Van Buskirk wagged a finger at the child. "You are supposed to be about your lessons."

The child made a comically annoyed face. "Herr Schmidt goes too slow!" she exclaimed. "I have learned my lessons for this week. I want to go faster!"

Van Buskirk blew out an aggrieved breath. "It would seem that once again I must mediate a dispute between my precocious granddaughter and her German tutor. Follow me into the hall, and I will direct you to Alex's cabinet."

We walked after them into a corridor that ran the length of the structure. In a room to our left, a gray-bearded man wearing scholar's robes snored softly in his chair.

The shopkeeper looked down at his granddaughter with rueful amusement. "Perhaps you are correct that Herr Schmidt is not equal to the task of keeping apace with you, granddaughter."

Naomi gazed up at him and said with complete seriousness, "He is very old."

Barely managing to keep a straight face, Van Buskirk said, "Awaken him gently, child, I will be with you in a moment."

When the girl went into the room, Van Buskirk released the chuckle he'd held back. "My granddaughter finds her tutor to be a trial."

"Forgive me for asking," Moira said, "but is the child ill?"

The man's eyes moved to Naomi who was tugging at the sleeve of her tutor's black robe. "She suffers from the phthisis," he said. "The cold brings on the coughing. She will be better when the weather turns warm."

He spoke the words with the desperate optimism of an adult willing an ailing child to get well against all odds.

"Sunshine and clean air are to her benefit," Moira agreed. "I will remember Naomi in my meditations."

"Thank you," Van Buskirk said. "Continue down this passage. My son-in-law's cabinet is the last room on the right."

Following his granddaughter, the shopkeeper began a loud conversation with the obviously quite deaf Herr Schmidt.

We moved several steps away before I whispered to Moira, "What's phthisis?"

"A disease of the lungs," she said. "The sickness causes a pale complexion and a failure to thrive in children. In time, Naomi will begin to cough blood. The disease is often fatal and was responsible for the death of the Queen's younger brother, Edward."

With a chill, I realized the alchemist had described tuberculosis; curable in my world, but deadly here — and contagious.

Glory and I exchanged a look. She understood what Moira described as well. In that instant, we made a wordless agreement to find a way to help Naomi if we could.

"What did Mr. Van Buskirk mean when he said Alex was in a cabinet?" Glory asked, scanning the length of the hall. "I don't see any cabinets out here."

"He refers to a Cabinet of Curiosities," Moira said. "You will understand when we go inside."

A man's voice answered Moira's knock bidding us enter. We stepped into a room overflowing with cases holding rocks and fossils, specimens of exotic animals and insects, dried plants, papers spilled out of packed folios, and an astonishing array of books. The space served as equal parts study, laboratory, and museum.

Alex Farnsworth sat at a cluttered desk peering through a brass magnifying glass on a stand. Ink stained his fingers. I saw a smudge near the neck of his white shirt where he'd absentmindedly rubbed the fabric.

His features and mannerisms reminded me of Lauren. Intelligence animated his gaze, and even under a proper Elizabethan beard, I recognized the strong jawline, but the gray in his hair and whiskers surprised me. Even my grandfather, who was hundreds of years old, didn't have that much silver at the temples.

Farnsworth's smile wavered when he saw Moira. I caught the flicker of recognition he instantly squelched. How could I have been so stupid? Of course, he would know this Moira — she was the image of *our* Moira, Lucas' aunt.

Recovering quickly and realizing he was in the presence of ladies, Farnsworth stood. "Good day. May I help you?"

"Your father-in-law kindly told us where we might find you," Moira said. "He is currently occupied settling a dispute between your daughter and her tutor."

His lips curved in an indulgent smile. "Better him than me," he said. "Although I have not said so, I agree with Naomi. Herr Schmidt is too old for the task of teaching. Good lessons are rarely imparted by instructors who slumber in their chairs."

Moira made the necessary introductions complete with our fake names and identities. After acknowledging each of us, Farnsworth motioned us to the circle of chairs across from his desk.

Reclaiming his seat, he asked, "Are you here to consult with me on a botanical matter?"

Moira looked at me. "Forgive me for being blunt," I said. "But does the name Axe Frazier mean anything to you?"

The guarded look in Farnsworth's eyes intensified. "Who are you?" he asked tightly. "Are you in the employ of the Ruling Elder?"

If I let a game of cat and mouse get started, we'd only waste time. I opted to take a leap of faith.

"No," I said. "My name isn't Jeane, it's Jinx Hamilton. This is my friend Glory Green. I'm the Witch of the Oak. My husband is Lucas Grayson. We've been thrown here from another time stream — your time stream. That is if you are Axe Frazier."

He didn't confirm what I said, but he didn't deny it either. Instead, he leaned back in his chair, clearly overcome, and covered his eyes with a shaking hand. We waited.

Finally, in a voice thick with emotion, he said, "I am Axe Frazier. It's hard for me to think of myself as that man any longer, but I am Axe Frazier. Do you . . . do you have any news of my sister?"

"Lauren is fine," I assured him. "She's in private security work now. She never believed that you were dead and she's never stopped looking for you.."

Axe's next question told me everything I needed to know about the events that sent Glory and me hurtling through time.

Meeting my eyes directly, Axe said flatly, "Let me guess. Morris Grayson didn't approve of your marriage to Lucas, so he decided to get rid of you in a portal 'accident,' too."

19

Londinium, 1590, Jinx

After asking Moira to cast a privacy spell on the room, Axe told us his story. Like me, he ran afoul of Morris Grayson's ambitions for Lucas.

"I was top of my class at the DGI Academy," Axe said. "Lucas didn't care. The three of us — Chase McGregor was our friend — never let competition get in the way of our friendship. Do you know Chase?"

We certainly didn't have time for *that* long story, but I thought it would help Axe to trust me if I told him at least the bare outline.

"I do know Chase," I said. "I dated him before Lucas and I got together."

Axe frowned, "But a witch and a werecat can't..."

I cut him off with a wave of my hand. "That was only one of our problems," I said. "Chase couldn't handle dating me and guarding me at the same time."

That only deepened Axe's confusion. "But Festus is the guardian of the Daughters of Knasgowa."

"Oh!" Glory said brightly. "Dad was retired back when Jinx first found out about her powers, but he's not retired anymore. He fired Chase so Chase can run his cobbler shop and be happy, but Chase still helps out if something big happens."

One detail from that staccato information dump hit Axe right between the eyes.

"*Dad?*" he said. "You call *Festus* 'Dad?'"

"Well," Glory said, "obviously he's not my *father* father, but see, *I'm* dating Chase now, and Festus lets me call him 'Dad' because he kinda likes me even if he won't admit it and my own father . . . well, he wasn't a nice person like Festus."

Obviously groping for a diplomatic response to that, Axe looked to me for some confirmation of Glory's rattling account.

When I nodded, he said, "*Wow*. Festus must have mellowed."

"Not really," I said. "There'll be plenty of opportunities to fill you in on all of that when we get back home."

Cautious hope passed over Axe's face. "You know how to get us back?"

My heart sank. "Honestly, I was hoping *you* would know how to get us back."

Irritation erased his momentary optimism. "If I did know how," he said, "do you think I would have spent the last 50 years of my life in an alternate version of the 16th century where Brenna Sinclair and the Creavit run roughshod over Fae society?"

He was right. I'd been spending too much time with Glory. That had been a stupid thing to say; one I didn't know how to correct.

Sensing my discomfort, Moira took charge. "Perhaps, Mr. Frazier, you should continue the narrative of your journey to this place, so Jinx and Glory might compare your experiences to their own."

"Right," he said. Then, looking at me, he added, "I'm sorry. I shouldn't have snapped at you."

"I shouldn't have asked such a thoughtless question."

We agreed to move on. The story Axe laid out sounded familiar. He related the events of the day of his "accident" in much the same way Lucas and Chase described the incident.

There was, however, one salient detail that neither man could have known.

"Before we left DGI headquarters to conduct the portal exercise," Axe said, "Director Grayson handed me a small brass disc. He told me to put it in my pocket and carry it through the opening after the stabilization spell. The disc was supposed to be the second phase of the test. It would cause an additional instability that Chase and Lucas would have to correct in order to get a passing grade. I'd known Morris all my life. I trusted him, and he double-crossed me."

"When did you stop trusting him? I asked.

"When I figured out that he'd given me a piece of the Copernican Astrolabe. Taking even a portion of one of the Temporal Arcana through a portal would activate a time jump."

Now he'd lost me. "What do you mean Temporal Arcana?"

Glory, who was batting a thousand in the "Let's Shock Jinx" World Series, caught on faster. "You mean like the Major Arcana in the tarot?" she asked.

Unable to contain myself, I said bluntly, "Who are you and what have you done with Glory?"

Delighted to be sitting at the head of the class for once, Glory giggled. "I study a lot of stuff I don't talk about. Our Brenna — she's good now in our world, Axe. Really. 'Cause she fell through the fires that separate the realms and landed in this big ole eagle's nest. He nursed her back to health and helped her find her good side, kinda like when somebody finds Jesus. But not the same. Anyway, Good Brenna has been teaching me to read Tarot cards."

Note to self. Get a nanny cam for the Lair in case somebody decides Glory needs to start playing with real fire.

To his credit, Axe plowed through the excess verbiage and settled on the one relevant word: tarot.

"Glory is right," he said. "The Major Arcana of the Tarot deck describes the sequential stages of a classic hero's journey or quest. That meaning, however, won't be attached to the cards for another century. Now, if you picked up a deck, the Major Arcana would be called the 'trumps.' They have significance in playing games, but not in deciphering metaphysical challenges."

My turn to cut through the word soup. "So the *Temporal* Arcana are navigational instruments that let people travel across the time streams — complete a journey — but with guidance instead of falling head first down the rabbit hole?"

For the first time, Axe laughed, a husky, rolling chuckle that instantly warmed my heart. "Yes, Alice. The Arcana tell you how to begin at the beginning and stop at the end."

"I love that book so, *so* much," Glory sighed. "If Dad smiled more he'd look just like the Cheshire cat, but not so fat. Don't ever tell him I said he was fat."

Moira, who had listened in silence to our conversation, said, "Though you all speak in riddles, I follow your meaning. If I may ask, Mr. Frazier . . ."

"Axe when we're alone," he said, "Alex otherwise."

"Axe," she said, "if I may ask, why did you take the disc through the portal at the direction of this man Grayson if you were aware of the workings of the Temporal Arcana?"

He scrubbed at his whiskers. "My awareness of the Arcana developed afterward through years of study. I work in secret with a *nonconformi* assistant. It's my belief that all time converges in the Middle Realm. Lashtazo has acquired documents and rumors that we've used to construct a future history of the Arcana and to expand our temporal understanding."

"To what race does your assistant belong?" Moira asked.

"Lashtazo is an Ebu Gogo from the island of Pulau Flores," Axe said. "He stowed away aboard a Portuguese trading vessel and made his way to Londinium. I took him in off the streets for his own good."

The Ebu Gogo, as Axe described them, look like the evolutionary missing link — short, even by 16th-century standards, hairy, dark complexion, with broad noses and flattened features.

"Why did Lashtazo undertake so perilous a passage?" Moira asked. "Surely he could have traveled through the Middle Realm more easily."

"He could have," Axe agreed, "but he wouldn't have learned as much. The Ebu Gogo have more native curiosity than any species I've encountered — so much so, that the trait gets them in trouble. Add in the caveman looks, and Lash wasn't safe on the streets. He far prefers living and working in my lab."

Axe described the underground rooms he and his assistant built together. "Lash enjoys being down there," he said. "When he isn't foraging for research material in the Middle Realm, he's got his head buried in experiments. The Ebu Gogo are friendly enough, but they do like their caves."

Together, the pair spent years cultivating their knowledge of the Temporal Arcana. "You have to understand that even in the Middle Realm there are layers of access," Axe said. "In the market at Cibolita, artifacts from all the realities and times are bartered and sold."

I could barely contain my excitement. "I've been to Cibolita," I said. "If you climb into the mountains outside the city and enter the Land of the Golem, there's an opening directly into the fairy mound under my store."

Axe let me down as easily as he could. "That door would

access some *version* of the fairy mound under your store. It could be in any time stream past or future."

"But you said all time converges in the Middle Realm," I protested.

"It does," he said, "but think of it like one of those mix master highway complexes in the 20th century. If you don't know which on ramp or off ramp to take, you can wind up driving hundreds of miles — or in this case, years — before you even realize you're going the wrong direction."

Moira considered his description. "You have become lost on such a circuitous route?"

"Once, yes," he said slowly, "but I found my way home — back here, I mean. I haven't gone into the Middle Realm again. Not since Naomi was born and Esther died. The last time I went in, I wandered lost for almost 75 years before I discovered the correct exit and came back to my wife."

The gray hair. He hadn't spent 50 years lost in *one* past; he'd spent 125 — maybe more — lost in multiple pasts.

Axe saw my understanding.

"I lost my nerve," he admitted. "Even though Lash and I continued to study for the pleasure of the pursuit, I couldn't go in there again. Esther didn't understand what happened to me. Why I came home with lines on my face and gray in my hair when she thought I'd only been away a matter of hours. When I put my arms around her again, I decided to make a life here. To be grateful for what I had and not to try to regain what I'd lost. That was ten years ago. Two years after I returned, the Universe gave me my daughter and took my wife."

No response could address what Axe Frazier had suffered. If we got home — *when* we got home — Morris Grayson was going to pay for his crimes.

I tried to stay on point. "How did you learn about the Copernican Astrolabe?"

"From Copernicus," Axe said, "or rather from one of his journals. Lash found it in Cibolita. Many of the pages are missing, but we were able to decipher Copernicus' more esoteric goals for the instrument."

Working from that clue, the two researchers developed a theory. "We think the temporal tools were first assembled in my — our — original timestream. Mariners from the In Between used them to explore the landscape of time. Then a hidden clause in The Agreement called for the items to be scattered across that landscape where they remain lost and unconnected."

(Insert profanity of choice regarding secretive Fae politics.)

"So the two pieces of the Astrolabe we have aren't enough to get us home?" I asked.

"No."

"Can I at least see the disc?"

"Sure."

Axe got up from the desk and walked to a collection of dried grasses hanging on the wall. Taking the frame down, he pressed a hidden button in the paneling exposing a recessed chamber. He drew out a black velvet bag, closed the hiding spot, replaced the frame, and returned to his chair.

Untying the strings holding the bag closed, Axe removed a shining circle of brass. In the bottom of the pouch hanging from my belt, I felt the brass rod straining to be set free. Unclasping the flap, I removed the linen bundle, unwrapped the fabric, and watched with fascination as the brass bar floated across the desk and settled in place alongside the disc.

"I was right!" Axe exclaimed triumphantly. "The parts of the Astrolabe do share essential magnetism."

Surprising me yet again, Glory said, "If that's true, wouldn't there have to be another part of the astrolabe thingy here in this time stream that your part was attracted to in the first place?"

"If there is," Axe said, "I've never been able to find it.

Honestly, your arrival is fortuitous. Not for me, but for Naomi. She's sick. Modern doctors could help her."

"It's tuberculosis, isn't it?" I asked.

"Yes," he replied. Only a father could pour so much desperation into a single word. "She'll die here. In the 20th century, she could be cured."

"Twenty-first," Glory said. "It's the 21st century now."

Axe shook his head. "It no longer matters how much I've missed. All I care about is saving my daughter. If we find a way to send you home, will you take Naomi with you?"

"If we find a way," I said firmly, "we're *all* going home."

Laying his hands flat on the surface of the desk, Axe said, "First things first. Security. Does anyone else know the truth about your origins?"

"No. We got lucky. Moira found us and kept us safe in her village."

He looked at the alchemist. "I know the woman who is your mirror image. She has great personal honor. I would trust her with my life."

Moira inclined her head. "I would hope that in all manifestations of my essence I would abide by the Druidic code. I will not betray their secret or yours and, if it is in my power to do so, I will help you."

"Thank you," Axe said. "Now, the three of you must stay here. Taking rooms outside Lime Street might call your presence in the city to Brenna Sinclair's attention. She may know already, but you're still better off being here. The Ruling Elder watches our comings and goings, but she has no spies in our community."

Thinking of the frail little girl and her effusive, elderly grandfather, I said, "Are you sure we won't attract attention and endanger your family?"

"Positive," Axe replied. "It's not unusual for visiting scholars to stay at our home. Noah will think nothing of it, nor will Naomi. They will both retire early after the evening meal. When they're asleep, I'll take you to meet Lash."

He showed us to a loft room with two large beds. The fire had been laid, but not lit. When Axe began searching for flint and steel, Moira said, "Allow me."

She gestured toward the logs and murmured, *"Ignium."*

The wood caught instantly, crackling to life in a cheery blaze of flame.

"I wish I could do that," Axe said. "The Seonaidh aren't good with fire."

"What's a sho-na?" Glory asked.

"A minor water spirit," he replied. "Think of us as first cousins of the Gwragedd Annwn. I can't make a fire catch, but you should see what I can do with a waterfall."

Glory nodded sympathetically. "I'm kind of a magical disaster," she admitted. "Back home I shrink and turn green a lot."

"That's a story you're going to have to tell me one day," Axe said. "Right now I need to tell Noah we have company and check in on Naomi. After that, I have a few errands to run, but I'll have cheese and fruit sent up to you. Rest after your long journey. I'll see you at supper."

When we were alone, Glory sank onto the hearth and held her hands out toward the flames. "He's been through so much," she said. "And poor, sweet little Naomi. We have to find a way to help her, Jinx. We just have to."

Wandering over to the window, I looked out at the foot traffic on Lime Street. "We have to find a way to help all of us." I said. "Nobody is getting left behind on my watch."

20

Shevington, Tori

T he phrase "pirate ship" makes me envision seafaring vessels that get from one place to another on water. I think you can see how I would go with that interpretation.

I expected the *Tempus Fugit* to somehow materialize on the surface of the merfolk lake.

I *didn't* expect a three-masted schooner manned by a two-person crew to shrink down to the size of a toy boat, squeeze through the portal, expand on the other side, float placidly toward the city in midair, and come to a hovering anchor outside the front gates.

And yet, that's exactly what happened.

Standing atop the wall with Chase, Festus, Rube, and Major "Ironweed" Aspid Istra recognition hit me as the anchor chain dropped out of the hawse-hole and sped toward the ground.

"That's the ship I saw out the window of my room at the inn in Cibolita," I exclaimed. "We were right in the middle of a pirate harbor in the Middle Realm, and we didn't even know it."

Chase leaned his elbows atop the stone wall and studied the *Tempus Fugit*. "We had a few other things to worry about," he said, "but I remember seeing that ship, too."

Those "other things" to which he referred included healing a massive wound in my leg, saving the Mother Tree's life, and thawing out the state of North Carolina from a deep-freeze brought on by Irenaeus Chesterfield.

I guess it's understandable we didn't put two and two together about the pirates.

Ironweed hovered near my shoulder, his incandescent wings shimmering in the sunlight. "She's a beauty," he said admiringly. "I miss the days of sail. Everything's so damned mechanical now."

"This from a man who prides himself on having the best fleet of micro GNATS drones in the business," Chase laughed.

The fairy bobbed up and down, compensating for the stiff breeze blowing over the Valley. "I didn't say I wanted to go *back* to the days of sail," he said, "but I do miss the majesty of it."

On cue, the *Tempus Fugit's* mainsail snapped smartly. From the deck, Miranda Winter spotted us and called out merrily, "Ahoy the town!"

Feeling silly, I shouted back, "Ahoy!"

Rube who had scrambled onto the wall to get a better view glanced over his shoulder at me. "You wanna do your pirate imitation again so I can get video and put it on Facebook?"

"I do not," I said firmly. "And what have we told you about posting videos on Facebook?"

The raccoon shrugged with self-deprecation, "Can I help it if the humans think us coons is adorable? All our videos go viral."

Instantly suspicious, I said, "Which videos?"

Digging his iPhone out of his waist pack, Rube opened the YouTube app.

Thumbing through his feed, he said, "The one of me pole

dancing is real popular like, but everybody loves it when we take cotton candy and act like we're confused about it dissolving in water."

In spite of my best intentions to remain firm about our "no social media" rule, I said, "Show me the pole dancing."

When he handed me the phone, I was regaled by the spectacle of Rube's ample gut and butt twerking around a pole. Two frames later, he appeared in a rainbow tutu turning circles on his hind legs, which morphed into an admittedly adorable series of scenes where he and Booger batted at soap bubbles.

Raising an eyebrow, I said, "I'm not sure the pole dancing part is appropriate for children."

"Aw, don't be such a stuffed shirt," Rube said. "Let me show you the one where the Wrecking Crew threw a pool party in this guy's backyard. His security cam caught the whole thing just like we planned."

"I've seen enough for one day," I assured him. "Just make sure you guys don't get caught on the business end of a shotgun near a chicken coop."

Rube looked wounded. "How many times do we have to tell you people we're totally reformed on the egg stealing thing. We turned over a new omelette. Honest."

Festus, who lay stretched out on the warm stone, said, "Don't be offended if we find it difficult to believe virtuous claims by a pack of trash pandas."

"Hey!" Rube said, "We're not just any trash pandas, McGregor, we're *your* trash pandas."

"However did I get so fortunate?" the werecat purred sardonically.

Completely missing the irony, Rube said, "Aw, we feel the same way about you, Hairball. Nothing but love for you, bro. Nothing but love."

Straightening, Chase said, "Not meaning to detract from this touching moment, but are we just going to leave those pirates floating out there?"

"We are not," Festus said, standing and stretching. "Ironweed, buzz on over there and ask them to join us for a drink at the Dirty Claw."

MIRANDA AND DRAKE accepted the invitation. Dropping a long rope ladder off one side of the ship, they climbed down and met us at the city gate.

Shevington's streets offer their fair share of exotic sights on a normal day, but people still turned their heads to stare when we walked past with the pirates.

At The Dirty Claw, Festus led the way to a round table tucked in a corner well away from the busy crowd.

After we claimed our seats and ordered our drinks, Drake suddenly ducked as a foam ball whizzed past his head. Miranda batted the projectile back toward the bar's new indoor tennis court.

"Human or feline rules?" she asked Festus.

"Feline," he replied. "First player to get three irretrievable balls under the refrigerator wins. See that hairless runt over there? That's Aloysius. I kicked his butt in this year's Christmas Tree Destruction contest so now he's organizing some lame foam ball tennis league thinking he can snag the inaugural trophy. He's been sniffing too much flea spray."

The pirate captain grinned. "I *love* werecat bars. The scratching. The hissing. The second-hand catnip smoke."

Across the table, her partner wiped at the sleeve of his black coat. "The damned cat hair sticking to everything," he muttered.

Rube sucked down his Litterbox Lager and nudged Festus.

"We got room in the budget to get the big bad pirate a sticky roller?"

"Back off you Fae bilge rat," Drake growled, only to stop when the point of a needle-sharp knife pressed against his jugular.

Hovering alongside the man's ear, Ironweed said, "That Fae bilge rat is a friend of mine."

Great. Not five minutes at the table and the boys weren't playing nice.

Miranda, who was sitting beside Rube, diffused the situation before I could say a word.

She threw back her head and let out with a belly laugh. "You like the feel of fairy steel at your throat, Drake?" she asked. "Ever expect to die by toothpick?"

Holding himself so still I couldn't see the guy breathe, Drake said, "No."

"Good," Miranda said using her command voice. "Apologize to the varmint"

He didn't like it, but Drake said, "No offense meant."

Rube's black nose twitched over the rim of his glass. "Better brush up on your definition of offensive there, Captain Kidd. We're good. For now. Back off, Ironweed."

The major sheathed his blade as Drake let out with an ear-splitting sneeze. The gust caught Ironweed off guard, sending him tumbling head over heels through the air.

Chase put up a hand and braked his roll. Ironweed caught hold of his index finger, executed a mid-air spin, and righted himself.

"Thanks man," the fairy said, adjusting his purple beret that had slipped over one eye. "Didn't expect that."

"No problem."

Festus slapped the table with his paw. "Holy hairball!" he crowed. "Drake's allergic. We just *love* the ones who are allergic.

How about I hop up on the table and send some dander your way?

Drake regarded him with watering, bloodshot eyes. The guy tried to glare. He really did, but he couldn't pull it off with tears streaming down his face.

"Don't get excited," the pirate said. The words came out in a mess of thick consonants thanks to his rapidly clogging nasal passages. "I'm only allergic to some species. There must be a werecheetah in here."

Chase surveyed the crowd. "Six by my count."

Miranda rolled her eyes. "I'm not going to sit here and dodge your snot, Drake. Get back to the *Tempus Fugit* and take a pill or something."

The pirate puffed out his chest. "I can't leave a woman alone in a bar full of drunk werecats."

All the men scooted back. They knew what was coming. I leaned my elbows on the table and enjoyed the show.

The air between Miranda and Drake chilled — literally. The lager in our glasses froze as our breath generated clouds of condensation.

Rube's grin split his black mask. "Man, you don't know much about dames, do you?"

Drake might have been slow, but he now realized his mistake. His eyes darted back and forth frantically searching for an out.

When Miranda spoke, her voice was low and dangerous, "Really Drake? And why is it, exactly, that you think I can't take care of myself here or anywhere else?"

Putting his hands up in a placating gesture, the pirate said, "Now, Miranda, don't get upset."

"This," she said levelly, "isn't upset. When your fingers start snapping off from the frostbite, I'm upset. Get back to the ship."

This time Drake didn't argue. He stood, tossed a handful of

coins on the table, and said, "Aye, Cap'n. This round's on me. A pleasure to have met you all."

With that, he hurried out of the bar, but not before a second furious round of sneezing sent a long-haired Persian backing away in disgust.

"For Bastet's sake man! Cover your nose when you do that." the werecat hissed.

As Drake apologized and stumbled out the door, Festus asked Miranda, "Why exactly do you keep that guy around?"

"He has hidden talents," Miranda replied, "but they're starting to wane."

Signaling Manfred, the lynx bartender for another round, Chase said, "You're an elemental elf?"

"On my mother's side," Miranda answered, waving her hand over our drinks to melt the ice. "The deep freeze tends to turn on when I'm angry."

Rube dipped one hand in his mug and pulled out a chunk of lager ice. For the record, the freezing temperature of beer is 28°F. I was impressed.

"Can you turn on the ice machine anytime you want?" he asked.

"Yes."

"Lady," he grinned, "you're gonna be handy in warm weather."

"I'm handy in all weather," Miranda replied in dulcet tones that left the raccoon speechless.

Festus laughed so hard he almost fell out of his chair. "Trust me, under all that black fur, the Trash Panda's blushing like a high school boy on his first date."

"I ain't doing no such thing," Rube protested indignantly.

Putting an arm around the embarrassed raccoon, I scolded the werecat. "Stop picking on him."

Rube scooted closer. "That's right," he said. "I'm just an inno-cent forest animal."

Festus made a reply, but I can't reproduce it here. Let's just say he doubted Rube's innocence and leave it at that.

"Even if you were blushing," Miranda assured Rube, "it would be adorable. Is The Dumpster Dive still open in Procyon?"

The raccoon brightened. "You know The Dumpster Dive?"

"Best raccoon gin joint in the trash panda home world," Miranda replied. "Nice sinks in the lady's room."

"Us coons is big on handwashing," Rube replied, "and hand sanitizer. You got any idea how many germs humans spread 'cause they go around with dirty paws all the time?"

"For the love of nip, Rube," Festus said, "you dig in garbage."

"Yeah," he said seriously, "and I wash my hands when I'm done."

Manfred appeared and dispensed fresh drinks. Raising her mug, Miranda said, "Drink and the devil be done for the rest."

Chase clinked his glass against hers. "Yo ho ho and a bottle of rum."

"Well," she said, "aren't you a surprise? Your girlfriend is the other missing woman?"

His face now serious, Chase nodded. "Glory," he said, "her name is Glory Green."

"She's a witch, too?"

"That," I said, "is a long story. Glory is a human victimized by witchcraft. She got in Irenaeus Chesterfield's way."

Miranda made a disapproving noise in her throat. "Now there," she said, "is a right bastard roasting in hell."

"Have to agree with you on that one," I said.

Staring into his lager, Chase ran one finger around the lip of the glass. "How does this work?" he asked. "How are we going after them?"

The pirate captain studied him. "You and the husband still insist on coming along?" she asked.

Chase looked up, eyes alight with fierce determination. "We're going. Period."

"Ditto," Festus said.

"Double ditto," Rube added.

Miranda looked at Ironweed. "And you?"

"Barnaby and Connor felt a military mind might be an advantage on this mission," the fairy said.

The pirate shook her head. "There has to be a straight line in there somewhere."

"Huh?" Chase said.

Rube, ever the jokester, wrote the line in his head. "Two pirates, two werecats, a coon, and a fairy walk into a bar . . . "

In spite of himself, Chase laughed. "Remember to tell Glory that," he said. "She'll love it."

Now Miranda looked at me. "And how about you?"

Blowing out a frustrated breath, I said, "I'm going back to Briar Hollow. Everyone has convinced me that we have to maintain a credible cover story there for the humans in our lives. That requires my presence. Rodney and I will return to the fairy mound as soon as you all set sail."

"Rodney?"

The rat stuck his head out from under my collar and waved at Miranda.

"Well, hello there," she said brightly, "you must be one fearless rodent to come into a werecat bar."

In response, Rodney flexed his biceps, which made Miranda laugh.

"Got it," she said. "Tough guy. No crossing you." She looked at Chase. "To answer your question about what happens now, we have Barnaby Shevington reopen the original portal where the accident occurred. Then we take the *Tempus Fugit* into the matrix with the piece of the Copernican Astrolabe Festus brought back from Londinium. The essential magnetism kicks in and we go for a wild ride."

"One that takes us to where Jinx and Glory landed?" Chase asked.

"That's the theory," she said.

Festus caught the equivocation. "Theory?"

"The way we jump across the streams without real instruments of temporal navigation is a crapshoot," Miranda said. "Nine times out of ten we hit the right stream. Half the time we nail our target in that stream. I'm hoping the astrolabe part improves those odds."

Nobody spoke. We all knew what could happen. They could get marooned in time too. Rube finally seized the bull by the horns, "So," he said, slurping his lager, "when we hitting the portal highway?"

It's hard to be upset by a question posed by a raccoon with a beer foam ring around his nose.

"As soon as Lucas finishes his conversation with Director Grayson," Chase said.

Rube shook his head sending flecks of foam flying onto the table, "I still think one of us oughtta be there when Hat Man talks with Uncle Mo. Otherwise, there's a good chance he's gonna go all homicidal murderous like on the guy."

"Connor is outside the door," I said. "He won't let anything happen."

"No disrespect to Con Man," the raccoon said, "but ain't none of you ever seen Lucas mad. He makes Pirate Lady here look like the Popsicle Fairy."

Tilting back his thimble full of lager, Ironweed warned, "Take it from someone with the battle scars to know. Don't disrespect the Popsicle Fairy. She's not as sweet as she looks."

"Neither's Hat Man," Rube said darkly.

21

Shevington

Lucas sat across from his uncle in Grayson's "accommodations" at the Inn. Connor and the triplets waited outside the door. Pushing his fedora back on his brow, Lucas crossed his arms over his chest and waited.

Grayson stared back at him without blinking. Minutes ticked by; the Director broke first.

"What does this ridiculous standoff accomplish, Lucas?" he asked. "You must accept that your wife is dead. The question now becomes, how you will continue with your life? Perhaps the Fates have intervened to give you the perfect opportunity to formally assume the Grysundl throne."

Leaning forward with his elbows on his knees, Lucas replied, "*Perhaps*, the Fates have intervened to reveal your true nature, Uncle Morris."

"I have never shown you anything but my true nature."

"Is that a fact?" Lucas said amiably. "So tossing a piece of the Copernican Astrolabe into the portal with my wife and friend was just you being you?"

The Director's mouth moved with annoyance. "I did no such thing."

"Oh," Lucas said, "but you did. There were multiple witnesses. A sentient pen and journal extracted the visual memory from Tori's mind while she slept. You threw the rule from the Astrolabe into the portal. Jinx caught it, triggering the artifact's essential magnetism."

"Essential magnetism is an unproven crackpot theory."

"I'll let you take that up with Stank Preston. For the magnetism to be triggered, another piece of the Astrolabe — the plate, to be specific, since it's also missing — has to exist somewhere in the timestreams. Who did you maroon in time before you went after my wife?"

Now visibly in a huff, Grayson said, "I have no idea what you're talking about."

"Don't you, Uncle?" Lucas asked pleasantly. "Let's use some visual aids."

Taking a tablet out of his satchel, he said, "Adeline, would you project the logs of Containment Vault 745."

"My pleasure," she replied. "On the wall or would you like a hologram?"

"A hologram, please."

In response, a three-dimensional image of a large ledger lying open formed between the two men. Lines of identical handwriting filled both pages.

"That's your signature, isn't it?" Lucas asked.

Ignoring the fine sheen of sweat on his forehead, Grayson said dismissively, "What if it is? I didn't go into the damned vault every time I certified the Astrolabe. No one does. Those artifacts haven't been touched in years. Why bother looking at them every six months to confirm their ossified status?"

Speaking to the tablet's screen, Lucas said, "Adeline, could you play the security footage, please?"

This time moving images filled the air. Grayson in his ubiquitous black suit entering the containment vault.

"Look at the date stamp, Morris," Lucas said. "That's the day before my wedding."

Unmoved, Grayson said, "I fulfilled my oversight obligation before I left Londinium to attend your nuptials. The footage proves nothing but that I met my responsibilities."

"Adeline, play the second clip, please."

A younger image of Grayson entered and left the same vault.

"*That*," Lucas said, "was footage recorded the day before Axe Frazier's 'death.'"

The Director threw up his hands. "Why are you letting Barnaby Shevington's people twist your mind?" he demanded. "Now you're accusing me of killing Axe? This is sheer insanity."

Lucas remained completely calm. "For your sake, Uncle," he said, "you better hope neither Axe nor Jinx is dead because if they are, I'll kill you with my bare hands."

Grayson made a "tsking" sound. "Threats do not become a king."

"Threats may not," Lucas said, "but actions do. You forget, Uncle, the moment Jinx married me she became the royal consort. I can order your death without a trial."

"Yes you can," Morris said, eyes gleaming, "and the instant you take such an action, you have claimed the throne. I am prepared to die as a patriot for my country if it will re-establish the Grysundl monarchy."

"And I," Lucas said, standing and gathering his things, "am prepared to become king for the pleasure of avenging my wife."

As he moved toward the door, the Director said, "Where are you going?"

Lucas paused with his hand on the doorknob. "To board a Sídhe vessel called the *Tempus Fugit* to go after Jinx."

Jumping to his feet, Grayson said, "You can't do that!"

"Oh, but I can. Festus brought another piece of the Astrolabe back from Londinium. Use the time I'm away to think about the things you've done, Morris. When we meet again, I suggest you tell me a better version of your side of this story if you expect to live. Either way though, I wouldn't hold out on being a free man again any time soon. The Ruling Elders want to discuss some matters with you when I'm ready to hand you over."

When the door closed behind him, Grayson sank into his chair, "I won't need a better story, my boy," he said softly. "I won't be here when you return."

Tori

Chase stood with one foot on the bottom rung of the rope ladder. The *Tempus Fugit* hovered only inches above the ground outside the city gate.

Above him, Festus and Rube rode in a basket connected to a winch, which Drake Lobranche cranked with jerking motions. Ironweed flew alongside offering encouragement to the nervous raccoon.

"Climbing is one thing," Rube said, "I was like *born* to climb. Look at these claws." He held up one foot and flexed his toes. "What I ain't liking is that these claws got nothing solid to grip."

Festus shifted his weight on purpose to make the basket sway, eliciting another panicked yelp from Rube.

"Live a little, Striped Butt," the werecat advised. "Ride the rollercoaster."

"I don't want to ride no freaking rollercoaster," Rube howled. "I want my paws on something solid."

From above them, Miranda called out, "Steady there, Reuben. You'll find your sea legs once you're aboard. Just a few more feet."

"How can I find my sea legs?" Rube yelled. "There ain't no ocean! You see anything wet around here? 'Cause I don't see nothing even counting as damp. Am I the only one bothered about this floating in thin air thing?"

Answering as one, Chase, Lucas, Festus, and Ironweed all said, *"Yes!"*

I tried not to laugh. I really did, but the sight of Rube's striped tail sticking straight out over the edge of the basket quivering with anxiety made me giggle.

"They're scaring him stiff," I said. "On purpose."

Chase looked up. "Don't worry about Rube. He'll be his old self when they get him out of that basket. I watched him pack for the trip. There's enough junk food in his duffle to soothe even the worse case of jangled nerves."

Standing on tiptoe, I kissed him on the cheek. "You be careful," I said. "Find Glory and bring her home, preferably full size and sans the green."

"Will do," he said. He reached for the first rung and began to climb.

Turning to Lucas, I held out my arms. When we embraced, I squeezed him tight and said, "Go get our girl."

"I will," he replied.

Rodney's head poked out of my shirt collar. He reached over and patted Lucas on the cheek, his paw looking extra tiny and pink against the 5 o'clock stubble.

Stepping back, Lucas put himself on eye level with the rat. "You take care of her, okay? I'm counting on you."

Rodney nodded, giving me a protective glance and Lucas a thumbs up.

When Chase swung his legs over the railing and dropped onto the deck, Lucas started up the ladder making quick work of the ascent.

With everyone accounted for, Miranda ordered Drake to raise anchor and deploy sail.

Above me, I heard Rube say, "Uh, point of order? Barnaby opened the portal right in the middle of town. We're too big to get down there."

Miranda replied, "Hold on to your fur. We're not going to be too big for long."

She bounded up the steps to the helm, grasped the wheel in one hand, and used the other to pull back a large lever mounted on the deck.

With a groan of protest, the ship and her passengers began to shrink until I found myself standing beside a sedan-sized version of the schooner.

Looking down into Festus' scowling, miniaturized face, I said, "You look like an itty bitty kitten."

The werecat backed his ears. "Even itty bitty kittens have claws."

As the ship passed through the city gate and floated down the High Street, Rodney and I trailed behind. Rube, his former fears forgotten, took up station near the bowsprit sporting the black tricorn hat Miranda had given him for enduring the ride up in the basket.

I have to say it went quite well with his black mask and white whiskers.

As the ship floated past Horatio Pagecliffe's shop, the raccoon put one leg up on the ship's rail and planted his paws on his hips.

"Not meaning to horn in on driving this tub," he called out, "but you gotta flower pot coming up on the right, Cap'n."

"Starboard," Miranda corrected. "The right side of a ship is the starboard side."

"Starboard, moonboard, whatever," Rube called out, "you're about to plow through a bunch of marigolds."

Miranda corrected course and brought the *Tempus Fugit* to bear on the portal Barnaby held open on the square.

Reaching for the lever again, she yelled, "Instigating secondary size reduction."

Cheers rose from the assembled crowd as the schooner diminished to roughly the size of a riding lawnmower. Using a bullhorn to magnify her voice, Miranda yelled, "Shield your eyes. We're going in!"

When the bow entered the portal, bolts of red lightning arced around the opening. With his fur standing on end from the static electricity, a tiny striped speck I knew was Rube scrambled down from his perch and joined the others at the base of the main mast.

The wind in the matrix picked up, making the sails whip and crack. The blast of light didn't trigger until the stern slipped through the opening.

Throwing up my arms to shield my eyes, I felt Rodney bury his face in my neck. When I looked again, the portal had closed. The *Tempus Fugit* was gone.

"Fair winds," I whispered after them, "and following seas."

Rodney snuggled closer; I put up my hand and stroked his fur. "They'll be back, Little Dude. All of them."

In my thoughts, I added, "Goddess, please make it so."

22

Londinium, 1590

Brenna Sinclair and Greer MacVicar reclined in the back of the barge, their legs covered by thick fur robes. The winter sun raised fiery highlights in their red hair. The beauty of the Ruling Elder and her chief enforcer, the baobhan sith, would have turned the heads of most men had those same men not feared a casual, lustful glance might cost them their lives.

Even in the cold weather, the watercraft plied smartly through the brisk traffic on the Thames. Both women had chosen conservative, dark dress for the day, mindful not to outshine Her Majesty Queen Elizabeth. The monarch was known for her vanity regarding her looks and her wardrobe.

The rowers' oars slapped the water with rhythmic efficiency. Both they and the helmsman labored under a discretion enchantment that allowed the women to speak freely.

"Bess favors the palace at Richmond for its warmth," Brenna said. "Thank the gods we didn't have to attend the Yule celebration and pretend to enjoy the human gaiety of the court."

The vampire studied the shoreline impassively, taking note of the clumps of ice clinging to patches of undisturbed bank.

"I have never minded the cold," she said. "As for the recent celebratory season, it afforded me copious numbers of young men in an advanced state of drink ripe for the taking."

Brenna snorted. "Londinium has no shortage of comely lads willing to accept your invitation for an evening's entertainment. They spare no worries for a different outcome."

Greer cocked an eyebrow, "I assure you they go away with false, but vivid memories, so long as I do not find them exceptionally flavorful of course."

"Do you even know how many you've killed?" Brenna asked.

"Do you?" the baobhan sith retorted.

The Ruling Elder thought for a moment. "I remember the first four — my father and brothers — with exquisite and pleasurable detail. Taking inconsequential lives grew more mundane and boring after that. If the river freezes this year, I suggest you stalk the skating parties. The groups will be filled with tender boys in the blush of their youth."

Greer made a scolding sound. "Even I have standards, Brenna. I prefer to wait until my dinner 'companions' have at least sprouted whiskers on their chins."

"The Queen does not share your scruples. With each passing year Her Majesty grows older and her playthings younger."

"Come now, you like your toys as well, and your age far exceeds hers."

"Yes," Brenna agreed, " but if Bess agrees to become Creavit, she can keep her youth and her throne for eternity."

"What progress on that front?"

Turning confident eyes on her companion, Greer said, "Bess is her father's daughter. Had Anne trusted my magic over her own paltry powers she would have given Henry a son and kept her head. None of the Boleyns escaped the curse of their arrogance. The Tudors are made of more practical mettle. The Queen will agree. She trusts me."

"As well she should, you have long protected her and influenced the course of her life from a distance."

Brenna grimaced in annoyance. "It would have been far simpler to bring a Fae halfling onto the throne had we not been forced to first orchestrate the death of her sickly brother Edward and the demise of her odious sister, Mary."

"The boy was an easy matter," Greer said. "A cold wind off the river was enough to do in his fragile lungs. We had but to arrange for an open window and wait."

Downstream, the turrets of Richmond palace came into view. "I did not lack sympathy for the boy king," Brenna mused. "He was but nine years when the humans put a crown upon his brow. In many ways, I believe we did him a favor hastening his way to the grave."

"You harbored no such sympathies for the Catholic Mary."

"I did not," she agreed. "Mary's affection for her mother's Spanish relatives would have brought the Inquisition down upon our heads. We have enough trouble with the human's religious weaknesses."

"And then the pox most conveniently threatened the new Queen. You have never told me," the baobhan sith said. "Did you afflict Elizabeth with the illness so that you might cure her or did nature put that fortuitous opportunity in your path?"

"Regardless of the manner of the infection," Brenna replied, "my ability to keep Her Majesty's ivory skin unmarked sealed her affection for me. She is now forever in my debt."

When the boat bumped alongside the dock, the helmsman offered his hand to assist the Ruling Elder and the vampire onto the platform. There, a plump, nervous lady-in-waiting greeted them.

"Her Majesty looks forward to your arrival," the woman said dropping a clumsy curtsy. "Please follow me."

Moving through the building's impressive entrance and crossing the interior courtyard, the lady-in-waiting escorted Brenna and Greer to the Queen's private study.

When they were announced, Elizabeth, resplendent in a gown of wine velvet studded with seed pearls, greeted them formally. Then she dismissed her ladies and bade the guards ensure that she and her guests remain undisturbed.

Once alone in the room, the Queen extended her arms and said, "Brenna, my dear sister, how fare thee?"

"Warmed to my soul in the reflected glow of Your Majesty's splendour," Brenna replied, returning the embrace.

Though pleased by the obsequious language, Elizabeth said, "Come now, when we are alone we are but Bess, Brenna, and Greer. Tell me, baobhan sith how did you find matters in France and Spain?"

As they talked, the women moved closer to the baronial fireplace heating the room. A woman of learning, in an age of educated men, Elizabeth maintained a proper cabinet of curiosities, stocked with gifts from foreign dignitaries and ambitious explorers seeking her favor.

Taking a chair alongside the hearth, Greer said, "The individuals whose activities caused Your Majesty vexation have been dispatched to their heaven or hell. I can speak only to the ending of their lives, not the state of their souls."

"And did you find time for personal amusement on the Continent?" the Queen asked.

A glowing ring of scarlet embers fired in Greer's eyes. "I did," she said. "I find the blood of the Spanish to be as astringent as their faith, but the indulgent French make for a richer meal."

Elizabeth laughed, a merry trilling sound. "I miss my Moor," she said, "but your methods are so much more compelling and entertaining."

"Sir Francis Walsingham was an effective spymaster," Greer said.

"He was," the Queen agreed, "but next to you, his methods were crude and unreliable. "

Brenna inclined her head to better study the monarch's features. "Do you not agree that Walsingham's great fondness for the rack blinded him to the nuances of men's souls?"

Elizabeth nodded. "I thought not to make windows into the souls of men until you, dear Brenna, showed me how much those windows might reveal."

"Ah," the sorceress replied, "but I possess the ability to craft windows whose utility exceed those broken panes created by Walsingham's torture."

The Queen poured wine into goblets and offered them to her guests. "I met with Dr. John Dee this morning," she said lightly, but the mention of the court astrologer put Brenna on the alert.

"I pray he saw nothing but good fortune in Your Majesty's stars,"

Elizabeth sipped at her wine. "He tells me of a disruptive event in the offing, one that lies simmering among my Fae subjects and involves the constellation Ophiuchus. Dr. Dee believes the token left in Dr. Lopez's quarters the night his journal was stolen to be an omen of what is to come."

The Ruling Elder sat her goblet on the table. "There are no disturbances among the Fae," she said. "Irregularities are brought to my attention immediately and handled decisively."

The Queen smiled, "Brenna, I do not doubt your control over your people, but you must agree the token is most strange. Have your alchemists divined its nature?"

"They have not," Brenna said, irritation coloring her features, "but they will if they wish not to find themselves turned into farm animals. The coin's material falls lightly in the hand. It is unlike any alloy known to us."

"And the deciphering of the words?"

Brenna removed a small book from her pocket, opened it to a marked page, and passed the volume to the Queen.

Elizabeth studied the page. "What manner of people use names like 'Bambi' and 'Topher?'"

"My linguists are uncertain if the pronunciation should be 'Bam-bee' or 'Bam-by,'" Brenna said. "They feel Topher to be a nickname for Christopher."

"And this Las Vegas?" the Queen asked, her expression darkening. "It has the sound of a Spanish outpost."

Greer shook her head. "As Your Majesty knows, in the language of the Spanish the phrase means 'the Meadows.' None of our people in Spain have heard a rumor of such a place figuring into King Philip's plans."

Brenna drummed the arm of her chair. "I care not for Bambi, Topher, and Las Vegas," she said. "I am intrigued by the phrase 'save the date' followed by November 15, 2017."

The Queen arched an eyebrow. "You believe this token to have traveled from a time 427 years in the future?"

"The old Seers spoke of time as the Fourth Realm," Brenna said. "If we are able to move freely among the human, Fae, and Middle Realms by the use of portals, is it so fantastical to assume time might not be accessed in a similar fashion?"

Elizabeth studied her closely. "More underlies your suspicion of time travel than the appearance of a strange token."

Brenna inclined her head. "As always Your Majesty," she said, "your intellect strikes deep at the heart of the matter. There is a man called Alex Farnsworth who works among the botanists of Lime Street. He employs strange methods in his work."

"Would you hold a man suspicious for an innovative manner of executing his profession?" the Queen asked.

"I would not," the Ruling Elder said, "but shortly before the death of his wife, Farnsworth is reputed to have been missing from his residence for no more than the space of a few days only to return with deep furrows in his face and hair gone to gray."

The Queen's eyes lit with interest. "You suggest he aged years in the span of but a few days?"

"I do," Brenna said, "but until the discovery of this token in Dr. Lopez's quarters, I had no corroborating evidence to suggest that Farnsworth might be conducting experiments in time travel. Experiments not sanctioned by me, which would make them both seditious and heretical."

The Queen laughed. "Such experiments will only remain seditious and heretical until they come to serve your purpose."

"Until they come to serve *our* purpose," Brenna said. "Our administrations work hand-in-hand to secure both your glory and the prosperity of the three realms."

Elizabeth considered the words. "If time travel were possible," she said, "how would we use it to our advantage?"

"Imagine," Brenna said, "if we could part the threads of time, would it not be possible for us to examine the outcome of our choices free of the limitations of waiting? Could we not move forward and backward correcting our decisions and altering the outcome of key events?"

The baobhan sith cleared her throat. "You must remember that I was alive in the time of the Seers," she said. "I have heard the stories of the Fourth Realm. They did not speak of a single stream of time, but of multiple eventualities in the great fabric of reality."

"All the better," Brenna said. "What stronger allies could we have than mirror images of ourselves?"

The Queen drank the remainder of her wine and sat the goblet aside. "You have this Farnsworth under surveillance?"

"I have, Your Majesty," Brenna said, "and there has been a development. Earlier today three Druid women entered Lime Street. The younger two seemed unusually amazed by the sites of Londinium."

"Londinium is a thriving and cosmopolitan jewel," the Queen said. "Why would they not be amazed?"

"The smaller of the two," the Ruling Elder said, "was heard to ask questions of the elder woman about commonplace things. The pattens upon the shoes of the people and the refuse flung from the windows. She asked after the stench of the city."

Elizabeth frowned. "It is your belief that these women are also displaced in time and thus unfamiliar with our world?"

"It is my belief that were they all to be arrested and brought to the Tower," Brenna replied, "we would soon enough extract answers to that question and perhaps many more."

"Then make it so," the Queen said. "Let us open a window into the souls of the strangers and find out what vistas they may lay before us. Perhaps they will tell us of Bambi, Topher, and Las Vegas."

Swirling the wine in her goblet, Greer said, "Las Vegas. I know not why, but the sound of it appeals to me."

23

Londinium, 1590, Jinx

After spending the afternoon in our room, we joined Axe — Alex — and his family downstairs for supper. Although Glory and I ate well during our time with the Druids, my mouth watered at the sight of roast beef and a surprising array of vegetables.

Normally I might have asked for water, but after our trek through the streets of Londinium, I understood why everybody in Elizabethan England drank ale or wine.

Naomi must have rested after her lessons, because in spite of her frail appearance, she was a lively presence at dinner.

I don't know how children were expected to behave in the 16th century, but this child was encouraged to discuss her day and share insights gleaned from her lessons.

The kid was polite about it, but she definitely felt that her tutor was over the hill. I listened while she and Axe launched into a detailed discussion of Roman history. Father and daughter dropped in and out of Latin as they spoke.

Although I had no basis to join in the conversation, Glory

did. There are times when Glory can seem like what Festus calls a "blithering flibbertigibbet" but there was no denying she had a way with young people.

Through a series of gently prompting questions, she drew Naomi into an animated conversation about her life. As they talked, I watched Axe's face. He openly adored the child, but the shadow of worry never left his gray eyes.

The man knew the orderly workings of his household well. Shortly after the meal ended, Noah yawned and suggested to Naomi that it was time for them to go to bed and leave the "scholars" to our conversations.

The little girl looked like she wanted to protest, but the burst of energy we'd seen through the evening had disappeared. Fatigue marred her pretty features betraying the extent of her illness.

Axe waited almost an hour before putting a finger to his lips and gesturing us to follow him down a cramped stairway to the cellar. There, he parted the curtain of a complex glamour that disguised the opening to a tunnel.

We went after him into the twisting and turning maze, only to discover after a few yards that we shared the space with a disturbing number of large gray rats.

The first one ran in front of Glory. She let out with a high-pitched, terrified squeal I was positive passersby in the street over our heads must have heard.

Realizing her mistake, she clapped a hand over her mouth, while a shudder ran through her body.

"I'm so sorry," she said, shrinking back against the wall. "It's not that I'm afraid of rats. I mean like, my best friend is a rat. But he's clean. And black and white. And his eyes don't go all red and beady in the dark. Anyway, I'm sorry. I won't do it again."

Axe gave her a tolerant smile. "My late wife was not fond of rats," he said. "I have seen a reaction similar to yours many times."

Glory gave him a wavering smile of thanks, and we continued deeper into the tunnels. Thankfully, we reached the underground workshop without having to leap over additional rodent-based hurdles.

I don't know what I expected, but the space that opened before us seemed to be a combination of natural cave and engineered construction. Some portions of the surrounding walls were laid bricks while others showed natural exposed stone.

The setting was perfect as a backdrop for our meeting with the Ebu Gogo, Lashtazo. Although he was dressed like a proper English gentleman of the period, there was no doubt that we were in the presence of a living caveman.

He smiled exposing a startling array of sturdy teeth and greeted us with a hoarse but cultured voice. When Axe explained that we, too, were time travelers, Lash could barely contain the flow of questions.

"Forgive his enthusiasm," Axe said. "It is Lash's fondest wish that we sort out the mysteries of time travel so that he might return to the future with me."

The Ebu Gogo's eyes glowed brightly in his dark face. "I wish to fly like the birds in an arrow plane," he said. "And see the box that makes pictures and tells stories."

"Lash," Axe corrected kindly, "it's 'airplane' not 'arrow plane.'"

Smiling complacently, Lash said, "But both fly through the air, why can't it be called an arrow plane?"

Glory giggled. "You're funny," she said, "and you'll love the box that makes pictures. It's called a television. I know all the best shows and movies. Those are longer stories that take two hours to tell. A TV show usually takes one hour. Well, 45 minutes when you take out the commercials. That's how TV people make money. The commercials. Wait until you see your first Elvis picture!"

"Who is Elvis?" Lash asked.

"Oh, my goodness gracious," Glory said, "he's just the best singer in the whole wide world."

Sensing that we could be on the brink of founding the 16th-century chapter of the Elvis Fan Club, I said, "So what exactly have you two been working on down here?"

Axe led me over to a work table and picked up a wooden framed instrument that seemed vaguely familiar. "Is that a sextant?" I asked.

"Close," he said, "it's an octant, and we've built it about 140 years ahead of its time. The frame comprises one-eighth of a circle. Two mirrors double the size of the angle and reflect light to the observer. It allows for viewing both the sun and the horizon simultaneously to determine latitude."

Adeline's words came back to me. *"A mirror cast into a tunnel of windows."*

"I kinda get what that means in relation to terrestrial navigation," I said, "but what about temporal navigation?"

Lash spoke up. "We hope the mirrors will align the identical windows so you know which one to go through."

Mirrors and windows.

A flicker of hope sprang to life in my heart.

"Windows to what?"

Picking up a bit of chalk, Axe walked to a smooth section of wall. "You came here through something like a tunnel, right?" he asked.

Glory piped up. "More like a vacuum cleaner hose. It was *awful.* We got sucked down this long black tube and then kinda hit a wall before we landed in the woods. That's where Moira found us."

The alchemist said, "The sky over the clearing broke open

with jagged fingers of light. When I went to investigate, I discovered Jinx and Glory."

"Interesting," Axe said. "No one witnessed my arrival."

"Did you land somewhere nice?" Glory asked.

Axe laughed. "Hardly," he said, "I was dumped into the middle of the Thames during a flood. Thankfully I used the incident as part of my cover story to explain why I had no possessions. I claimed to have been traveling from the north when my horse and belongings were washed away. Noah pulled me out of the river and brought me home. But my experience in the tunnel was the same as yours."

I turned to Glory. "You saw the openings flash by on the sides, right? The ones with scenes from places we know?"

She shook her head. "No. I kept my eyes closed the whole time."

Using the chalk, Axe sketched out a main tunnel with lateral branches. "What you saw, Jinx are the junction points of different time streams. The scenes were variations of familiar realities."

An image of the Lair with all the furniture in the wrong places popped into my head. "Yes," I said, "I recognized everything I saw, but the details were wrong."

"Correct," he said. "The problem when you are in the tunnel is getting back to where you are supposed to be properly located in the fabric of time. We believe the octant will allow the user to take a line of sight down the tunnel and align their course with the window that matches their temporal coordinates."

He strode across the room with animated steps. "Lash gathered these charts in the Middle Realm. The coordinates are based on an intricate system of exact times and dates with an index number that correlates with an individual time stream. You plug in the date when you fell into the portal and use that to backtrack to your point of origin."

"So that means you could go back and live the life you were supposed to live?" Glory asked excitedly. "You could come right back out of the portal and be there with your sister, and Chase, and Lucas again?"

"I suppose I could," Axe said, "but I would arrive as I am now. Older, knowing everything I know. I would prefer to pick up my life at the point it would have naturally evolved — in your time."

"Your sister would like that," I said. "So would Lucas and Chase."

He leaned against the table. "They're all still friends?"

I owed him the truth, painful though it might be. "Everyone has believed for years that you died in the accident. Lauren blamed Lucas and Chase. She hasn't spoken to them in years. She quit the DGI and got into private security work. I don't know everything about her business, but she has dealings with a band of antiquities thieves who brought back a sketch of you in some journal."

A strange almost sick look came over his face. "Dr. Lopez's journal?"

Shrugging, I said, "I have no idea. Would that be bad?"

"It would be *very* bad," Axe said. "The theft of the journal has been the talk of Londinium for weeks. The thieves dropped some sort of strange token that pointed to potential Spanish spies. Brenna Sinclair's alchemists have been trying to decipher its origins for the Queen. Where are my sister and these pirates based?"

"Las Vegas," I said. "Lauren works with the high Sídhe nobles."

That news stumped him. "What are the Pretty People doing in Vegas?"

"Being pretty," I said. "That's a thing now. Being famous for being famous."

He shook his head. "Add that to the list of things I need to catch up on. The important thing now is that if these thieves dropped an item that points to another timestream, the Ruling Elder's interest could be piqued. That's the part that could be bad for us."

From the other side of the room, Lash said, "I'm afraid it may already be bad."

The Ebu Gogo stood beside a translucent sphere that showed the junction of the main thoroughfare and Lime Street. A group of men moved forward in the darkness, their passage lit by glowing orbs.

"Who are they?" Glory asked.

"The Ruling Elder's secret police," Lash replied. "They have watched Alex's house for many years, but never before have they entered the street en masse. Why would they come now?"

"Because of us," Moira said. "Our arrival this morning must have interested Brenna Sinclair sufficiently to cause her to order your arrest."

Axe sprang into action. "Lash, get Naomi."

The air around the burly man shimmered, and then he was gone.

"Wow," Glory said, "how did he do that?"

Shoving the octant and charts into a leather satchel, which he handed to Moira, Axe said, "The Ebu Gogo have mastered the ability of personal teleportation. It's how he enters the Middle Realm without a portal."

As he finished speaking, Lash returned, cradling a sleepy Naomi in his arms. The befuddled girl looked up in the Ebu Gogo's face, "Uncle Lash, I'm not supposed to be out of bed this late."

"Your Papa sent me to fetch you, sweet girl," Lash replied, putting her down carefully.

Naomi, only half awake, stumbled toward Axe. "Have I done something wrong, Papa?"

Axe scooped the girl up in his arms. "No, you haven't," he said, "but I need you to stay here with Uncle Lash and these ladies until I come back. You'll be safe here. There's a nice cot by the fire." He looked at me, "Would you?"

"Of course," I said, as he passed the child to me. "Come on sweetheart, let's get you back in bed."

As I tucked the blanket around Naomi, Axe caught hold of Lash's hand. "He'll take me up top and then come back here. No matter what you see through the sphere, stay below ground. I'm entrusting you with my daughter, Jinx, and with the octant and charts. Don't let me down."

Our eyes met. Somehow I knew it would be for the last time. "I won't let you down. Naomi will be safe, now and always."

The shimmer returned, and the men were gone.

24

Aboard the Tempus Fugit

Miranda steered the ship into the portal forcing the vessel into a steep turn to port. The sails caught in the crosswind and propelled the *Tempest Fugit* through the matrix membrane and into the time tunnel.

Straining to control the wheel, the pirate captain reached for a second lever that ignited a pulsating bubble that expanded to envelop her craft.

Inside the protective shield, the wind on the deck died away but continued to fill the sails. As the forward progress slowed, Miranda called out, "I've got her in hand now. Should be smooth sailing from here on out."

Craning his neck in a circle to examine the pulsating translucent barrier, Rube said, "*Suh-wheet!* It's like we're inside a freaking fishbowl!"

Miranda turned the helm over to Drake and joined them on the lower deck.

"This," she said, gesturing toward the bubble, "is what I like to call the secret sauce. Instead of plummeting down the time channel like a bat out of hell, we can maintain a steady course and speed. That's how we reconnoiter the scenes in the adjacent branches and pick our voyages."

Festus hopped onto a barrel and surveyed the passing tableau of Trafalgar Square. "Something's not right," he said. "Isn't Lord Nelson looking the wrong direction?"

Miranda moved to stand beside him. "Not in there he's not," she said. "I've seen the Admiral with and without his sword, holding a telescope, and even on horseback — damned silly for a naval man. Each temporal branch we pass gives us a window into an alternate version of reality and events."

Lucas joined them. "So when Jinx and Glory came into the tunnel they fell into one of these branches?"

"Yes," the captain said. "This is the world where I make my living. Down every one of those junctions is a treasure waiting to be found."

Ironweed took up a fluttering position alongside her shoulder. "How do you find your way to your destination and back again?"

Miranda considered the question. "Normally," she said, "I wouldn't answer that, but you people are so squeaky clean even a pirate can trust you. We have proprietary charts."

The fairy nodded. "I suspected as much. Maps and an understanding of terrain are critical to any tactical maneuver. You did the surveying yourself?"

The captain nodded, "Me and generations of my family that came before. We guard the maps with our lives."

"Has anyone ever tried to take them?"

"A few years ago a duplicate set went missing," Miranda said. "We didn't get the charts back, but I assure you the crew members who sold them on the Middle Realm black market didn't live to repeat the deed."

On the starboard side, a view of the Coliseum in Rome

floated by. "How many of these branching tunnels will we see?" Chase asked.

"Hundreds. Thousands. Maybe hundreds of thousands," Miranda replied. "It's impossible to count. That's why being a time pirate is so much fun."

Rube shook his head. "Lady," he said, "you got yourself one twisted idea of fun."

"You run a tight ship," Lucas said. "I admire that. The miniaturization trick was unexpected.

"Yeah," Ironweed said. "How do you pull that off?"

The pirate motioned to the fairy. When he flew closer to her face, she said, "Hate to blow your fantasy about security, Major, but a few years ago we liberated some GNATS drone tech from the fairy guard depot in California."

Ironweed's arm shot out until his index finger almost touched Miranda's nose. *"You!"* he accused. "You're the one behind the San Francisco heist!"

Rather than look guilty, Miranda appeared delighted. "Yeah," she said. "That was some of our best work."

"You know," the incensed fairy sputtered, "the statute of limitations won't run out on that job for another thousand years."

"Do tell," Miranda said. "I'm assuming since we're here to help you get your witch back, I'm not going to be fending off any Fae law enforcement officials in the near future."

Lucas intervened, catching hold of the back of Ironweed's commando sweater and pulling him out of Miranda's face.

"Nobody with a badge is going to come after you," he assured the pirate. "Our deal stands. You help us get Jinx and Glory back in exchange for immunity and all or part of the Astrolabe."

Satisfied with the answer, Miranda leaned toward Ironweed again. "Be sweet, little man," she advised, "and I might give you some information on how to make those GNATS drones of yours even better."

Torn between outrage and curiosity, the fairy grumbled, "How would you do that?"

"Your drones are manned by remote crews working across dimensions," Miranda said. "One bad burst of transmatrix static and you're out of business. We miniaturize our vessels down to the size of insects with live crews on board. We're not tethered to some central network. I would, however, recommend avoiding fly swatters and roach traps."

Ironweed didn't look happy, but he did say, "We'll talk."

Festus jumped down from the barrel and sharpened his claws on the deck boards.

"Stop that!" Drake yelled. "That's a teak deck."

Unfazed, the werecat flexed his feet and stretched. "Yeah, I know. Sucks as a scratching post. Now, if everyone is done negotiating extra angles to this deal, could somebody please tell me if the Astrolabe latitude plate is working?"

Miranda called up to Drake, "How's she handling?"

Still scowling, the first mate said, "The Astrolabe part is pulling us on a heading, but the ship doesn't feel like herself. She's wallowing in the wind."

Miranda took the steps two at a time and claimed the wheel. Holding the handles loosely, she tested the play of the vessel.

"He's right," she said. "Something has changed the balance of the stream's flow."

Lucas followed her up to the helm with Chase, Rube, and Festus following behind. "Do you think it's Jinx and Glory?" He asked. "Could they be doing something to try to find their way home?"

"Maybe," Miranda conceded, "but if they are, they could be throwing a monkey wrench into our rescue operation."

"I don't care *how* they get home," Lucas said. "I just want them to get home."

"And you want *us* to get home," Miranda reminded him. "We didn't factor in the possibility that your wife and her friend might do something to destabilize the timestream. It's not going to do you much good to get your Jinx back if you wind up lost in time instead."

"Whoa, whoa, *whoa!*" Rube interjected. "When you say' lost,' that's like one of them meta-fours, right? You don't mean stuck in here with no way how to get home, 'cause if you do, that ain't what I signed on for."

Festus' paw shot out and slapped the raccoon across the snout.

Yelping, Rube jumped back. "Hey! No hitting!"

"Don't whine and I won't have to slap you," Festus said. "What you signed on for — what we all signed on for — is to get Jinx and Glory home. If there are complications, we'll deal with them."

Rubbing at his sore nose, Rube said, "Look, I want Jinx and the Pickle back same as you do, but I was intending on getting home myself at the same time."

"The Pickle?" Miranda asked.

"On account of Glory was once about the size of a cocktail gherkin," Rube explained. "Then she did some mojo and now she just goes green around the ears. Sometimes. Like when she's stressed. Which could mean we're looking for a chartreuse dame needing a ride home."

Miranda looked down into the raccoon's black-masked face. "You," she said, "are rapidly becoming my favorite. Don't worry about getting lost. That doesn't happen to us. Okay, there was one time, but that involved a temporal typhoon, so it doesn't count."

Rube's eyes went round with alarm. "Wait a minute!" He said. "You mean there's weather in here?"

From his position leaning against the rail, Drake said, "There's weather all right. Miranda is talking about a typhoon that blew us into the Sahara desert, except we landed in the Mesozoic era. You have no idea how big the dinosaurs were until you've got one craning his neck over the mast."

The raccoon started backing up holding his paws in front of his body as if he was holding back an enemy.

"Not only no," he said, "but *hell no*. I ain't gonna be no hors d'oeuvre for a Triceratoposaurus."

Festus scratched absently at one ear with his hind leg. "I don't think you're big enough to be a dinosaur hors d'oeuvre. Besides, remember what the dragonlets said. Coon meat is stringy. I can just see a T Rex picking you out of his dental work now."

"That ain't funny, McGregor," Rube said, "and how come I'd be the one to get eaten anyway?"

The werecat yawned, "Standard operational protocol. Sacrifice the vermin first."

"Dad, for Bastet's sake, stop it," Chase said. "He's just giving you a hard time, Rube. Nobody is going to let you get eaten by a dinosaur."

Rube gave him a grateful look. "You're a nice guy, Chase. You must get it from your Mama 'cause your Old Man's a pain in my striped butt."

Laughing along with the others, Miranda said, "Drake is embellishing the typhoon story. That was a once in 10,000-year storm."

Somewhat mollified, Rube said, "Okay, them's long odds. I can live with that. Geez. I'm a nervous wreck. I gotta eat something."

Festus snorted. "Eating something is your answer to everything."

"I got a policy," Rube replied, "don't never pass up a meal in case it's your last. I packed chips and salsa. Anybody want some?"

As he started back down to the main deck, the *Tempus Fugit* shuddered. Miranda tightened her grip on the wheel.

"What the hell was that?" she said, struggling to right the ship.

Moving to join her, Drake said, "We're picking up speed."

"Increase shield intensity," Miranda ordered. "Slow us down."

He grasped the lever, straining to shove it forward. "It's not working," he yelled over the rising wind as the translucent dome sputtered and blinked out. "Too much resistance."

"We've got a strong pull to port," Miranda said. "Hold on. I think we're going into a junction."

Bracing himself, Lucas said, "Is it where the Astrolabe wants us to go?"

"No," Miranda said grimly, "it's not."

The masts groaned against the shrieking of the sails. "Steer into the turn, Miranda," Drake shouted. "You'll snap a mast if you don't."

Miranda altered course. "Aye that," she said. "We need her intact where ever we wind up."

As she twisted the wheel, the strain on the vessel lessened. Ironweed, who had lashed himself to a bit of rigging, put a hand over his eyes. "This is not good," he yelled.

Straining to hear, Lucas said, "What did you say?"

"I said," Ironweed repeated, "this is not good. Look."

Blinking away tears from the force of the wind, Lucas looked.

"Oh crap," he said, "is that the Great Pyramid?"

25

Londinium, 1590

E ven though Naomi fell right to sleep when I put her down on the small bed, I worked a slumber enchantment over her before Lash returned. I didn't want the child to wake up and witness what we watched through the remote viewing magic.

The secret police pounded on the shop door. Axe met them with Noah standing in the shadows behind him. The commander of the squad immediately read a warrant charging Axe with the practice of seditious and heretical research. He was to be remanded into custody immediately by order of the Ruling Elder.

We saw it all. The ransacking of the shop and the house. The questions regarding us. Our origins. Our whereabouts. The police asked about Naomi but found her room in perfect order. The bed made as if no one had slept there in weeks. A light coating of dust on the furniture. The fireplace cold and clean.

Axe told me he possessed only the mild magic of a lesser water spirit. He must have implemented the complex protective measures long ago, in place and set to trigger at a moment's notice. For all his confidence and self-assurance, Axe Frazier still lived the life of a temporally displaced and thus endangered man.

With the intuitive understanding of a parent, Axe knew Naomi could be used as leverage against him. He told the commander the girl had been sent to the country, far away from the foul odors and contagion of greater Londinium. When he spoke of the fragile condition of his daughter's lungs, the words rang true because they were.

Our Brenna, the Brenna who would have used her abilities to soothe if not heal the ailing child, once told me, "The most convincing lies are those infused by truth." Axe spoke convincingly about sending his daughter away for her health because that solution was precisely what Naomi needed to live.

We weren't a component in Axe's careful plans, yet again and again, he told Brenna's henchmen the identical story about our presence in his home. We were traveling Druid scholars paying a call on a noted botanical expert. He enjoyed a pleasant morning's conversation with us before we went about our way not specifying a destination.

When the police came into the basement and beat on the walls looking for a sign of a tunnel or hiding place, we held our breath. The sounds of the search penetrated our subterranean refuge, but the glamour held. To the ears of the men, their blows fell on solid rock.

Axe managed to dissuade the captain from arresting Noah, pointing out that the old man had been a noted merchant in Lime Street, and a loyal subject of Her Majesty for his entire life — and he was human.

Did the Ruling Elder want the religiously volatile human population of Londinium to think the Fae were rounding up the non-magical?

"I came to Londinium a stranger and Noah took me in," Axe said. "There are no mysteries about my father-in-law's origins, but mine are a different matter. His only crime is that he gave me shelter and welcomed me into his family. If you have suspicions, let them fall on me, not on him."

When the squad took Axe away, Glory began to weep. "What will they do to him?" she asked. "Where will they take him?"

Lash, his dark eyes stoic and sad, answered. "They will take him to the Tower. There he will be questioned by Brenna's head of security, the baobhan sith, Greer MacVicar."

The announcement shouldn't have left me stunned. Intellectually I knew that all things being equal Greer must also be alive in this alternate version of Elizabethan England. Of all my Fae friends, she was by far the oldest.

My Greer was more than capable of extracting information from recalcitrant individuals, but she was also a woman of tremendous kindness and honor. A vampire living in a modern world, she managed her appetites modestly and in settings where her activities called no attention to herself.

Once or twice a month, she disappeared on a Friday or Saturday night, bound for a convention in some city in America or Europe. There, she selected a man, dined with him, and gave him the memory of a next chapter to the evening that never occurred.

Greer called the men her "evening companions." Men who awakened the next day lightheaded from what they assumed was a hangover, unaware of the blood loss and convinced they had romantically conquered a gorgeous redhead with fiery green eyes and a knockout personality. She came away satiated with blood, they with a metaphorical notch in their belts.

But if the fire in those emerald eyes went to ice?

If the glamour of the baobhan sith remained unspun?

If those ivory fangs sank into pale flesh without benefit of magical anesthetic?

Greer MacVicar could be the answer to a man's most fevered dreams or a monster straight from the nightmare depths of hell. It sickened me to know which woman waited for Axe in the Tower.

As soon as we were certain Brenna's men were gone, I asked Lash to teleport me upstairs.

The experience was completely unlike passing through a portal. I grasped the Ebu Gogo's strong hand. A shimmering cloud of tiny colored bubbles passed over my vision. It felt as if the cells and energies that comprise my body were disassembled and carried along a direct beam to a chosen location where they were put together again.

When the glittering aura faded, we stood in the hallway between the living quarters and the shop. In a flash of *Star Trek*-inspired understanding, it occurred to me I had experienced the closest thing to a science-fiction transporter I was likely to encounter in my life. Tori would be *green* with envy.

Lash and I found Noah quietly tidying up his business, sweeping herbs scattered across the floorboards and re-shelving bottles. The old man didn't flinch when we appeared, nor did he react when I muttered *"praetexentium conspectu nostro"* to cloak our presence from anyone passing by on the street.

The incantation didn't stop Lash from taking up a watchful guard post by the door.

"You have my granddaughter in a secure location?" Noah asked.

"We do," I assured him. "She is safe, warm, and sleeping peacefully. She doesn't know that her father was arrested."

When I started to offer further details, the old man stopped me. "Don't tell me," he said. "I can't divulge information I've never known in the first place."

The words made me go cold. "Are you afraid they'll come back for you?"

"With the Ruling Elder," he said, "anything is possible."

"You know the truth about Alex?" I asked.

Noah sat down heavily on the stool. "I know that my son-in-law is not of this place. I know that he was a good husband. He is a good father. He is a good man."

He paused and put his face in his hands gaining control of his emotions before going on. "There was a time when Alex went away. He was gone only a day, two at the most, yet he came home with the heavy weight of years upon his countenance and silver in his hair. I have no magic. I am what I seem — a human fascinated by the healing potential of the natural world — but Alex is more than that, isn't he?"

"Yes," I said, "and so are we. I don't know if we can help him, but we're going to try."

Looking at me with haunted eyes, Noah said, "I will say to you what Alex would say. Do not worry about him. Do not worry about me. Save Naomi."

I promised, doubling my obligation willingly. I gave my word to father and grandfather that no harm would come to the child who was the light of their world.

When Lash returned us to our subterranean hiding place, I stood looking down at that girl sleeping by the fire in oblivious peace. I dreaded telling her that her beloved Papa had been taken to a dark prison from which he very well might not return.

Apart from the emotional weight of our circumstances, we could have stayed underground for months. Lash had enough provisions to keep us well fed. He had the ability of teleportation. If we chose, we could disappear into the Middle Realm at any time.

Instead, I insisted that the Ebu Gogo educate me on the mechanics of time travel as he understood them.

"When Axe described the octant to me," I said, "it sounded as if he expected to use it in the time channel that brought us here, but you've discovered that all time streams converge in the Middle Realm. Why try to re-enter the channel?"

"Alex — Axe — could not decipher how to differentiate the levels of the Middle Realm," Lash said. "You have been there. The rules of Creation itself are fluid in the In Between. Axe wanted a direct way home, but he arrived in the middle of the Thames. We have been attempting to locate evidence of a portal near the spot he remembers entering the river but to no avail."

Go back the way we came. That made sense.

"If his theory is correct," I said, "we could return to the clearing where we landed, open a portal, enter the channel, and use the octant to navigate back to our correct timestream?"

Lash nodded. "Yes," he said, "but I will have to go with you. You do not understand how to operate the octant, and I will not leave Naomi."

"Of course you'll go with us," I said, "and if I have anything to say about it, so will Axe."

Moira, who had been listening to our conversation, offered a plan of her own. She wanted to arrange a meeting with Barnaby Shevington.

"Adeline will have reached him," the alchemist said. "He is a moderate member of the Council of Ruling Elders. I assure you that he opposes Brenna Sinclair's ambitions, but he finds it more useful to work against her from the inside than from without. He does not wish to see her plan to wall off the Middle Realm become a reality."

"Are you talking about The Agreement?" I asked.

"How could you know of this?" Moira asked. "Was such an arrangement implemented in your time stream?"

"It was," I said, "and it was an abomination. There is no justification for walling off an entire realm simply because the humans might see a *nonconformi* and be upset."

"Brenna Sinclair has far more audacious plans than segregating the realms. She wishes for Her Majesty the Queen to become Creavit."

We definitely wanted to be out of Londinium and back to our own time before that happened!

"How do you think Barnaby can help? I asked.

"He can tell us if any eventuality exists under which Alex Farnsworth will be a free man or if our only hope is to fulfill our promise and save his child."

The starkness of the statement only strengthened my determination to act.

"Fine," I said, "but I'm going with you."

26

Londinium, 1590

We decided to wait until dawn to attempt a meeting with Barnaby. Grateful for the delay, I moved to a quiet corner and spent several minutes concentrating on deep, cleansing breaths. The space overhead, freshly violated by Brenna's secret police, left me feeling raw and exposed.

Over the previous few months, in an effort to gain control of my psychometry, Myrtle and I began regular guided meditation sessions. The aos sí taught me to search for what she called "the center of the wheel. That still circle around which all life turns."

For the most part I'd been satisfied with my progress. I could once again enter an antique shop without every relic in the place flooding me with unwanted visions. I am, however, still vulnerable to intense environmental energy.

Brenna's thugs left a toxic waste dump of residual badness upstairs that left me shaken and unsteady inside.

They didn't know Axe. They didn't care if he was guilty or innocent. But they *relished* their license to intimidate and ransack. None of us could risk being at their mercy, especially Naomi.

When I rejoined Moira and Lash, the alchemist was asking a question I hadn't even considered. "Did they search the stables? Are our horses safe?"

"The police found our stables empty as Alex intended," the Ebu Gogo replied. "Your mounts are housed in a livery blocks from here, their board paid for under a name that will raise no suspicion with the Ruling Elder."

I'm ashamed to admit I'd forgotten about the animals — a sure sign of my growing stress levels. I *never* forget about animals.

Over Moira's shoulder, I saw Glory sitting on the hearth watching Naomi sleep. The odd, remote expression on her normally sunny face worried me.

Moving to sit beside her, I asked, "Hey, are you okay?"

Even though the slumber enchantment I'd placed on the child remained in place, Glory kept her voice low when she answered me.

"I started losing people in my life when I wasn't that much older than she is," Glory said. "Oh, Jinx! Naomi is just the sweetest little girl I've ever met, and she's so smart. I don't want her to be lonely the way I was or to doubt for one single second that she's special and loved. We have to take care of her."

Equal parts sympathy for Glory and worry for Naomi tore at my heart. "We're not going to let anything happen to Naomi," I said, putting my arm around my companion's shoulders. "You're not alone anymore, Glory, and you are loved."

Leaning into me, Glory whispered hoarsely, "What if we can't help her father? How are we ever going to explain that to her?"

I had no answer, but Lash did.

"Naomi will understand more than you think," he said,

looking down at the girl with dark eyes gone deeper with the force of his devotion to her. "Though young in years she is old of soul. Do not hide the events of this night from her. Honesty will soften the truth more than kind subterfuge."

In other words, *The kid can take it.*

If I could have let Naomi sleep through it all and awaken her when we'd put her world back together, I would have, but some broken things can't be repaired.

Mumbling words to gradually reduce the enchantment, we all moved away to let the girl come slowly to consciousness. Since we didn't plan to hide anything from her, we sat around the table and discussed how to arrange the meeting with Barnaby.

Moira explained that this version of my grandfather maintained a set of rooms close to the Council of Ruling Elders' central offices.

"It would be best if I were to approach Barnaby first," she said. "Adeline will have prepared him for a potential encounter with us, but we should still proceed with caution."

After Moira determined I could safely join her in Barnaby's quarters, she would signal Lash who would teleport me into the room.

"I cannot, however, walk the streets of Londinium in Druid robes," the alchemist said. "Brenna's people would spot me immediately."

A small voice from the cot interrupted our discussion. "My mother's dresses are still in the cupboard in the room she shared with Papa. Her gowns will fit you. Would that help?"

"Thank you, sweetheart," I said, motioning for the girl to join us. "That will help a lot. Now that you're awake, there are some things we need to tell you."

Naomi sat up sleepily, wrapping a quilt around her thin shoulders before she shuffled over to stand beside my chair. She rubbed at her eyes, and put her weight into me much as Glory had done a few minutes earlier. Without thinking, I pulled her onto my lap.

"My Papa said if he ever told me to stay in this room it would mean he was in some kind of trouble," she told me with with earnest eyes. "He said Uncle Lash would know what to do."

The Ebu Gogo laid a gentle hand on her back. "What you must do," he said, "is listen to these ladies. They promised your Papa they would look after you."

Naomi didn't cry, but the faltering doubt in her voice brought tears to my eyes. "Won't Papa come back for me, Uncle Lash?"

"I have never lied to you, Naomi," he said. "Your father will try to, but he has been arrested by the Ruling Elder's secret police."

A small gasp escaped the child's lips. "That is *bad* trouble."

"Yes," Lash agreed gravely, "it is."

When Moira called her name, Naomi twisted slightly in my arms so she could look at the alchemist.

"What do you know of your father's life story?" Moira asked.

"He told me that he is from a place far away," the girl replied. "He wants to go back now that Mama is dead. My Aunt Lauren lives there and there are doctors who will make it easier for me to breathe."

Goddess, how many ways was the Universe going to ask this child to grow up before her time?

"That's right," Glory said. "Your Daddy made us promise that we would take you there with us."

Swiveling her head around the circle of concerned faces that surrounded her, Naomi said, "The place you want to take me is in another stream of time, isn't it?"

Growing up, I never understood why my mother would look at me, shake her head, and say, *"Norma Jean, you're too smart for your own good."* Naomi's question cleared that up fast. A child's precociousness can be both a wonderful and terrible gift.

"How did you figure that out?" I asked.

"I listen," she said, "and I watch. Papa and Uncle Lash make instruments for navigation, but neither of them has ever gone to sea in a ship except for the time years ago when my uncle came to England from his island."

She looked at the Ebu Gogo. "You travel into the Middle Realm all the time, Uncle Lash. I heard you tell Papa that you bought charts for 'temporal' navigation in Cibolita from pirates. 'Temporal' means 'time' from the Latin *temporalis.*"

Smiling in spite of the seriousness of the conversation, I said, "You *are* too clever for Herr Schmidt."

Naomi nodded solemnly. "I truly am, but I don't understand how anyone, even the Fae, can travel through time."

"I don't understand either," I said, "and I've done it. My name isn't Jeane. It's Jinx, and this is Glory. We know your Aunt Lauren. We're from your father's original time stream."

Cocking her head like an inquisitive bird, Naomi said, "Jinx is an odd name."

"It's what my father called me when I was born," I said. "He told me my mother jinxed me when she named me Norma Jean."

"I like Jinx better than Norma Jean."

"So do I."

Naomi swallowed hard. "Have they taken Papa to the Tower?"

"Yes, honey, they have."

Her eyes filled again, but still the tears didn't fall. "If Papa is in the Tower then speaking with Elder Shevington is a good idea. Papa says he is an honorable man."

At that moment, Glory stepped in, assuming the fallback position of any southern woman in the midst of crisis; she decided Naomi needed to eat something. When she ushered the child into the makeshift "kitchen" to inventory Lash's pantry, Moira and I exchanged a grim look.

"We should begin our preparations for the dawn," the alchemist said. "We have no time to spare."

What she meant was *Axe* had no time to spare.

Lash transported to the master bedroom, and came back with a simple blue frock and matching cloak. Moira changed clothes and then, studying herself in the mirror, applied a disguising glamour.

The alchemist's lean face grew short and broad, the jawline disappearing into a layer of jowls as her lively eyes took on a dull, listless blankness. If anyone saw her on the street they'd take no notice of a plain, unremarkable woman out on an early morning errand.

We opted for a simple plan. Lash would carry Moira to an alley across from Barnaby's rooms. The Ebu Gogo would wait there, edging himself into the first phase of the teleportation process but no further. It wasn't quite as good as Darby's invisibility trick; anyone looking into the alley would see a patch of undulating air, but the concealment would work for a few minutes.

When Moira determined I could safely join her, she would come to the window and lay her hand on the glass. Lash would then return to the workshop and carry me directly into Barnaby's rooms.

As the alchemist prepared to leave, I said, "In my world, I know Barnaby Shevington. Although it's several generations removed, he's my grandfather. The two of you play important roles in one another's lives there. Do you think this Barnaby will help us?"

"If it is in his power to do so," Moira assured me, "Barnaby will render his aid."

LASH AIMED for the back of the deserted and filthy alleyway. No one witnessed the shimmering light that signaled the active teleportation. Putting his finger to his lips, the stocky man moved with surprising agility to the opening onto the street and glanced quickly in both directions.

Few people stirred at such an early hour. Lash waited for an instant when the thoroughfare was almost deserted and motioned to Moira. The alchemist walked briskly out of the alley and crossed the cobblestones to the boarding house.

When she placed her inquiry to the proprietress, the red-faced women looked Moira over with a suspicious and appraising eye. "Elder Shevington has a wife," she said flatly.

"Adeline," Moira replied. "A delightful woman of my acquaintance."

Still suspicious of Moira's intentions, the landlady warned, "Proceed with care, Mistress. Adeline Shevington's a right powerful witch. Dally with her man, and you could find yourself turned into a toad or worse."

Smiling tolerantly, Moira said, "Will you please announce me?"

"Sign your own death warrant," the landlady said. "I'll play no part in the Elder's wenching. You'll find him in the room at the head of the stair."

Holding her skirt tight against her body, Moira ascended the narrow staircase and rapped three times on the door.

A voice inside said with no small degree of annoyance, "I told you I wish no breakfast today."

"I do not come for breakfast, Barnaby," the alchemist said. "It is Moira, from the woods of Kent."

Boots sounded on the hardwood floor, a latch rattled, and Barnaby Shevington threw open the door.

"Moira," he said cheerfully. "Adeline wrote that you would be in the city. Please, come in."

After she stepped over the threshold, Barnaby closed the door, pausing to move his hand along the frame sealing the opening against prying ears.

Then and only then did he turn to embrace Moira.

"How fare thee?" he asked, kissing her on the cheek. "Adeline sent a cipher telling me of your strange visitors from another time and place. Has ill fortune befallen the women?"

Slipping out of her cloak, Moira draped the fabric over the back of a chair and moved to warm her hands by the fire. "They are in hiding," she said. "Do you know of the arrest last evening in Lime Street of a man called Alex Farnsworth?"

Barnaby moved to his desk and picked up a piece of correspondence. He passed the paper to Moira, explaining its contents as she scanned the words.

"Each of the members of the Council of Ruling Elders received notice this morning of Farnsworth's arrest. Brenna Sinclair charges him with the conduct of seditious and heretical experiments against the safety and integrity of Fae society. What has this to do with the time travelers?"

"Farnsworth himself is not of this time," Moira said. "Brenna Sinclair and Her Majesty the Queen have apparently kept his home under surveillance for some months now. Something must have occurred to deepen their suspicions thus triggering the arrest. I fear it was our arrival at his door."

Barnaby nodded. "You are correct," he said, "but Farnsworth's apprehension was inevitable. Brenna believes Dr. Lopez's journal was taken because it contained a sketch of Farnsworth rendered during a reception for botanists hosted by Her Majesty some weeks past."

"Why would Lopez believe the journal to have been taken for this reason?"

"According to the good doctor," Barnaby said, "Farnsworth was displeased when he learned his likeness had been captured. A token dropped at the scene of the theft pointed to a possible Spanish connection. Lopez assembled these facts into the theory that Farnsworth is an agent of King Philip's."

Moira held up her hand. "Do not tell me more until one of the time travelers joins us. Her name is Jinx Hamilton. In her reality she serves as the Witch of the Oak, a fact to which Adeline attests."

"Of course I will speak with her," Barnaby said, "but it would be too dangerous for her to be seen entering my place of residence."

"Do not be troubled, we have the assistance of a most unusual confederate."

Moving to the window, Moira put her hand flat against the pane. Across the street, a patch of air at the mouth of the alley rippled and was gone.

"We have but to wait a moment or two," she said. "Do not be alarmed when they appear."

Barnaby's brow furrowed. "When who appears?"

No sooner had the words left his throat than a luminous curtain descended in the center of the room. The light faded to reveal a young woman standing beside a dark-skinned man with a muscular, menacing stance.

"Barnaby Shevington," Moira said, "allow me to present Jinx Hamilton and Lashtazo, an Ebu Gogo late of Pulau Flores."

I STARED at the man standing before me in Elizabethan dress. He wore a white shirt with puffy sleeves that stood open at the neck. His velvet pants disappeared into tight leather knee boots. He was thinner than my Barnaby, younger and stronger, but with the same moustache and goatee I loved.

Thankfully this doppelgänger possessed my grandfather's unflappable response to surprises. Sixteenth century Barnaby greeted Lash and me warmly and invited us to take chairs by the fire.

"Moira has told me of your journey," he said. "Please do not blame yourself for the arrest of the man called Alex Farnsworth. It was only a matter of time until Brenna Sinclair ordered him taken to the Tower."

"But why?" I asked. "What has he done?"

"You must understand that here all intellectual inquiry undertaken by Fae alchemists and scientists must be sanctioned by the Ruling Elder," Barnaby said. "There have long been rumors that Farnsworth traffics in oddities from the Middle Realm, and that his interests are not confined to the simple study of botany. Now, due to the theft of a journal belonging to the Queen's physician, Farnsworth's name has been linked to Spanish espionage."

Conspiracy theories grow in the dark, fertile ground of suspicion. None of the "facts" Barnaby cited lined up, except in the minds of the people who needed and wanted to believe them.

"That's ridiculous," I said, "Alex's real name is Axe Frazier. He's from my world. All he wants is to go home and take his daughter with him. She's sick. Our doctors can heal her."

This Barnaby might spend most of his time wrangling Fae politics, but I recognized grandad's maddeningly pedagogical streak when he asked, "Do you play chess, Mistress Hamilton?"

Bracing myself for what I hoped would be a short "lesson," I said, ""Call me Jinx. I don't play, but everybody around me does."

"You are familiar with the phrase 'check and mate?'"

"It means one player has made a move that puts the King in a fatal position on the board," I replied. "There's no escape."

"Correct," Barnaby said, "and I fear your friend Mr. Frazier finds himself in precisely that position."

There's a good reason why I will never be a politician. My mind doesn't work in a convoluted, bureaucratic way. I still believe the shortest distance between two points is a straight line.

"Chess is a game," I said stubbornly. "In life, there's always a way."

Barnaby smiled at me approvingly, but with knowing caution. "I applaud your ethics, Jinx, but beware they do not cost you your head."

Not the response I expected. When I didn't answer he continued.

"I am not a father, but were I in Mr. Frazier's place, I would immediately understand that only my silence would ensure my child's safety. He cannot speak to his captors for to do so would mean confirming the potential of time travel to Brenna Sinclair."

"Knowing time travel exists doesn't mean she could do it," I said.

"You have landed, Mistress Jinx, in a world rife with political intrigue. The Ruling Elder seeks to confine the *nonconformi* species to the Middle Realm because she sees them as lesser beings too obsessed with the preservation of natural magic. She wishes to turn Her Majesty to the Creavit heresy. Can you imagine what havoc such women might wreak were they to be free to traverse the fabric of time?"

Images of evil versions of Brenna and Greer loose in multiple worlds flitted through my mind. I sagged in my seat. "Isn't there anything you can do?" I pleaded. "Naomi needs her father."

"Were I to attempt to intervene," Barnaby said, "I would raise

Brenna's suspicions and most likely come to share Frazier's cell. I am sorry, but there is too much at stake here in my world. My associates and I represent the last bastion of moderation on the Council. We represent old and noble Fae families. Brenna needs the aura of legitimacy our presence on the Council imparts, but I assure you, were we to give her the opportunity, she would dispose of us in a mere heartbeat."

Which meant Brenna intended to kill Axe. "Then he's doomed?"

"Few who enter the Tower and pass into the hands of the baobhan sith live to see the light of day again."

I looked at Lash. "Why can't he teleport into the Tower and get Axe out?"

"Brenna has armed the prison with overlapping spells and alarms. Any magical incursion will set them off and bring the guards down on your head."

The logical part of my brain told me that everything he said made sense. We'd given our word to protect Naomi. Axe would want us to get her out of Londinium and back to our time, but the idea of leaving him behind after all he'd suffered was unimaginable.

"I need to speak to him," I said. "You're on the council. You must have people inside the Tower. Surely you can get me 5 minutes."

Barnaby considered my request. "If I arrange this meeting," he said at last, "will you leave Londinium and use whatever means at your disposal to return to your world?"

"Yes."

"Then come back here at midnight. I will make the necessary arrangements."

27

Aboard the Tempus Fugit

F estus sat on the stern of the *Tempus Fugit* copying Bastet's famous regal pose. He wore the headdress of a pharaoh, and rewarded the cheering crowds outside the portal opening with a credible imitation of the royal wave.

"*Fes-tus, Fes-tus, Fes-tus.*"

Chase, who stood at mock attention beside his father said out of the corner of his mouth, "You're enjoying this entirely too much."

Still making short choppy motions with his paw and nodding to his adoring Egyptian public, Festus replied, "Be glad they took one look at me and decided I'm Bastet's celestial emissary."

Rube, who reclined out of sight on the deck eating cheese puffs, said, "It didn't hurt none that you showed up on a flying three-masted schooner and buzzed the pyramids or that you had yourself a talking raccoon, and a commando fairy in a purple hat."

"Details," Festus said, "details. My innate majesty sealed the deal, which is a good thing since nothing on this temporal tub works the way it's supposed to including the miniaturization gizmo."

Miranda scowled and crossed her arms. "I would appreciate it, *Mr. McGregor*, if you didn't refer to my ship as a tub."

"Get us through the portal, *Ms. Winter*, and then worry about your wounded feelings," Festus shot back. "My ears itch, and I'm getting a cramp in my paw."

Overhead the sails caught the wind inside the matrix. At the helm, Drake steered the ship to starboard and activated the shield. The energy crackled weakly to life, dimmed, went out, and then caught.

As the voices of the chanting Egyptians died away and the portal opening closed, Festus batted the headdress off and scratched furiously at his ears.

"That's better," he said, giving one last vigorous swipe with his hind foot and shaking his head. "They may be smart enough to worship cats, but their fashion sense leaves something to be desired."

The ship chose the exact moment he jumped toward the deck to roll violently forcing the werecat to sink his claws into the wood to gain traction.

Rube slid by on his backside clutching the bag of cheese puffs against his chest while Chase made a quick grab for the rigging.

Glaring up at Miranda, Festus said, "Will it offend your Pirate-ness if I say your ship *steers* like a tub?"

"It will," she glared back. "The vessel's not at fault. None of this is supposed to happen. The time junctions are pulling on us like we're magnetic. Something is destabilizing the channel. If we could miniaturize she wouldn't be wallowing like a pig in mud, but the energy in here keeps randomly spiking off the charts. Are you sure you brought us a piece of the *real* Copernican Astrolabe?"

Steadying himself as the ship pitched again, Festus sneered, "Naw, I popped into a pawn shop in Londinium and picked up a cheap knock off 'cause I don't really care about rescuing the Witch of the Oak and my son's girlfriend. *Of course* I brought you a piece of the damned Astrolabe. Silly me for assuming you'd know what to do with it."

Lucas stepped between them. "Not helpful, people. *Not helpful.* Come on Miranda, you do this for a living. What do you think is going on?"

The pirate scrubbed at her face. "The old salts always referred to time as a fabric. We were never meant to make lateral jumps through portals and enter these channels. Time is supposed to converge in the Middle Realm and be accessed with proper temporal instruments. Maybe the . . . I don't know . . . *weight* . . . of time is having a destructive effect on the portal network."

Rube wiped neon orange crumbs off his whiskers. "I ain't liking the sound of that. How are we supposed to get home if the portal network blows a gasket?"

"More importantly," Chase said, "how many daily portal users are we endangering every time we go into one of these junctions and possibly increase the extent of the damage?"

Blowing out a long breath, Lucas said, "What are the possible ramifications of what you're describing?

Miranda shrugged. "Worst case scenario? Time implodes."

The raccoon's eyes almost popped out of his mask. "Geez *Louise*, lady! How 'bout we dial it down from Arma-*freaking*-geddon to something we can work with?"

"Okay," the pirate said. "Second worst case scenario, all access to the alternate time streams collapses."

Shoving his hat back on his head, Lucas said wearily,

"Which means Jinx and Glory are lost for good. Do you have a 'best case scenario' in the mix?"

"I do," Miranda said. "We get ourselves into the Middle Realm, make port in Cibolita, find out if other crews are having problems, and come up with Plan B."

Lucas looked at Chase. "What do you think?"

Before he could answer, the *Tempus Fugit* floated past an opening showing a spectacular view of Machu Picchu — with a flying saucer floating in the sky over the mountain.

Rube jumped up and almost swatted Ironweed overboard in his elation.

"I *knew* it!" the raccoon exclaimed. "I told you them Incans was little green men just like the TV show said. Pay up, Sparkle Wings."

"This is what I get for binge-watching *Ancient Aliens* with a varmint who likes to gamble," the major mumbled. "Will you take FairyDust?"

"Do I look like Tinkerbell?"

"A little," Ironweed admitted. "She's let herself go."

Chase cleared his throat. "To answer your question, Lucas, I think Miranda has a good plan. We don't really have another viable option at the moment."

Lucas looked down at Festus. "How about you?"

"I'm good with it. If we keep rolling and pitching around like this I'll be hurling hairballs all over the deck."

Miranda paled. "We have buckets for that," she said. "Use them."

The werecat's eyes danced with amusement. "And miss seeing you and Dirk step in cat barf with your pretty pirate boots? Not a chance."

From the helm, the first mate yelled, "*Drake!* My name is *Drake!*"

Ignoring them, Lucas looked at the fairy hovering near his shoulder. "What do you say, Ironweed?"

"The plan makes tactical sense."

"Rube?"

Opening a bag of potato chips, the raccoon said, "As long as the Pirate Queen ain't using words like 'implode' and 'collapse' count me in."

Lucas nodded to Miranda. "Okay. It's unanimous. Take us to Cibolita."

LONDINIUM, 1590, Jinx

Lash and I materialized in Barnaby's rooms at the stroke of midnight. The fire burned low and a single candle flickered beside the Elder's chair.

"You're on time," Barnaby said. "Good. In exactly 15 minutes, Lash, I need you to take Mistress Jinx to The Tower. I have a map of the prison for your reference."

The Ebu Gogo held up one chunky hand. "I don't need a map. I can take us directly to Alex."

"Very well," Barnaby said. "Stay no more than five minutes. I cannot guarantee your safety beyond that."

As we waited for the time of our departure, I said, "Thank you, Barnaby. I know you — a different you — in my world. You're my . . . my friend. You've never let me down. Not there and not here."

"My dear," he said, "I devoutly hope that to be true."

On the second jump my vision cleared in a dank stone prison cell. A pitiful fire glowed in the hearth. A ragged figure in torn clothing huddled close to the grate seeking its meager warmth.

"Axe?" I said softly. "Is that you?"

He turned toward us, a shaft of moonlight from the narrow window falling on his battered face. Coagulated rivulets of blood coated his neck and stained his shirt.

"Lash," he said, his bruised throat constricting as he tried to speak. "Have you lost your mind? You shouldn't have brought her here."

I moved to him and sank to my knees, cupping his cheek in my hand. "What has she done to you?"

With a thin smile, Axe said, "She's a baobhan sith. What do you think she's done to me? You can't be here."

"Barnaby Shevington called in some kind of favor," I said. "We don't have much time. He wants us to leave you here and get Naomi out of the city. He says there's nothing we can do for you."

"He's right. Get my daughter to safety and take all my research with you. Brenna and Greer know I've been experimenting with time travel."

"But how?"

Frustration replaced his haggard exhaustion. "Because I'm a damned vain fool. I never should have joined the other botanists Elizabeth summoned to court. When I saw Dr. Lopez sketching me, I overreacted. Then they found the token."

"Token. What token?"

He started to answer, but a fit of coughing racked his body. I put my hands on his arms and tried to steady him.

"Thanks," he said, rasping for breath. "I'm okay now. Those time pirates you told me about? The ones from Las Vegas? One of them dropped some kind of poker chip in the doctor's quarters. There's writing on it. Something about 'saving the date' for Bambi and Topher — November 15, 2017. They think my reaction to the sketch and the name 'Las Vegas' mean I'm developing time travel as a weapon for the Spanish King Philip."

If I hadn't been afraid of attracting the attention of the

guards, I might have screamed. People have died for foolish reasons, but surely none as foolish as this.

"Come with us," I begged. "We can get you out of here."

Axe shook his head. "They'd catch us before we crossed the Thames. I have to stay here and say nothing. You have to keep your word and get my daughter back to the 21st century where she can get the medical help she needs. You promised, Jinx."

Tears rolled down my cheeks. "Can I do anything for you?" I asked.

"Tell my daughter and my sister I love them. Lash?"

The Ebu Gogo stepped closer. "Take what you can and destroy the rest. Make sure Noah is safe before you go. I want you to see the arrow plane and the box that tells stories."

Lash nodded solemnly, clasping Axe's hand. "I will guard your daughter with my life and when I see these wonders, I will share them in my heart with you."

"I know you will, old friend," Axe said. "Now go, before the guards come back."

"We can't leave you here," I choked. "How will I ever explain this to Naomi?"

Now his tears left tracks through the grime coating his cheeks. "My girl has had to grow up fast," Axe said. "She's stronger than she looks. Now go. Get out of the city before dawn. I'll hold out as long as I can. They don't know where you are. Leave your horses. Teleport with Lash."

Outside the door, the sound of a guard's laughter and the clank of something heavy had the Ebu Gogo pulling urgently at my arm. "We must do as he says, Mistress Jinx."

"But we don't know how to use your research," I protested. "We don't know what to do."

As the colored motes of light signaling the transport filled my vision, Axe smiled weakly, "Neither do I," he said, "but I'm not the Witch of the Oak."

28

Londinium, Jinx

Instead of aiming for the main room, Lash returned us to the dim corridor outside the underground workshop. "I must get Noah before we go in," he explained. "He should be with us when we tell Naomi about her father."

The Ebu Gogo disappeared again. I leaned my forehead against the cool stone and wept. For the sake of an innocent child, I had been forced to leave a good man to face an unjust death.

When the air behind me stirred, I hastily scrubbed the tears off my cheeks. Lash and Noah materialized. The old botanist blinked rapidly. "My friend," he told Lash, "you did not adequately prepare me for that experience."

"Jumping from one place to another is a thing that cannot be described," Lash replied. Then his voice broke, "Alex said the lights of my travel are like something in his world called 'glitter.'"

Choking back another sob, I said, "He's right. I'll show you what he meant when we get home."

Noah read the truth in my eyes. "Have they killed him already?"

"He was alive when we left the Tower, but we must take Naomi and get out of the city before sunrise. Come with us Noah."

Crossing his arms over his chest, Van Buskirk leaned against the wall and stared down at the toes of his slippers.

"My life has been spent in Londinium," he said slowly. "Adventures of the kind you describe are for the young. I have my shop, my plants. Brenna Sinclair will not come after me."

"How can you be sure?"

"The Ruling Elder covets nothing in my possession," Noah said. "Many others on Lime Street are Fae. Throughout the day the shops have rumbled with talk of Alex's arrest. Brenna dare not offend us all. We are the makers of tinctures . . . and of poisons. There are many kinds of magic in the world, young woman."

In a rush of frustrated rage, I hoped someone did poison Brenna. She deserved to die a hard death in payment for her cruel tyrannies.

"Think of Naomi," I urged, still unwilling to leave him behind. "You're her family."

He looked up. "I think she needs you more. In your world there is a cure for the illness that afflicts her lungs?"

"There is," I said. "We'll get her the help she needs."

"And you will continue her education?"

"My grandfather runs a university," I said. "She'll be up to her ears in education."

That brought a smile to his thin lips. "Naomi will love that. God has gifted her with an exceptional mind and the kindest of hearts. I trust you to hold both in safekeeping."

"I will," I said. "Naomi has an aunt, Lauren, who will be part of her life."

Pushing away from the wall, Noah said, "Give me a few minutes to speak with the child."

"Of course," I said. "I'll wait here."

Instead of using teleportation, Lash led Noah down the passage. A few minutes later the Ebu Gogo returned with Moira and Glory.

Without speaking, Glory put her arms around me and began to cry. "You couldn't save him," she finally choked out.

"I couldn't," I said, rubbing comforting circles on her back, "but we are going to save Naomi."

Noah stayed with his granddaughter a long time. When he signaled for us to join them in the workshop, I could see the child had been crying, but now she was composed and oddly resolute.

"Grandpapa says that I am to go with you and Uncle Lash," Naomi said. "Are we going to a nice place?"

Glory went down on one knee to put herself on eye level with the girl.

"The nicest place in the whole world, sweetheart," she said. "I was like you. Well, not quite like you, but I got myself in a lot of trouble because I made bad decisions and was all alone in the world. Everybody in Briar Hollow and Shevington forgave me and helped me. They took me in and made me family, and they'll do the same for you. And we have doctors who can make you well so you won't cough anymore."

Naomi nodded. "I would like that," she said, and then faltering slightly, added, "and so would Papa."

After he embraced his granddaughter for the last time, Lash carried Noah upstairs. Together they packed a small bag for Naomi. When the Ebu Gogo returned, he busied himself gathering papers and instruments into a compact travel case. The rest he tossed into the fire.

When he was satisfied that he had everything he needed,

Lash told Moira, "I cannot take us all at once. Mistress Jinx and Naomi will go first, you and Mistress Glory next. When we leave this place for the last time, can you collapse the workshop?"

The alchemist nodded. "I can," she said, "and do no harm to the structures above."

The Ebu Gogo reached into his pocket and removed a brass disc — Axe's piece of the Copernican Astrolabe — and handed it to me. When I put it away in my pouch, I felt its magnetism pull toward the matching rod nestled in the roll of linen.

On his first jump, Lash deposited Naomi and me outside the city. As we stood watching the sun come up, I prayed for Axe to be freed from his torment before the day ended.

"Will I ever see Londinium again," the child asked me suddenly.

I put my arm around her shoulders and drew her closer. "You'll see another Londinium," I promised, "and it will remind you of home."

The answer seemed to satisfy her. We didn't speak again, lost in our private thoughts as we waited for the others.

Even with the ability to teleport, our journey to the Druid woods took all day. Lash leapfrogged us across the English countryside, always picking secluded landing spots well away from the prying eyes of humans or Fae spies.

Right at dusk we stepped into the sheltering trees. I felt the the Veil descend over us. For the first time since we left the Tower, I took an easy breath.

When Orion trotted out of the shadows, Lash moved to stand in front of Naomi.

"Oh, no," Glory said. "It's okay. Orion is a nice wolf. The nicest wolf ever, and he's my friend. Orion, this is Lash and Naomi. Lash and Naomi, this is Orion."

The massive black wolf approached Naomi with gentle care. He sat down at her feet and held out one front paw.

The child looked at Glory in confusion. "What does he want me to do?"

"He wants you to shake his paw," Glory said. "He's telling you that he wants to be your friend."

Tentatively Naomi grasped the wolf's massive front foot and gave it a shake. Orion grinned and wagged his tail.

Even the heavy sadness of our departure from Londinium couldn't dim the girl's delight; she had a new friend, and bless her, she needed one.

When we reached the outskirts of the village, Newlyn met us. "Fare thee well, Moira?" he asked. "And you, young mistresses? I see you have brought us guests."

"We have," Moira said. "Forgive me, Newlyn, but we must speak with you in the privacy of your hut."

The village elder looked at her curiously, "You know of the stars that fell through Ophiuchus last evening?"

The alchemist shook her head. "I do not, but I believe I know what the omen portends."

For the record, no good ever comes of the word "omen."

We told Newlyn the whole story. I have to say he took it well, but then I think Newlyn like all of the Druids maintained an elemental connection with the will of the Universe.

According to him, the sight of meteors streaking through the constellation Ophiuchus the night before — at roughly the same time Axe told us goodbye in the Tower — meant a tremendous change was about to occur.

The elder kindly suggested, in so many words, that it might be time for us to get out of Dodge.

"Do you know how to open the portal that will give you a doorway back to your world?" he asked.

"Opening the portal is the easy part," I said. "Once we're inside, finding our way home is a different matter, but we don't have a choice."

Newlyn rested his hands atop his staff. "All journeys begin with a single step, young witch. Take that one and each that is to follow will occur in the proper order. Tree witches rarely lose their way."

I would have to take his word about that last part.

Lash spoke up. "I have maps to ensure we do not wander lost in time," he said. "I will show you."

The Ebu Gogo unrolled several intricate charts and spread them across the elder's scarred worktable. Newlyn studied the material with interest.

"These are the constellations that marked the passage of the sun through the year," he said. "I know them well. What have they to do with time travel?"

"Do not all mariners navigate by the position of the sun and the stars?" Lash asked.

"They do," Newlyn said thoughtfully, "from one fixed point to another. Mistress Jinx, do you know the exact date you fell through the portal and became sucked into the stream of time?"

"Of course," I said, "it was my wedding day. The summer solstice. June 20, 2017."

Muttering to himself, Newlyn produced quill and parchment. He began making calculations, his pages adding to the litter atop the table.

Leaning toward Moira, I said, "I thought Druids didn't write things down."

"We do when we have need of the tools," she said. "It is possible for a people to both honor their traditions and be practical."

"And to change the rules on the fly when it suits them," I thought, but I kept that observation to myself.

At last, Newlyn set the quill aside. "Gemini," he told Lash. "I believe you are to set your sights on Gemini."

After a brief debate, Lash agreed.

With no time to waste, we followed Moira out of the village toward the clearing where we landed on our first night in 1590.

When we emerged from the woods at the familiar spot, I grasped Moira's hands.

"I don't know how to thank you," I said. "You believed us, took us in, and risked your safety to help us get home. No matter in what century I meet you, you're always my good friend."

The alchemist drew me into a tight hug. "Rendering aid to you has been my honor, Witch of the Oak," she said. "The knowledge that our destinies have intertwined in this world and beyond gives me great happiness."

As Glory said her goodbyes to our friend and protector, I stepped into the center of the clearing and spoke the words of the portal opening spell. The matrix responded slowly, but the magic worked.

"Glory, stay close to Naomi," I ordered, "Lash, you're with me."

The Ebu Gogo stepped with me into the opening leaning into the stiff wind and using his travel case for ballast. He took Axe's octant from the pocket of his coat and then did something I'd never thought to do inside a portal — he looked up.

Following his gaze, I discovered we stood beneath an ebony canopy ablaze with diamond-bright stars. The beauty of it took my breath away, and diverted my attention.

When the first tremor shook the portal, the force threw me off balance, knocking me onto one knee. A bolt of greenish-blue lightning hit the spot where I'd been standing.

Throwing his hands up to protect his eyes, Lash yelled, "Something is not right. The matrix is unstable. I cannot get a fix on Gemini. We must go to the Middle Realm."

"Can you do that from here?" I yelled back.

The Ebu Gogo nodded. "Yes. I will open a secondary portal. Follow me through when I signal you to come."

I turned one last time to look at Moira. The Druid knelt on the ground talking to Orion. As I watched, she kissed the wolf tenderly on the forehead before the beast turned and leaped into the main portal a fraction of a second before the opening snapped shut.

Orion landed beside Glory and shielded Naomi with his muscular bulk.

"Oh," I thought, *"Festus is* not *going to be happy when we show up with him."*

Lash raised his hand. I started forward, but stopped when something caught my attention at the edges of my peripheral vision.

At first, I thought I was looking into a mirror, but then I realized it was a window.

The me in that scene walked hand in hand with a toddler through the deep, soft grass in the big meadow below Shevington. Bright fairies played among the flowers and enchanted kites dueled in the skies.

Giggling merrily, the child looked up, saw me, and waved a tiny, chubby hand.

I met the eyes of that other Jinx who stood beside that precious baby. We smiled at one another, and in that instant I knew that bright-eyed child was my daughter yet to be born.

29

Inside the Temporal Channel

Over the howling wind I heard Lash shouting. Reluctantly, I pulled away from that summer bright vision of the Valley ripe with the promise of new life. If I wanted that child, I had to go home to her father.

The Ebu Gogo stood beside a second opening — not a proper portal, but a ragged gap between the time channel and the In Between. Strange though that middle world might be, I had been there before and come back again.

The In Between didn't frighten me nearly as much as being stranded in an alternate version of the 16th century where thoroughly evil incarnations of Brenna Sinclair and Greer MacVicar had reasons to hunt me down.

On my first step, the tunnel began to spin. Instinctively I searched for a handhold before I realized the churning motion centered on me. Golden lights danced around my body in a whirling circle.

They coalesced into a disc. For a wild moment I thought,

"How did a DVD get in here?" Then the disc levitated above my head, tipped on edge, and dropped down blocking the way between me and Lash's opening.

When I tried to go around the glowing dial, energy barriers kept me from moving. Unable to join my companions and cut off from the 16th-century version of reality we left behind, I had nowhere to go.

Through the center of the disc, I saw Naomi looking at me; I knew what I had to do.

"Go!" I yelled. "Get into the Middle Realm. Tell Lucas I'll find him."

Glory opened her mouth and began to talk rapidly, punctuating the words I couldn't hear with wild, desperate gestures beckoning — begging — me to overcome the implacable obstacle.

Unable to deny the pleading in her eyes, I raised my hands and sent a bolt of energy toward the disc only to duck as the magic ricocheted back at my head.

With their attention trained on me, Lash and Glory forgot about Naomi — forgot that though a child, she possessed equal free will. Before they could stop her, the girl walked toward me with Orion at her heels.

The barrier that refused my magic parted like a curtain for her. Naomi and Orion stopped in front of me. The voice of the wind fell silent. The temporal channel disappeared.

Reality shrank down to a witch, a child, and a wolf.

Searching Naomi's face, I said, "Do you know what this is?"

Over her shoulder, the disc's rotation slowed as a ring of symbols appeared along its outer rim. "Don't you know?" Naomi asked. "Those are the astrological signs. Herr Schmidt taught me about the constellations. Her Majesty keeps an astrologer at court to read the future in the stars."

A *horoscope*? After everything we'd been through our futures hinged on a horoscope?

As we watched, a lone symbol materialized above the dial — a "u" with a horizontal curved line running across it.

"Why is that one floating above the others?" I asked.

"I don't know," Naomi replied, "but it has a funny name; Ophiuchus."

The word sounded like "Off-ee-you-cuss." A Rube-esque comeback popped into my head, *"I don't know, how often do you cuss?"*

That did it. The last traces of panic or confusion disappeared from my mind. "Do you know what Ophiuchus means?"

The child nodded. "It's Greek for 'serpent barrier.'" Then she looked down at the wolf. "In the sky it lies opposite Orion. He's the celestial hunter and Ophiuchus is the healer."

This time my mother's voice rose in my thoughts. *"There are no coincidences, Norma Jean."*

"What do you mean Ophiuchus is the healer?"

Like the good student she was, Naomi answered, "Ophiuchus is associated with Asclepius. In Greek mythology Asclepius can bring the dead back to the land of the living."

The hunter. The healer. The living land.

"Where does Ophiuchus belong on the wheel?"

The girl's brow furrowed. "I'm not sure. Before or after Sagittarius, I think."

My birth sign.

No coincidences.

"Stand back, honey."

Extending my arms, I closed my eyes and willed myself to enter the calm center of my being, the place where Myrtle told me my strongest magic lies. I conjured the image of Ophiuchus and slowly drew it toward the wheel.

The symbol crossed the border of the disc and slipped between Scorpio and Sagittarius. Our protective bubble disappeared. The howl of the wind picked up again. I opened my eyes and saw masses of roiling water heading at us from all directions.

Grabbing Naomi's hand, I yelled, *"Run!"*

With Orion loping beside us we plunged through the opening into the Middle Realm, shoving Lash and Glory clear as the surging current hit the disc and shattered it.

The symbols rode the waves through the matrix and shot into the heavens, scattering through a crackling spider web of lightning. The sky tore open beneath each sign releasing thirteen rivers to flow into the valley basin where an ocean began to form.

Beside me Glory gasped and caught hold of my arm. "Jinx," she breathed. *"Look."*

Beneath the symbol for Gemini a three-masted schooner descended on the current and came to rest on the surface of the sea. A familiar voice echoed across the valley.

"Suck it up, McGregor. Ain't you never rode a freaking roller coaster?"

By the time we climbed down the rocky path and reached the shoreline, the vessel had weighed anchor. A dinghy lowered over the side. The oars pulled against the waves on their own delivering my husband to me.

I didn't wait. I waded. Up to my knees in the warm, clear water.

Lucas jumped out and splashed toward me, throwing his arms around me and lifting me clear of the water.

When we kissed, I heard Rube say, "Geez you two. Ixnay on the kissy face already. There's a kid watching over there."

"I found you," Lucas said.

"Not so fast, big guy," I grinned up at him. "*I* found *you*."

Cupping my cheek he caressed my jawline. "We found each other."

"Okay," I conceded happily. "I can live with that."

From the bank, I heard Festus roar, "Put me *down* you idiotic Pickle. I risked eight of my lives to rescue you, and you show up with some stinking mutt?"

Lucas and I both started to laugh.

"I think our diplomatic skills are needed on shore," he said. "Come on, before Festus takes his claws to Glory. What's up with the wolf?"

"Long story," I said, "but his name is Orion."

By the time we reached the beach, Glory, tucked into the protective circle of Chase's arm, had launched into an effusive round of apologies.

"I'm sorry I picked you up, Dad. I know you don't like that, it's just that I'm so very, very, *very* glad to see you and Chase and *everybody*. This is my new friend Orion. I know he's a dog — okay, technically a wolf, but he's really nice, and I promise he'll grow on you."

Grooming furiously, Festus paused mid-lick to eye the wolf. "At least tell me he's housebroken."

Orion whined, plopped down, put his head on his paws, and looked up at Festus from under his eyewhiskers.

"Good move, Fido," the werecat said. "I'm the Alpha around here, and don't you forget it."

At that, the wolf put his paws over his eyes and whimpered.

"Now look at what you've done, Dad," Glory scolded. "You're scaring the poor puppy dog."

"Good," Festus said, turning to Lash. "Where'd you get the caveman?"

Lash gave him a toothy grin. "Ebu Gogo."

"Ga-zoont-height," Rube said cheerfully.

Festus rolled his eyes. When Naomi giggled, the werecat gentled his tone. "Hi, kid. I'm Festus McGregor. You look like you've had a rough trip."

Naomi stared down at him with wide eyes. "Excuse me, sir," she said. "But are you a werecat?"

"I am."

"You don't look like the other werecat with the stripes and the mask."

"For which I give thanks to Bastet daily," Festus assured her.

Rube waddled forward and extended one black paw. "I ain't no werecat. Just your garden variety Fae raccoon. Don't mind ole Hairball, here. Ain't you never seen a critter like me before?"

"No, sir," Naomi said, now looking at Ironweed with enraptured fascination. "Are you a pixie?"

Normally confusing a pixie with a fairy is a great way to start a fight in a bar, but Ironweed has a soft spot for children.

"I'm a fairy," he said. "My name is Ironweed."

"My name is Naomi. Glory told me this would be a wonderful place."

Digging in his waistpack, Rube came up with a chocolate bar, which he offered the girl. When she took it, he instructed her on removing the wrapper.

"Yeah, there you go," he coached, "just rip off the paper to get to the good stuff."

Lucas and Chase exchanged a look. Kissing Glory on the temple, Chase moved over to join us. "Who is she?" he whispered.

"Axe Frazier's daughter."

I felt a quiver pass through my husband. "Axe is alive?" he asked.

Shaking my head sadly, I said, "No. That's a longer conversation. Let's get home first. Naomi is sick. Tuberculosis. We need to get her to a doctor."

A blonde woman I didn't recognize said, "Pardon the intrusion. You must be the Witch of the Oak. Welcome back."

"Honey," Lucas said, "this is Captain Miranda Winter and her first mate Drake Lobranche. They are Lauren's . . . business associates."

Naomi overheard the introduction and spoke up immediately. "You know my Aunt Lauren?"

With a demeanor far kinder than her leather-clad dagger-sporting appearance might suggest, Miranda said, "Your aunt is a good friend. Would you like me to take you to her?"

"Yes, please," Naomi said politely. "My father said she would take care of me now."

Rube's head swiveled from us back to the girl. I saw the wheels working in that fertile brain of his. He reached out and caught hold of Naomi's hand.

"Don't worry, Kiddo. We're all gonna take care of you. We're family. That's what we do."

MIRANDA WOULD HAVE TAKEN the long way back to Briar Hollow via Las Vegas. I had a different plan in mind. "If you can get us to Cibolita, we can enter our fairy mound through the Land of the Golem."

"*Oh*," the pirate grinned, "you I like. Full of surprises already."

"You ain't got no idea," Rube assured her. Then he leaned in and said, "The kid looks beat. Maybe we oughta crash at the Inn for a few hours. Let her catch some shut eye."

He was right. Black circles had appeared under Naomi's eyes. Her chest moved irregularly with the effort of breathing. When a violent fit of coughing overtook her, I saw flecks of blood on the white handkerchief she used to cover her mouth. Miranda saw them, too.

"Consumption?" she asked quietly.

"If that's another name for tuberculosis, yes."

The captain took a small device out of the pocket of her vest. With a few taps on the screen, she raised her vessel's anchor, levitated the hull off the water's surface, and brought the ship floating toward the beach.

Festus cocked an eyewhisker. "*Now* you get the tub working?"

We flew to Cibolita aboard the *Tempus Fugit*. As the ship reached cruising altitude, I had my first good view of the thirteen rivers.

"I'm guessing this is also a long story," Lucas asked, threading his arm around my waist and pulling me back against his chest.

Leaning into him, I said, "A really long story. I'm almost as exhausted as Naomi."

Miranda came to the rail. "I don't know what you've been through," she said, her eyes on the coursing River of Aries, "but you've returned the Rivers of Time to the Middle Realm. Expect a hero's welcome in Cibolita."

She wasn't wrong. We made port to the welcome of a 21-gun salute and cheers from the crowds gathered on the docks. Miranda lowered her vessel into a berth and dropped the gangplank.

With his arms still protectively locked around me, Lucas

said, "I know I promised you a honeymoon in Paris, but will you take a night in the Crow's Nest?"

"Is that the place with the sign that says, 'Travelers Welcome. Brigands Beware?'"

"The very one."

Jerking my head toward Miranda and Drake, I said, "I think we have brigands with us."

Lucas shot me a crooked grin. "Yeah, but they won't be in our room."

30

Epilogue, Briar Hollow

Miranda dropped us off atop the mountain ridge bordering the Land of the Golem. We had a nice reunion with the Golem himself before he obligingly opened the door into the fairy mound.

As the latch on the heavy wooden door closed behind us, confetti and streamers rained down from the ceiling. "Hi," I said, looking up, "good to see you, too. Don't give us away. I want to surprise everyone."

The fairy mound let out with a low whistle I assumed was conspiratorial assent. Leading the way, I took the group along the winding path through the stacks and stepped into the lair at the same moment Tori started down from the store above.

I'll never forget the shock on her face or the way joy instantly replaced the stunned reaction. She pounded down the last few steps and threw her arms around me with such force we fell back into one of the sofas laughing.

"Hey!" I said, hugging her back. "Slow down. I'm fine. We're all fine. Honest."

Duke, Beau's ghostly coonhand, approached Orion cautiously, wagging his tail in greeting. To my immense relief, the wolf threw his front paws down playfully and the two went galloping off toward the treehouse.

No sooner did Tori release me than Rodney hit me in the chest like a guided rodent missile. "Hiya, Little Dude," I said, holding him up to eye level. "Sorry I scared you."

Tori called my parents, who arrived in such a rush my father still had shaving cream on one side of his face.

"Really, Dad?" I said, brushing my hand over his features. *"Clean radi."*

The white stuff disappeared leaving a freshly shaven cheek behind. He didn't even notice, engulfing me in a tight embrace. I felt his chest shake and realized with a start that he was crying.

"It's okay, Daddy," I whispered. "I'm back. All in one piece. I promise."

"Don't you *ever* do anything like that to me again," he choked. "Not *ever*."

My mother was the first to notice Naomi. "Hi," she said, offering her hand to the little girl. "I'm Kelly."

Meeting her gaze, Naomi recognized the maternal vibe. "Hello," she said in a small voice. "I'm very tired."

"Then let's get you right to bed," Mom said, leading her toward one of the spare rooms. "Have you had anything to eat?" She didn't wait for an answer, calling out, "Darby, chicken soup, please."

The delighted brownie showed up long enough to throw his arms around my knees and say, "Welcome home, Mistress Jinx. I was ever so worried," before blipping out to get the soup.

After that, everyone started showing up at once. Greer blew in on the flight of the baobhan sith, Jilly came through the door from Londinium, Brenna and Gemma arrived from the apothecary, and Myrtle materialized through the Shevington portal with Connor close behind.

Following a consultation about Naomi's health, Mom and Gemma stirred up a potion to temporarily ease her coughing. After meeting everyone, Lash insisted on sitting with the child in case she woke up and was afraid.

That freed the rest of us to talk long into the night. We had a lot to cover. Connor delivered the most shocking news. That morning, the triplets found Morris Grayson dead in his room at the inn in Shevington.

"He left a note addressed to you, Lucas," Connor said, taking a folded sheet of paper from his pocket and passing it across the table.

I saw the tremor in my husband's hands when he opened the note. He quickly scanned the contents and then read the message aloud:

My Dear Boy,

I hope in time you will forgive me for dispensing with your wife. With age and experience you will understand that she, like Axe Frazier, only served to impede your life's course. You were meant for greatness, Lucas. I only hoped to see you embrace it.

Word has arrived from the Ruling Elder that I am to be tried for tampering with Blacklist items. I do not intend to be present to witness the public denigration of my lifetime of service by bumbling fools incapable of grasping the higher purpose in my actions.

Should it give you comfort, I learned last year that I suffer from the wasting disease of the Gwragedd Annwn. That is why I so clumsily tossed the rule of the Copernican Astrolabe into the portal. I lacked the control of my muscles to achieve the stealth of which I was once capable.

My last request to you is that you ascend to the Grysundl throne. If you feel you do not owe this respect to me, do it for your late father. Until we meet again in another place.

Your uncle,
Morsyn Grysundl

"He took belladonna," Connor said. "We didn't find him in time to administer the antidote. I'm so sorry, Lucas."

Lucas' voice broke when he answered. "Everything always had to be on Uncle Morris' terms," he said. "He wouldn't have had it any other way."

It's amazing how fast life can go back to normal after a major crisis. Within a day I was back at the counter in the store, and Lucas was commuting to Londinium to start sorting out the mess at DGI headquarters.

We'd get our honeymoon in Paris later. Right now, I didn't want to leave Naomi. The day after we arrived home from the Middle Realm, Festus showed up in the lair with a lung specialist from Raleigh who happened to be Fae.

Rather than subject the child to more dislocation, Dr. Engelman brought the necessary medicines and equipment to us. Greer went to Las Vegas to get Lauren. Together she and her niece are grieving Axe's death. They both have a lot of healing to do.

Ruling Elder Hilton Barnstable shed light on my encounter with the glowing disc in the time channel. In order to suspend time travel, the Fae who forged the secret portion of The Agreement, removed Ophiuchus from the Zodiac rendering accurate

temporal navigation impossible with or without the proper
instruments.

When I pulled the missing sign back into the dial, the horizontal channels connecting the portals shut down. Now, all the
time streams pass through the In Between where they belong —
just as Axe knew they should.

There are, however, infinite numbers of unique threads,
each one a tributary of the thirteen Temporal Rivers, and each
one calling to explorers like Miranda Winter.

She and the members of the temporal resistance in Cibolita,
successfully petitioned the Ruling Elders for the return of the
Temporal Arcana. The Elders put Festus in charge of the task
force to locate the items. He and Jilly are hard at work combing
the Blacklist archives to figure out where to begin.

A few nights after we returned, I asked my grimoire to
absorb all the entries I penned in the 16th century. When the
book finished, I carefully shelved the small journal above my
desk, my fingers lingering on the soft leather of the spine.

"Thank you, Moira," I whispered softly. "At least we were
able to help Naomi."

My Phoenix pen rose from the surface of the desk and
scratched three phrases in the grimoire.

The hunter. The healer. The way home.

"I guess it would be too much to ask you to explain that," I
said.

In response, the pen drew Orion and two girls under the sign
of Ophiuchus.

Naomi and my unborn daughter.

AUTHOR'S NOTE

Thank you for reading *Mirrors of Time*, the most epic adventure our characters have ever experienced.

From here, our world will be opening up in new and exciting directions. The next book that will appear in our universe is the third "Wrecking Crew" novella, *Tigerstone*, which will set Festus, Jilly, and the others off in search of a Temporal Arcana artifact.

If you haven't read the first two "Wrecking Crew" novellas, *Moonstone* and *Merstone*, now is the perfect time to start! Both are available as ebooks on Amazon.

These humorous shorts will give you insight into Festus McGregor's secret life leading to his new assignment as a Blacklist agent.

The next full-length Jinx Hamilton novel, *The Never Sky* will be in your hands before you know it!

GET EXCLUSIVE JINX HAMILTON MATERIAL

There are many things I love about being an author, but building a relationship with my readers is far and away the best.

Once a month I send out a newsletter with information on new releases, sneak peeks, and inside articles on Jinx Hamilton as well as other books and series I'm currently developing.

You can get all this, a **FREE** copy of the prequel novella *Granny Witch*, and more by signing up at JulietteHarper.com.

ALSO BY JULIETTE HARPER

In the Jinx Hamilton Series:

Witch at Heart

Jinx Hamilton is ready to trade in waitressing for becoming her own boss. The shop she inherits from her eccentric aunt in Briar Hollow, North Carolina seems like the perfect fit. As Jinx handles the enchanted inventory and the unruly clientele, she discovers her aunt also willed her magical powers without an instruction manual!

As if that weren't enough, she's forced to deal with four cats, several homeless ghosts, and a potential serial killer. With a little help from her best friend and a dreamy new neighbor, Jinx must keep the business afloat and the murderer at bay. And it'll take more than clever bookkeeping and spellcasting to keep the store... and herself... from going under.

Witch at Odds

Jinx accepts her new life as a witch and is determined to make a success of both that and her new business. However, she has a great deal to learn. As the story unfolds, Jinx sets out to both study her craft and to get a real direction for her aunt's haphazard approach to inventory. Although Jinx can call on Aunt Fiona's ghost for help, the old lady is far too busy living a jet set afterlife to be worried about her niece's learning curve. That sets Jinx up to make a major mistake and to figure out how to set things right again.

Witch at Last

A lot has changed for Jinx in just a few months. After the mishaps that befell her in *Witch At Odds*, she just wants to enjoy the rest of the summer, but she's not going to be that lucky. As she's poised to tell her friends she's a witch, secrets start popping out all over the place. Between old foes and new locations, Jinx isn't going to get her peaceful summer, but she may just get an entirely different world.

Witch on First

Jinx walks out the front door of her store in Briar Hollow on a Sunday morning only to find her werecat neighbor and boyfriend, Chase McGregor, staring at a dead man. Under the best of circumstances, a corpse complicates things, but Jinx has other problems. Is her trusted mentor lying to her? Have dangerous magical artifacts been placed inside the shop? Join Jinx and Tori as they race to catch a killer and find out what's going on literally under their noses.

Witch on Second

The story opens just a week before Halloween. Jinx and Tori have their hands full helping to organize Briar Hollow's first ever paranormal festival. Beau and the ghosts at the cemetery are eager to help make the event a success, but tensions remain high after the recent killings. Without a mentor to lean on, Jinx must become a stronger, more independent leader. Is she up to the task in the face of ongoing threats? Still mourning the loss of Myrtle and her breakup with Chase, Jinx finds herself confronting new and unexpected foes.

Witch on Third

The books opens on the the last night of Briar Hollow's first annual paranormal festival. With Chase still stinging from the breakup and Lucas Grayson more than a little interested, Jinx has plenty on her plate without a new evil trio in town. As the team works to counter Chesterfield's newest scheme, something happens in the Valley that changes everything for the Hamilton family.

Christmas in the Valley

Join Jinx and company for the first Jinx Hamilton / Shevington novella. In this short read of approximately 75 pages, Jinx, Tori, and the gang head out to spend their first Christmas in the magical Valley of Shevington, a place where anything is possible.

Everything seems perfect, but on Christmas night, Jinx finds herself at the base of the Mother Tree thinking about the one thing she can't have . . . or can she?

The Amulet of Caorunn

Creavit wizard Irenaeus Chesterfield is back, with a bigger, badder plan to go after Jinx and company. In the weeks leading up to Christmas, Jinx starts having dream visions about the mysterious Amulet of Caorunn. Trying to get more details, she and Tori try a dicey double enchantment with shocking results. Join Jinx, Tori, and the gang as they work to recover the Amulet, stop Chesterfield, and enter the mysterious Middle Realm.

To Haunt a Witch

Jinx, Tori, and the gang have settled down to enjoy some "normal" time after their adventure in the Middle Realm. Then Cezar Ionescu walks through the front door of the Witch's Brew asking for a favor. An abandoned house owned by the local Strigoi clan is attracting the attention of the Haunted Briar Hollow web series. Can Jinx and company relocater the spirit?

As usual, there's more to the abandoned house than anyone imagines. When the group brings home a "helpful" spirit, Jinx finds out more about Fae politics than she wanted to know, and discovers a completely hidden element of her already complicated family history.

To Test a Witch

Book 9 transports readers to Fae Londinium. As the Conference of the Realms convenes, Jinx and the gang settle into adjoining rooms at Claridge's determined to find a way to end The Agreement segregating the In Between.

In the three days before the opening ceremony, Lucas assumes the role of tour guide, taking Jinx to Hampton Court and the British Museum. But it's the sites he doesn't show her that prove to be the most critical after an assassination attempt puts Barnaby's life in danger and leaves Jinx in charge of the Shevington delegation.

From encountering the ghosts of Henry VIII's wives to meeting a troop of gargoyle guards in the Fae Houses of Parliament, Jinx and her friends take the town by storm.

To Trick a Witch

In Book 10, *To Trick a Witch*, Jinx answers the age old question, "What did you do over your summer vacation?" Her story beats everyone else's by a mile.

The Conference of the Realms may be over, but the trouble is just getting started for the crew in the lair. There's an outbreak of cryptids in the human realm, threatening witch hysteria in Briar Hollow, and a covert coven reunion in the works.

Jinx finds herself juggling Fae politics while grappling with new career aspirations and relationship complications — all with SpookCon2 looming in October.

To Teach a Witch

The opening of the magical sanctuary of Tír na nÓg has rocked the foundations of Fae society. Isherwood sits in the Tower of Londinium awaiting trial. Jinx and the special ops team circle the globe dealing with *nonconformi* incidents.

Behind every layer of evil lies another bad guy waiting to be unmasked. A crime witnessed by a raven sets in motion a journey into the mists surrounding a hidden island. There, in the company of a king and an order of gallant knights, Jinx will do battle with the woman who started it all.

To Love a Witch

After accepting Lucas Grayson's proposal, Jinx finds herself trying to figure out how to throw a wedding for friends and family in three realms without offending anyone. Yes, even powerful witches struggle with etiquette.

With a new coven member in town and the unexpected arrival of an angry spirit in the courthouse, unsolved murders add to the already complicated situation. What can we say? It's crazy business as usual in Briar Hollow, but look for the twist because it's coming.

To Love a Witch is the 12th book in this urban fantasy series that has grown from its cozy, paranormal beginnings into a world some readers compare to Harry Potter or The Dresden Files. Filled with intrigue, hilarious hijinks, family devotion, and sweet romance, you'll fall in love with the world Juliette Harper has created in Briar Hollow and beyond.

Other Works By Juliette

The Lockwood Legacy

Previously released as a six-book series, *The Lockwood Legacy* returns in three updated and combined editions. The first, *One Silent Bullet*, is available now on Amazon. Edited for clarity and continuity, these re-releases come in advance of the long-awaited continuation of the series in *Four Hearts Bleed*.

One Silent Bullet

A single bullet destroyed a life of lies.

When family patriarch Langston Lockwood allegedly commits suicide, his daughters Kate, Jenny, and Mandy suspect foul play. As the twisted details of their father's life emerge, the girls uncover generations of family secrets that lead them to a mysterious treasure hidden in Baxter's Draw.

Will the Aztec gold lying in their father's private cave bring his girls even greater wealth or will they be the next to die?

The Selby Jensen Paranormal Mysteries

Descendants of the Rose

Selby Jensen's business card reads "Private Investigator," but that seriously downplays her occupation. Let's hear it in her own words:

"You want to know what I do for a living? I rip souls out. Cut heads off. Put silver bullets where silver bullets need putting. You think there aren't any monsters? . . . I have some disturbing news for you. You might want to sit down. Monsters walk among us. I'm looking for one in particular. In the meantime? I'm keeping the rest of them from eating people like you."

Juliette Harper, author of The Jinx Hamilton Novels, creates a cast of characters, most of whom have one thing in common; they don't have a pulse. The dead are doing just fine by Selby, who is determined never to lose someone she loves again, but then a force of love more powerful than her grief changes that plan.

Join Selby Jensen as she and her team track down a shadowy figure tied to a murder at a girls' school. What none of them realize, however, is that in solving this case, they will enter a longer battle against a larger evil.

The Study Club Mysteries

You Can't Get Blood Out of Shag Carpet

Wanda Jean Milton discovers her husband, local exterminator Hilton Milton, dead on her new shag carpet with an Old Hickory carving knife sticking out of his chest.

Beside herself over how she'll remove the stain, and grief-stricken over Hilton's demise, Wanda Jean finds herself the prime suspect. But she is also a member of "the" local Study Club, a bastion of independent Texas feminism 1960s style.

Club President Clara Wyler has no intention of allowing a member to be a murder suspect. Aided by her younger sister and County Clerk, Mae Ella Gormley; Sugar Watson, the proprietress of Sugar's Style and Spray; and Wilma Schneider, Army MASH veteran and local RN, the Club women set out to clear Wanda Jean's name — never guessing the local dirt they'll uncover.

ABOUT THE AUTHOR

Juliette Harper is the pen name used by the writing team of Patricia Pauletti and Rana K. Williamson. As a writer, Juliette's goal is to create strong female characters facing interesting, challenging, painful, and at times comical situations. Refusing to be bound by genre, her primary interest lies in telling good stories.

For more information...
www.JulietteHarper.com
author@julietteharper.com